Tom Nash was brought up in East Bergholt, Suffolk, where John Constable grew up. He worked as a rural architect and an artist, and has taught drawing courses at Flatford Mill. He has written five novels, four plays, all performed, and numerous short stories. He has an MA in Fine Art and lives in a small, south Norfolk village.

VILLAGE STORIES

T P NASH

Troubador Publishing Ltd
Unit E2 Airfield Business Park,
Harrison Road, Market Harborough,
Leicestershire. LE16 7UL
Tel: 0116 2792299
Email: books@troubador.co.uk
Web: www.troubador.co.uk/matador

ISBN 978 1805142 287

British Library Cataloguing in Publication Data.
A catalogue record for this book is available from the British Library.

Printed and bound in Great Britain by 4edge Limited
Typeset in 10pt Minion Pro by Troubador Publishing Ltd, Leicester, UK

To Sarah

STUMP

I t wasn't much more than a stump. An eight-foot high stump, weathered limestone, a base of two rows of steps. Standing in the middle of Market Street. Always been there, taken for granted. Now and then, someone would put a traffic beacon over the top of it, or drape some streamers around it. You know, Christmas time, that sort of thing. And now and then, those that lived near, would swear that they heard horses and armour at night, with nothing to see. They didn't get much credit; I ask you, horses and armour! We put it down to drink, and over-active imaginations. But whenever they said that they heard them, a little more stone would be wasted away, the stump a little shorter.

I walked down to the shop, saw a digger standing right up to Stump. Didn't look right, didn't look good. In the shop, there was muttering about it, the usual sort of random views without anybody doing anything. Mavis, the shopkeeper, who is always early, said she heard this roaring and clanking about half seven, and looked out. Blimey, there was a digger, sitting right up to the Stump as though it meant business. Pretty early for any action by the Council, she said. The driver seemed to avoid talking to anyone, and was in the café next door. I did my shopping and went to have a look.

A big man, scoffing his second breakfast by the looks of it: egg, bacon, black pudding, tomato, mushroom, all the trimmings.

1

He had his head down, as though he was concentrating on his food, and he looked like the kind of man who did concentrate on his food. But I reckoned he was keeping his head down to duck the flack. Because there was plenty of it flying around. I sat down to enjoy it.

There must have been at least ten of us in there all talking at once, as though the driver was deaf. Comments about the Council, comments about diggers parked in the middle of the road, comments about the driver himself, who didn't dare say a word. Just kept his head down. I wondered at his bravery, coming in here; perhaps he didn't realise that he had raised a storm.

What he had said, when he came in and before he got a lot of flack, County Highways had deemed the stump a dangerous obstruction. He was to demolish it, load it onto a truck – coming later – and level the ground, all ready for the tarmac boys. He had been genuinely amazed that it could cause any fuss. What was so special about a bit of ruin in the middle of the road? And then ordered his food, got his head down and kept it down.

There was no way that some busybody, Council or no, was going to come into the village, and decide to remove an historic bit of it. Not that anyone could tell you what the history was. That wasn't the point; we look after our village, and its history. But who was going to do anything about it? There was considerable discussion; someone said the police, others the Parish Council, and there was a voice for the Vicar. Poor old boy, the Vicar; can't imagine he would like to get mixed up in all this fuss. Well, someone went running and came back with the Chairman of the Parish Council. He walked in, all self-important, and asked what the fuss was all about. Can't you see? Just about everyone yelled, pointing out the window. He hummed and hawed, coughed a few times, and went to speak to the tractor driver. It was a

2

quiet conversation, couldn't hear a word of it. But he stood up, demanded the telephone and extracted a stay of execution from County Highways, citing Planning Laws, Historic Buildings, and so on. And it was only just a stump.

The digger driver didn't wait to be sent away with a flea in his ear. Didn't even wait to pay his bill, but stepped up to his digger. Couldn't get in. Door jammed. Almost broke the key off trying again. He was muttering that some village boy had got at it, not that he would have had a chance, the digger parked in front of the café window. After a while, he got the door open, but couldn't start the motor; it wouldn't start. He was winding away, got down, looked under the bonnet, swore something terrible. Seems the digger was new, nothing wrong with it. I saw a few people smiling; wondered what they had been up to. Maybe it was just justice. In the end, he called a taxi and disappeared, leaving the digger standing there like some monster that Stump had defeated.

It is amazing how fast the word can get around in our village. It was not as if there was any kind of organised broadcast but within an hour a poster went up summoning the village to a meeting, 10.30am on the Monday. I should have said that it all started on a Friday, before a Bank Holiday; perhaps Highways thought they would get away with it, the Historic Buildings people being off all that time. They had not reckoned with the village people.

Over the weekend, there was a constant trickle of people, mostly village, coming down, looking at Stump – well, that's what it was called – taking selfies with it, dropping in to the café to hear the gossip, and so on. Café did a roaring trade. Someone even wrapped a scarf around it, as though to say it was a much-loved member of the village. And then the press appeared, photoed it with the scarf, went in the shop and café, asking

3

personal opinions, picking up the vibe. We expected television, but they didn't come.

There was something funny, sort of odd; those selfies, they all had a shadow of another person behind Stump, sort of hiding and yet not hiding. I had a look at one; difficult to make out, a short person, old-fashioned clothes. Lot of nonsense, the owner of the selfie said; just shadows and sunshine, that's all. I couldn't say.

Monday morning arrived. It had been a busy weekend. Stump was now decorated with flags and streamers, like a Nepal prayer offering. A parking beacon had appeared on the top, but disappeared overnight. Someone said serve them right; disrespect. Of what, someone asked. And nobody knew the answer but Stump had been there for ever and that earned a degree of respect. Like the Church, Castle and Market Cross – which isn't a cross but that's another tale.

The Village Hall hummed. The early judo class had been sent away, and chairs hastily put out. But there were far more people than chairs. The kitchen took the opportunity of brewing up, and charging for coffee and tea. It was more like a party, until it was felt time to get going. There were even a couple of reporters, getting in on the action, hustling around, quizzing people over Stump, and what sort of village it was, and how we knew each other, and what we thought… on and on.

And that was when a further rumpus started. Who was chairing the meeting?

Of course, the Parish Council Chairman said that he was the Chair. But the Village Society Chair said that it was a village affair concerning an historic part of the village, and she should chair it. Whereupon the Hall Committee Chair said that as they were not charging for the meeting – they didn't know who to charge – they should chair it. And then the Sheriff stood up and said as Stump was their responsibility, he should chair the meeting. But when he was asked why it was in such bad condition, why it hadn't been maintained as an important historic structure, and perhaps he could tell us what it stood for, he sat down and said nothing. And all factions had supporters, who argued noisily to little effect.

Into this pandemonium strolled the Vicar. I should explain; he was a good old boy, retired farmer, an easy Christian soul who saw the good in everyone. Can I help, he asked in his usual meek voice. There was a hush, a pause, and then the Parish Council Chair said would he be so good as to chair this meeting. And Vicar obliged. I'm not sure he even knew what it was about; I think he'd only dropped in for a cup of coffee. The Parish Chairman said that it was no place for reporters, and they were ushered out, none too gently.

I don't know how Vicar did it, and I was there myself. But there was quiet, and all the old boys lining the walls gave up chattering, about tractors and crops and all the things they always talked about whenever they got together. So Vicar says, What is the question? And a great squall of eager voices broke out, and the sound swept up to the roof until the walls were shaking as everyone it seemed had their say. Vicar waited. And waited. Then he clapped his hands and all were quiet.

He turned to the Parish Council Chair, and said, What is the question?

The Chair looked round, as though to get everyone's agreement, and said, Do we keep it, or do we let it be removed? By whom? asked the Vicar, whose diction was always correct. County Highways was the answer. And what are the arguments each way, asked Vicar, because he was not so foolish as to stick his oar in one way or tother.

Of course, there was a great tumult of noise again, mostly

5

in favour of one or tother, and some pleading some other cause altogether. After he had allowed them to get rid of some hot air and exhaust themselves, he clapped his hands and they all went quiet. Could someone tell me why it should be removed? He asked, meek and mild as usual.

A big ol' boy stood up; everyone knew him. He had the biggest farm around here, and the biggest equipment. And didn't we know it! The noise, the mud in the road, and the queues of cars held up. I can't get my new combine down Market Street, he said. Not without driving all over the pavement, and you don't like it. He was turning around, trying to catch everyone's eye. And I can't get my new beet harvester down the street either, an if that one goes on the pavement, you'll have a bloody great hole. And then he went all quiet, a bit pale, and he said he was sorry and slid out of the door. That was a rum go; nobody had ever heard him say 'sorry' before.

There a great muttering and moaning. 'Cause it wasn't as if we didn't wish the best for our farmers, but they can't go driving all over us. Vicar clapped his hands and asked if there was anyone else who wished it removed. And this little man stood up, and started talking; it was so quiet, we couldn't hear, the Parish Chair told him to speak up, apologising to Vicar for interrupting.

He was a little man; we could hardly see him. And we couldn't hear him even when he spoke up. Well, there was a big ol' girl next to him, and she bent down to hear him and didn't look too pleased with what he said. But eventually, she told us, He's a driving instructor, and he says we don't have Keep Left signs in front of it, and it makes the road narrow either side, he said, she said, and it's dangerous, he said. That made a great deal of laughter and chat, some raucous comments about learner drivers. Vicar let it go on a while, and blast me, but didn't the

6

little man go pale and slide out of the door too.

Vicar clapped his hands. Was there anyone who wished to keep the monument? He said. Sounded funny calling Stump a monument.

A buzz broke out. Comments like, It ain't right, and Who says it must go, and Tell them to get their hands off our village, and such like. But at last one man stood up, in the middle of the floor. A quiet looking old man, old tweed jacket and balding; gentle smile. The vicar smiled at him, greeted him like an old friend. Joshua, can you help us here? And everyone went quiet; if Vicar rated this man, he must be some kind of authority. He said to us, This is Joshua Reynolds. He is an archaeologist and wrote the history of the village. Oh, years ago, wasn't it Joshua? Come up here by me. And this old boy went up the front. Tell us all about it, would you?

He had a mild sort of voice, but it was very clear; we could hear every word. Well, he said, I had been wondering when the Stump would receive a little attention. It's been in poor condition for a long time, and it is interesting to hear that the Sheriff's Trust is responsible for it. But I'm not sure how a repair would proceed; what authority and permissions, quite apart from the technique.

I don't think anyone had mentioned the thought of repair; it was taken for granted that Stump was a weathered old bit of stone. What could be done to it that wouldn't raise more questions, more difficulties? There was no-one there, I reckoned, that would have any idea what to do with it. Vicar asked him, Can you tell us its history?

There was a hush there, because some had ideas that it was an old market cross, and others that it was planted from space, and some that it was not old at all.

The history is not clear, said Joshua. We don't know how

7

old it is, but there are records that it was erected by a lord of the manor in the fifteenth century as a memorial to his daughter. She was only twelve, and would have been married in a couple of years. There was some grinning and comments from the old boys round the walls. But she was knocked down and killed by a troop of the King; it was a time when the Lord in the Castle, not the Lord of the Manor, was not very popular with his King, and there was talk of a siege. Our Lord, of the Manor, put up the memorial as some kind of visual complaint against his King, a reminder of his loss. These records are not very clear; they are in the County Records Office. It is always difficult interpreting such old records; they are rarely in good condition and if they are not in Latin, the Old English can be open to misinterpretation. But I have come across this tale in a number of places, and it seems that there must be some truth to it. Some say that she is seen still, and the troop heard, but I can give no credit to such tales; I deal in facts.

It seems surprising that it remained so long, if it was a personal memorial, said Vicar. You would have thought that it would be in the Church. Well, said Joshua, the Church hasn't always been popular, you know. The Vicar looked a bit grumpy, and then laughed. But that's not the end of the story, said Joshua. There are better records that it was converted, if that is the word, to a War Memorial. There was a buzz of talk, until one man stood up and said that the War Memorial was in the Church. Ah yes, said Joshua, so it is. But which War are you talking about? And that silenced the man. I think it goes back to the beginning of the century, he said. Some young ones wondered about a beginning only twenty years old, most thought about a century about a hundred years back. Would that be for the Boer War? asked someone. Joshua smiled. I was talking about a bit earlier than that. Gosh, said the Vicar. Did they have War Memorials

8

then? But certainly, said Joshua. I believe this commemorates the dead of the Napoleonic Wars; there were many killed from around here, by all accounts, taken for soldiers and sailors. And they don't show up in the Church. The Vicar looked thoughtful. They ought to be remembered in the Church, he said. And then he pulled himself together. Is there anyone else with an opinion on this matter?

That was a mistake. A woman stood up, and in a very loud voice started talking about a cat trust, and would everyone contribute to it, and she was getting going when a loud clamour broke out and she was hushed. And then someone said how good it was to have the village assembled, and to remember the Harvest Festival, contributions gratefully received, and they all went to a good home. And again, a hubbub of chatter drowned her out.

I was feeling rather weary by then; there was such a crush, and everybody talking now when they liked, that I slid out of the door and went home for lunch. And the funny thing was, when I next went down to the shop, nobody could tell me if a decision had been reached at the Village Hall, whether Stump was coming down or staying, or was to be renovated.

I went down to Market Street, and Stump looked just the same. No streamers, scarves or Keep Left signs. But one couldn't help feeling different about it, about the lord's daughter who was killed, about the dead and wounded in the Napoleonic Wars. How could they demolish it now?

And as I turned away, I thought that someone had brushed my arm, in a familiar sort of way. But there was nobody there.

THE GIANT

We were carving a new route through the blackness of unknown. Wild country, dark mountains and narrow valleys that led to difficult places or, unexpectedly, brought one across known tracks. Great stretches of water glinted in the morning sunshine. The map would show it all white, unmarked and unclaimed by explorers. Perhaps, a few dotted lines, suggestions of seasonal rivers, rising God-knows-where in the hinterland.

Tramping through a bog filled with fluorescent weed: the shush of waves, scaring the crocodiles, giant rats and water snakes. Reeds and threatening thorn obscured the way ahead. I came to a stop. My lieutenant paused, looked back, continued on his way, tale wagging.

My boot was lodged tight. Not in glutinous mud but as in a vice. Held. And then my foot was wet. Water or blood? Or both? I called out; he paused, came back to me. At that moment, my foot was released and we continued together.

Back at base, I examined my foot. The left one. A bloody sock. The boot was holed, a clean incision, too large for a thorn or rat. Perhaps a croc. Fresh blood flowed onto the floor. I tasted it; there was the light rankness of sock and the iron of fresh blood. Associated with wounds, extractions, battles.

My wounds were dealt with and plastered. Thought no more of it; added it to the forgotten scars.

The next day, we followed the same route. I hadn't mapped it, a mental record to survive the season, and liked to experience a route three times: the first for the pure essence of exploration, unhindered by any preconceptions or limitations; the second for recording, learning the wayposts, orientation and aspects; the third for familiarity so I should know it in the future from whatever angle I came across it.

As we came round a small hillock, there was something not observed before; an undiscovered outcrop, standing tall, much taller than me, fringed with thorn, green flanks, precipitous, unexpected.

We halted.

Had our memories failed us? It could not be, it was too abrupt. A halt for a con, observation, a search through the records. Nothing.

A gutteral sound seemed to come from the outcrop. My lieutenant sidled behind me, tale between his legs. I held my ground, seeing but not believing.

You know how sometimes you can make out a face in the clouds or on the condensation on a window glass. You can try to change it, turn it into something else or lose it. But it remains rigidly the same. I could make out now the elements of a face. The 'mouth' opened again, another dribble of meaningless sounds. Above was what might be seen as a nose, eyes, black pits that twinkled with an ancient intelligence. The cheeks were creased and folded like a mountain range and all around was a grey growth like a beard that trailed into the undergrowth and tawny hair tipped with lichen and sunbeams.

Mesmerised by the sounds, I began to hear words and after a while phrases and sentences. I could never swear that the words meant anything to me or that it was a language that was known. And yet I understood it well as though the message was being transmitted directly into my brain. I did not wonder who or what he was and how he came to be there; my surprise at his appearance held me in thrall.

'I come from a land of giants. Giant mountains pierced by great fjords, a hard land and a hard giant people.

'My name is Kari the Kingmaker, son of Audbjorn, son of Ulf the Fearless. When I was twenty, I became a Viking and went raiding.'

'A Viking!'

He ignored me; perhaps he could not hear.

'A few years ago or so it seems, we came up a river into a soft, green land. So flat that you could see the people running from us, so fat that we could feed ourselves and settle for winter and go a'viking along the coast in the spring.

'But a hard time came. The winter was long and cold, the river frozen, and we were threatened by warriors from the South. One day, near spring, our ship was fired; we were using it for shelter and the cooking fire took it. So, come the spring without our ship and no means to build a new one or take another, we went a'viking into the land, moving on to avoid attack from the South. And it was a good time, easy living, rich settlements, until we settled here in this place.

'There was no settlement here, but wood and water; we built shelters, settled for a while, raided the area around, thought we were barons, the local lords. Until one night...'

He paused; his eyes seemed to dull, his head to drop. My companion became restless, wanted to leave but I stood still and waited. After a time, the giant lifted his head.

'It was about a woman. A comely wench; I had taken her from a hovel on the way for a slave but when I left her behind, she followed me, stayed with me, became my bed-warmer. But there was another who desired her, who pestered me day and night. Said we should share and share about. His name was Leif Arufsson. One night he gave me drink plied with herbs; I knew it not. But slept like a winter tree until woken by the covers dragged off me and my woman taken. I reared up, full of sleep but angered at this falseness, this theft among brothers. And then I saw that Leif had sided with the Southern warriors who surrounded our settlement; a traitor to his people. I wielded my great sword, felling three of the South people but was slain, a sword to the gut.

'Until you woke me. What is your name, elfling?'

'Jonathan.'

'That is not a name. Give me your name.'

I stared at him, turned to leave.

'No, don't run. I will not harm you. But you must have a name; Ulf or Leif or Kari or Bjorn… what is it?'

'My name is Jonathan.' I spoke it slowly, so he should hear me clearly. As one would speak to savages in darkest Africa.

'Jon-a-thon… jon-a-thorn. How apt. I don't know this name; how shall I know you?'

'John. You can call me John. Like Mother does.'

He smiled, I think. There was a creaking of the thorn around his head, his mouth opened and closed, his eyes twinkled.

'Jon, son of… son of what?'

I didn't know what to say.

'Your forebears; they must have names.'

'Fore bears?'

'Who bore you? Who holds the house name?'

'We live at the Warren.'

'Well then, John-a-thorn son of Warren, I need your help.'

'Help?' How could I help him? As if he was a human and I wasn't sure about that.

'John-a-thorn, son of Warren, help me to go home.'

13

'Home?' I wondered what he meant. How could I help him? What would Father say? Or Mother? I started to back away, confused by this spectre, this abrupt interruption to my exploration; I had not bargained for real savages. 'I'll come back. Tomorrow.'

He stared and before my eyes seem to fade back into the substance of a thornbush, no identifiable face or human form. We left, my lieutenant and I, and went home to tea and television.

And yet, even as I watched a particularly good Bugs Bunny (and Bugs Bunny is never bad), I began to wonder who this giant was and how I might help him 'go home'. It would be a mistake to involve Mother or Father. He was my giant; mine alone. Not for sharing. And Father would only muck it up.

It was a few days before I could return to the wilds. On a Saturday, accompanied by my trusty four-legged lieutenant, I returned to that corner of the wilderness, walking with slow precision along the same route that I had traversed before. The thought of being armed, a spear or dagger, had crossed my mind but the giant had not threatened me or moved.

I stood before him; the bush gave a slight shake in the sunshine and resolved itself into a face, as before. He greeted me with what I could only feel was warmth, like an old friend. The sun twinkled out of his eyes and I felt a great peace but there was something not quite right.

'You have returned to me, elfling Jon.'

I was silent. My companion was scouting around, exploring the area, checking for traps and dangerous devices.

'My tale was too brief. There was a man, Leif Arufsson, who took my woman in the night and when I rose to claim what was mine, received a sword blow in the guts.'

'Yes,' I said. 'You told me this but what can I do for you? Would you want me to find others, your relations? Or call the police?'

'I have no need of others. Those that are bound to me are all far away and I am lost to them. But I might see them again if you help me. You alone, for only you do I trust.'

I stared, wondered how I alone could help him.

'My tale has not ended. The South people took me as I lay in the mud and tied me to a throne, calling out "Kingmaker, Kingmaker", laughing in my face as I watched my life draining out of me onto the ground. They left me there for the bushes and the trees to take me.

'But I died in battle, elfling, and I would travel to Asgard and pass through the gates of Valgrind to the great hall of Valhalla, the house of Odin, where I would rest at last with Thor and all great warriors who have fallen in battle.

'I see the great roof of Valhalla in my dreams, the golden shields dazzling in the sunshine. Let me be taken there.'

I didn't understand: the dying, the journey and the foreign places. He looked at me and saw my confusion.

'You are young and have little experience of those who have died.'

'My grandfather. He died and is buried in the churchyard; I can't see him.'

'And did you not all bid him farewell and fire his coffin high above the ground so that he could see his way home?'

I stared at him. Did he mean burning the coffin? Who would do that?

'Where is your grandfather now?'

'Why, in the churchyard.'

'But where does his spirit lie?'

All the stories and religious teaching that we had had swept over me in a rush so that I was silent, staring at him, beginning to understand my parents, especially my Father who told me when I was weeping that Grandpa would be looking down on us, and the priest who spoke of Heaven, and then I thought of ghost stories and how I had asked a teacher what a ghost was and she had looked serious and said that they were spirits that had not yet come to rest and waited for some living person to put something right and help them to go to a place of peace and how it seemed to make sense and began to think that the giant might not be dead and yet was dead and so might be a ghost and that ghosts might not be the unpleasant and frightening things that stories told us they were but simply lost people or rather spirits. My mouth dropped open.

The giant smiled, a gentle creasing of the folds in his face, and spoke to me.

'You understand now?'

I nodded. A peace fell on us; a lark sang high above answered by another a mile away. A great tit bawled its repetitive notes and flashed away as a buzzard hovered, riding the gentle wind like a seasoned sailor.

'It is a good place, this, but it belongs to you, not me. I must be gone, now or soon. For I have a longing to join the others with Thor.'

'What can I do?'

'Build me a longship and send me on my way with fire. That is all.'

'All?' was all I could say. A longship? I knew what they looked like, huge powerful greyhounds of the ancient seas, the Viking warship. I could not even build a dinghy or a raft.

'It is in the spirit of it, young Jon-a-thorn. The spirit of a longship but the fire must be real.'

'A fire here? It would bring all the men from the village who would rush to put out the flames, would drown your fire before you can sail away.'

'We must be private and speedy. Elfling, we shall do it. You shall do it.'

He told me what to do and guided me as I worked. There was an old oak gate, collapsed but not rotten, and I pulled timbers from it. There was a barrel not far away, some lost dream of a farmer; the staves came away in my hands. From fields nearby I found binder twine and lengths of wire. One piece only I could not locate and that was the carved prowhead, the dragon's head that would lead the ship home.

He directed me as I laid the keel, stretching away from his 'throne'; I ploughed a clear space on the ground, kicking away the turves and dragging the undergrowth aside.

A glint from the boggy ground; I scraped around it. And uncovered a sword, massive in length and weight, heavy with rust but strangely preserved, jewels shining in the pommel. As I held it up and wondered at it, rubbing the mud free of the handle, there was a great roar.

'The Kingmaker. My Kingmaker. With this sword I strode through the armies of enemies, of lesser peoples, to make Kings of our leaders. With this sword I went a'viking across foreign lands until I fell here. With this sword...'

His head was bent; I lifted the great blade and laid it in his lap, the handle towards where I imagined his right hand to be. While I worked and he waited to be sent on his final voyage, he told me tales of his journeys and of all the things he had seen.

'There were great birds in the sky, not so long ago. Silver with wings that never beat the air but flew faster and higher than any birds I had seen. There were long cold winters when the very air froze, a fog hanging heavy over the land and men came

17

scavenging for wood to burn, any stick they could find. And before then, men came on horses, armour shining, long spears, and drove the little people to work, digging, carrying, putting stone on stone, and a great building rose up there towards where the sun sets, an earth mound as high as a small hill. A square building all white like a sail. And those little people would come here, digging in the ground for stones and sand; why did they want stones and sand?'

He directed me as I worked.

'The keel. Good. The hearthstone of my ship. No, it is not too short, it will do well. Now a frame, a shaped timber to hold the planking. Yes, that will do well...'

I had offered up a curved ash bough, stripped of leaves and twigs.

'Next, the planking, stout boarding to hold all together...'

There was an old plank near the gate, rotten at one end, but oak, a durable wood.

'No... no, not like that. It must hang from the frame, form the gunwale, allow openings for the oars.'

Binder twine from a sheaf lying in a hedge bound the plank to the frame. A barrel stave supported the prow, another the poop at the stern. A board became a rowers bench, another the steering oar, pierced with an ash branch as the tiller that he tucked under his arm.

The prowhead evaded me; he had spoken of a bird or a noble emblem to fly before him. For a time I despaired of finding anything; I searched dustbins and rubbish pits and was sent away with a flea in my ear by the dustbin men as I tipped up bins searching, hunting for anything suitable. There were a few things that I dragged up to the wilderness but they were always dismissed with a shrug of his thorny head.

One day, I was in the garage at home, pumping up the tyres

of my bicycle. As I returned the pump to the shelf, I noticed an old metal cap. I didn't know what it was; it didn't come off the car and it was too large for the lawn-mower. It had a brass figure standing up, a Red Indian chief in full headdress. I slipped it into my bag and hid it in my bedroom; it was so dusty I didn't think Father would miss it and I was so desperate that I could not risk losing it.

I mounted it on a stave and presented it to the Viking. He smiled and nodded.

'A warrior of another people. He has a proud look; he cannot have been beaten in battle. He will do well. By Odin, I have waited a long time for this.'

And the prow was assembled, binder twine and thorn branches, sore hands and long hours. I stood back; it seemed to be the ghost of a ship, hardly enough to bear the heavy load of such a spirit. But it was made. He smiled his approval, casting his eyes over his 'ship'. And now, I could see it too, stretching away from him into the future, my prow glinting in the sunshine.

'You have done well, Jon-a-thorn. I name you Jon the Deliverer; you shall deliver me from this place so that I may set to sail for Valhalla.'

For many days I had worried about the fire. Whatever the Viking said, I knew that the flames in the wilderness would bring men and water and quench the dreams. I waited for the longer nights, darkness and oblivion, when few might see the conflagration.

And the time came. Guy Fawkes Night. A huge bonfire in the village, rockets and loud bangs. Another fire at a distance would be seen to be a similar celebration. It was obvious. I delayed telling the Viking (I couldn't call him Kari, it sounded like the name of a woman in the village); he would not understand, neither my fears nor the history and the bonfires that carried no spirits to their resting place. He had become restless, bending in the breezes, bowed down by autumnal storms. The twinkle in his eyes had faded. I feared that he would collapse into a storm of pieces, taking his ship with him.

The day came at last. 'It is tonight,' I told him.

At once he became erect and the twinkle glowed in his eyes. He looked around his ship, had me straighten a gunwale, prop the prow yet higher and hand him the tiller.

'You have done well, Jon-a-thorn the Deliverer. Valhalla shall hear of your deeds and I shall welcome you there myself in good time.'

I left him until darkness had fallen. Father and Mother expected me to be with them at the bonfire. I slipped out early saying that I was helping with some friends, passing round food. They smiled, patted me on the head and did not comment on my bag in which I had concealed the matches and dry kindling.

The path was dark and I cursed that I had not thought to bring a torch. But the night was bright, the Milky Way a brushmark of a million million stars across the sky. There were some awful rustlings in the bushes on either side and an owl soared close over me, making me jump. I had left my trusty lieutenant behind, thinking to bid farewell to the Viking alone. Once I stopped, listening to my heart beating; there were no pursuing steps. I pressed on.

He was waiting. 'Jon-a-thorn, let it be now. I am ready.'

I built a small pyre of kindling beneath him, following his instructions. And set it alight.

'Farewell, Jon-a-thorn. You have done well. I shall reward you in Valhalla. Farewell.'

At first, there was no sign of flame apart from a close smoke that clung to the ground. The fire caught, blazing through the thornbush; I saw the Viking set alight, a glowing spectre that took human form. His legs were encased in great boots and there was a blue cloak thrown over one shoulder, held with a shining brooch. His beard flowed over his chest and on his head was a shining helmet with raised cow horns. The long sword hung at his side and a battleaxe was by him. I stood back, staring. He grasped the tiller, pushed it away from him and the ship rose glowing in the night, complete, boarding, mast and sail.

A shouting came up the hill. There was a crowd of torches flashing in the darkness and calls for water. The wilderness has been fired, save the wilderness.

I looked back to the ship. Kari the Viking looked down at me and smiled.

The ship lifted above the bushes, above the trees towards the sky, a Viking ship, a great bearded cloaked warrior at the stern steering his way to Valhalla. As it rose, the ship faded and became a ball of fire climbing towards the stars.

Men were beating down the flames on the ground; they had not spread. The fire was dying out already, leaving a blackened patch that would be grown over by spring. A hand fell on my shoulder. My Father. What was I doing up here, setting a fire in the wilderness? What was I thinking of? I looked up at him; there were no words that I could use, no way to tell him of the Viking and his journey home. I gazed up into the heavens; the ball of fire had become another star.

MURDURUR

"MURDURER" it said.

The paint was still dripping onto the road, like a scarlet necklace in the morning sunshine. And on the car, giant letters, rough capitals of different sizes. I stared at my car and wondered how, my God how did this happen?

There I was, lying in bed reading as I did every morning, the dog at my feet. There was this scraping sound just outside on the road; a can mostly empty it sounded like. I forgot about it until I had got up and breakfasted. And then went out wondering what it was. It was a beautiful morning, the early sun over the pub, birds twittering in the privet, dogs barking in the distance, and all the day before me. How I would spend it, in walking or reading or writing? No, it needed an activity, some way to fulfil this glorious day, especially as the autumn approached. I went down to my car. Yes, a drive to some good walking country.

I was stunned, gob-smacked.

In this village, of all places. Why? Why? What had I done to earn this? I couldn't imagine.

Rushing indoors, I got on the 'phone, called the police. Yes Officer, the paint is still wet – I can't touch anything? – But it will be dry, and I won't be able to wipe it off – So… so, if I wipe it off, there's no need for you to come out, and there's no investigation?! – OK, OK, I'll leave it. When can you come? I'm in all morning. – Tomorrow?! Tomorrow?! – Yes, but the crime is fresh, wet paint, and you going to wait – OK, OK, I'll wait! I'll wait! But meanwhile some idiot is going around spreading some false rumour – Hullo? Hullo?

I went down to the shop to pick up some breakfast. Pam served me, gave me a look, asked me if I was OK and asked after my wife; I said she had been struggling, she didn't ask why or what, I didn't like to go on about it, then some village man came in. I recognised him, didn't know his name, had seen him in the pub. He looked at me, asked Pam if she was serving me, said he was surprised that I was being served, I didn't need serving, didn't she know, he wasn't going to spell it out.

I didn't know what the hell he was talking about; asked him outright and he said if I didn't know, the police would certainly make that clear. And walked out; he hadn't even bought what he came in for. Pam looked at me, shrugged her shoulders.

Lunchtime and I was in the pub; got as far as the bar and Jem looked at me, a weary look, and said that he couldn't serve me, would be grateful if I left. I was stunned, asked why, I'd been going there for years and now I was a stranger; wasn't a matter of credit or anything, I always paid my way. He shrugged, said hadn't I heard? There was a muttering behind me, somebody said 'Who does he think he is, a criminal that's what he is;' couldn't have been about me. I walked out in a muse and felt destroyed, utterly alone in a place that I knew well and thought knew me well enough. Thought about bunging a stone through the window, but what would that serve? And I liked Jem.

I mean, my missus and I aren't exactly the sociable types; we don't party or do the church or anything, we tend to keep to ourselves but we are known, we do our bit here and there and we know people. Well, pretty much everybody; we are not a large village.

On the street, I bumped into Alf, asked him what was going

on. And do you know what? He looked at me and ducked past, almost at a run. Hoy, I said, cat got yer tongue, and he didn't even look back at me. Known him thirty years, man and boy. What the hell is going on? What have I done, or not done?

At home, I sat down to think. There must be some mistake; some stupid idea someone had uttered, probably in the pub. I'll go back to Jem; he'll tell me.

But he didn't. Just showed me the door.

And so it went on; everybody really, put me in Coventry, like the old school system. People would cross over or disappear into doorways or… well, anything to avoid eye contact. Some boys threw stones at me as I was walking down the street. And I had to go out of the village for everything, food, milk, papers, the lot. Driving the paint corrupted car; used to park in the corner of the supermarket car park and still get funny looks when I drove out.

And they never told me what it was all about.

When Alf passed me again, on the other side of the road, I shouted at him, Here Alf, what's the matter with you? Would you tell me what's going on? Why are you avoiding me, you b…? And he muttered something about well if I didn't know… and was gone. Fat lot of use.

My home became a sanctuary, free from abuse and accusation, and a prison, for I could go nowhere else near home. But had to drive away, some town or other where of course I was not known.

After a few days, the police did come round and I showed them the car but they were not so interested in it; I couldn't believe it. That was why I had called them. But they said they had received some information, wouldn't tell me who from, my wife had disappeared. Disappeared? I said. What were they talking about? What was this to do with the vandalism on my car? When were they going to pursue that, find the man who had ruined my car?

They said that of course they would pursue the business of vandalism and admitted that it was a crime. But could I reassure them about my wife?

'What about my wife?'

'Well, where is she?'

'Why, what business is it of yours?'

'Come come, that attitude doesn't do you any good.'

'What attitude? I report vandalism and you want to talk about my wife. I don't understand.'

'Perhaps you had better come down the station.'

'Why? What have I done? On what charge?'

'Please, could you just tell us where your wife is. I gather that she hasn't been seen in the village.'

'So who told you that? Come on, who is spreading rumours? They won't serve me in the pub or the shop. Nobody talks to me, and I have no idea why; nobody asked me about Sally. Who is making up evil rumours?'

'You know we can't tell you that! Please, it's simple enough, where is your wife? We are beginning to think that you know very well where she is and perhaps she is no longer alive.'

'You're accusing me of murder? Of murder?! My God, I report a case of vile vandalism and next I'm accused of murder. What has become of this country? There was a time when one could depend on the police, and now—'

'Enough. One more chance before we take you down the station.'

'But you have no proof and you would still do that?'

'In view of the information received and your reluctance to give us any sound evidence that she is still alive, I think we are justified in taking you in.'

There was a long silence; I was still furious about the rumours, my treatment in the village, the lack of progress on my car and now accusations of murder of all things. But I could see that nothing would be helped unless I told them about my poor wife.

'She's in London. An old friend is ill, and she is looking after her.'

'Can you provide evidence of that?'

'Don't you believe me? Isn't it bad enough that we have a crisis on our hands and the police want to arrest me for murder? My God, you want blood, don't you!'

'Please.'

'All right, all right, here is her phone number.'

'May I?' He picked up the phone, dialled and stood to attention for some minutes. 'No answer. Is this really the number?'

I looked at the phone; he had made a mistake. Idiot! I used the phone memory, heard it ringing and passed it back to him. Again, no answer.

'It's not looking very good, is it?' he said. I couldn't help it if they were out shopping or something.

'Do you have an address for this friend? And her name, if you would be so good.'

And they went away at last with the address and told me not to go anywhere. As though I could with all that was going on. And what about the car I said. Still covered with paint. I couldn't go anywhere. I sat at home and fumed; a car vandalised and an accusation of murder. Of all things.

Nothing changed; I would slink into my paint spattered car, drive to the supermarket, ignore the cocky comments, drive home and hide in my home.

And then it came to the village fete. Now, I had been helping out there for over ten years, always the same stall, White Elephant; you know, loads of off-loaded desirable objects (my wife called it junk!) rummaged through by a patient crowd, mostly women. There were always some characters that I recognised who used to give me a bit of chat. And there were the unusual purchases, like the woman who bought all the mugs, whatever the pattern on them; we never got rid of mugs before nor since. And the one who went through all this old jewellery and bought half of it; that was a big purchase for us.

So I thought, to hell with the lot of you, I'm not letting Jane down. When I went in, Jane gave me a smile, kitted me out with the change bag and told me where to stand.

But I'd only been there five minutes, and sold a couple of handbags I may say, when a covey of men came in, all villagers, all looking at me in a distinctly unfriendly way.

'Just clear off will you,' one of them said in a low tone. 'We wouldn't want to be creating a scene here would we, with all these visitors.'

'What business is it of yours if I'm helping out here? I don't see you helping out, just behaving like a bully boy.'

He didn't like this. 'Just get out of here quick, and there won't be any more trouble. Just now though you've got it coming, by all accounts. Now –'

'What do you mean, "got it coming"?' I said.

'Don't be smart with me. Do we have to eject you? Say you're drunk and cheeked a customer? Now, git!'

There was no mileage in carrying on. I went over to Jane and told her I had to leave; she gave me an old-fashioned look and I said I had a bad headache; didn't like to embarrass her going through it all.

And I still didn't see why the villagers couldn't come out with it. Just ask me.

At last, I received a brief phone call to say that the Metropolitan Police had interviewed my wife and ascertained that she had been detained in London all that time. What about my car, what about the village rumours, I asked. They said they were continuing investigations but didn't hold out much hope; there seemed to be a large number of villagers who might have been involved. Was I particularly unpopular?

What a question; it brought me down to earth. Perhaps it was time to move.

Two days later, Alf gave me a cheery Good Morning, and told me that Pam had been keeping the papers for me; did I want to pick them up? In the shop, she said that she had put aside some strawberries for me; she knew I liked them.

So I tried the garage, to get my car resprayed. Wilbur gave me a look, said I had been giving them the runaround; what do you mean, I said. Well, nobody had seen your missus for weeks and you had never said she was away. Anyway, there'll be no charge; it's taken care of. And to whom am I indebted, I said, not that anybody had asked me where she was. It doesn't matter now, he said. Best forget it if I was you.

Not that simple.

When I went to the pub, Jem pulled my pint as if nothing had happened. I didn't know what to say but down the end of the bar, two ol' boys were talking.

'It was wrong, really, wasn't it?'

'Yeah, shouldn't have gone so far. Why didn't somebody ask him?'

'What was Gabriel thinking of?'

'Oh, was it him?'

'Well, I don't know about that, but I heard him say…'

I couldn't hear anymore, but I gave Jem a hard look.

'All right,' he said. 'Old Gabriel, he said it wasn't right, your wife had disappeared. And somebody else said there's the perfect murder and why didn't the police take care of it. And there were no right thinking ol' boys in the bar that night and I guess it got out of hand.'

And that was that. People started nodding to me, bought me the odd drink, said they were sorry I was having such a hard time. Old Gabriel, I didn't see him for weeks; got the idea that Jem said he wasn't welcome. Well, I knew what that felt like. I found it hard for a while, couldn't trust people and preferred to walk alone. But that was nothing new.

AN AFTERNOON OUT

They thought it would be a nice thing, a kindness.

And now they are on the way to the coast. Barney had thought it would be a good thing to take Grandpa out for a ride, wouldn't it? He has always been good to them, money at Christmas, sweets when they were young and on one occasion, the Circus; it didn't come to town often. It gnaws at him, all this goodness and they hadn't done a sodding thing about it. So when he said why don't we take him out, it's a lovely day, we ain't on shift at the mill till six and blast we owe him some don't we, Jeff thought about it, wondered whether he can miss going down the pub, and agreed.

Grandpa looked surprised, looked at Barney's car, asked is there room for three and will it make it to the coast, and was not happy to be shoe-horned into the back seat; it's only a two door. But Barney told him, it's the best seat; and prayed that there were no stains from when he took Michelle out. They set off about two, making for the coast; reckoned it will take them about an hour to get there, if the car behaves.

Grandpa sat there, not saying too much, just looking out of the window. He didn't ask where they are going, when they will be back, how will they manage for fuel, or any of the things that Ma usually asks. He just sits there.

Are you all right there, Grandpa?

You shouldn't have put him in the back. Can't be so comfortable.

Ah, come on! You know that's front seat is shot. You're fine there, aren't you Grandpa?

He can't hear you, this ol' rattletrap. Why didn't we bring his car?

He doesn't have it anymore.

About half way there, just going through the forest, though they don't think it's much of a forest, more scrubland, better for keeping hogs on, Grandpa chirps up. Really, it's more of a groan and would they mind stopping, he has to go. Barney pulls off the road, a good firm springy piece of grass, with heather, gorse and a few stunted trees around, and the sun shining down. They extract Grandpa from the back seat and watch him as he staggers over to some trees and wrestles with his trousers. The car ticks in the heat, bonnet too hot to touch, the smell of hot metal.

There doesn't seem to be much happening.

After a while, he comes back; he doesn't look happy. His trousers are undone. Barney says to Jeff your turn and Jeff says no he had to do double last time and Grandpa stands there looking kind of lost just gazing into the distance and then his legs give way falling towards the car too hot to touch. Both lads jump and Barney holds him while Jeff does his flies. They put him back in the back seat; it isn't easy, Grandpa is not helping, he doesn't seem to be with it. He looks from one to the other and asks if they're going home now but Barney says, A bit of sea air will pick you up, it won't be long before we're there.

And it's not too long, not over half an hour. The town is crowded and they have to go round and around before they find a parking place. Engine stopped, they breath a sigh of relief; the air tastes better already and they look round to see Grandpa enjoying it.

He's asleep.

What? We've just got here.

Barney, look for yourself.

I am. He's sodding asleep, after all that.

What shall we do then?

I dunno. Don't like to leave him here alone; you know what he's like. We'll get back and find half the town wondering why we left him there alone, a poor ol' boy and us enjoying ourselves, just look at them they ought to be ashamed of themselves, and all that.

But what shall we do then?

Wake him up. That's best, kindest. We'll get him a cup of tea; that'll pick him up.

A few minutes pass.

Barney, I can't wake him up.

What do you mean, can't?

Look, I'm shaking him and he won't wake up.

Let me try. Here, where's his pulse?

I dunno; missed the Health and Safety talk at work.

I've heard you can do this thing with a mirror. Have you got one?

What the fuck do you think?

I wonder… can we get the rear view mirror off?… Yes, that's got it. Here, hold that in front of his mouth.

His mouth is closed.

Well his nose then.

A long pause. Barney is looking around; there are people getting out of cars, getting into cars, looking for cars. He doesn't want a scene; his mother is always going on about avoiding a scene, especially after Dad comes home after the pub a bit loose with his fists.

There's nothing.

What do you mean nothing? Come on Jeff, hold it up properly.

I was. You try.

A long pause. Barney holds the mirror, looks at it, puts it back under Grandpa's nose, looks at it, swears under his breath, and slowly, gently, puts his hand under Grandpa's coat. Grandpa is wearing a heavy coat and at least two jerseys and a shirt and goodness knows what else. Probably long johns.

Nothing. He pushes harder and Grandpa slumps sideways, his glasses falling to the floor, his mouth sagging open. There is no sound, no groan or sigh.

Jeff looks at Barney. He's dead, ain't he? He's bloody dead!

Barney doesn't answer. He is feeling Grandpa's wrists, his chest, his head. He shakes him, slowly like an annoying sister.

Jeff is bleating. What do we do now then? Bloody hell. He wants to get out, to get away, to escape the nightmare, have an icecream and be an innocent tripper. But he's not and he knows it.

What do we do now?

I don't know Jeff. Any suggestions, bro?

Er… why don't we take him to the hospital, say he's just fainted and scarper.

And when they say why have you brought a dead man here and call the police, what are you going to do then?

What do you mean?

Come on Jeff. How do you think the coppers are going to think when two boys turn up with a dead man and say he's just fainted? I don't want to be there, I'm telling you. Not after that time I spent in the cells after you took that tractor and drove into Cable's shop window.

Well… are you saying… we have to get rid of the body? You can't be serious, how the hell do we do that?

I think… yes. We'll have an accident. Put him in his wheelchair and push him off the pier. So it looks as if he's drowned.

33

My, you're quick this afternoon, ain't yer?

They pull the unresisting Grandpa out of the car; they have to stop twice when there are people around. One woman says your old man doesn't look too well and Barney says that they are just getting him to the pier for a shot of sea air. After a while, Grandpa is in the wheelchair, his head propped up; he looks as if he is asleep. Jeff pushes the chair, Barney walking casually beside, chatting to Grandpa, what a lovely day, did you see the seagull, it's a grand view isn't it, look at these old buildings, no thanks, I won't have an icecream just now, maybe after we've been on the pier.

On the pier, the breeze is strong. They stop to tuck up Grandpa, ask him to tell them if he is cold and walk to the far end. There is a gate, for access to boats or something. Barney looks around, Jeff hangs back.

Go on then, open it.

Jeff starts to open the gate. A fierce voice calls out. What do you think you're doing, lad? That's dangerous. Leave it alone.

Barney turns the chair towards the voice; it is a man in some uniform, striding towards them. He explains, he only wanted to see the sea, without all these railings in the way.

Then take him on the front. The pier is not for opening railings, or diving or swimming. What would we do if there were an accident?

Barney smiles, thanks the man and pushes the wheelchair back towards land.

Why did you thank him? Officious bastard!

Do you want us to be remembered, you idiot?

Jeff shuts up. After a while, he says, What are we going to do then? Just leave him here?

Somebody will see us. The forest; plenty of hiding places.

They return to the car. The day is cooler. The car is no longer hot as they lift Grandpa out of his chair and into the car. Halfway through this manoeuvre, there is a loud fart. Jeff jumps, almost drops Grandpa. He's alive! He's alive!

Don't be a stupid sod. It's just air escaping.

How do you know that?

Come on. Let's get out of here.

In the car, Barney looks at Jeff. Jeff is weeping silently, tears streaking his cheeks, a look both appalled and defeated.

Let's go to the police. Please Barney.

The forest. It will be all right, bro. Hang in there.

Jeff is silent as Barney drives out of town, back down the road to the forest. The sky is getting darker, heavy clouds covering the afternoon sun. They pull off where they stopped before. Jeff jumps out and walks away into the trees.

Come on, I can't do it alone, Jeff.

I'm just having a pee.

Barney waits, looking into the trees, thinking of anything but what they have to do soon. Jeff wanders back; he looks a little better. They open the car door. A police car pulls in beside them. An officer gets out, stretching. Lovely day. You on the way somewhere nice?

Been to the seaside, on the way home. Barney is leaning against the car, between the officer and Grandpa.

Jeff gulps and goes to the other side of the car. The officer notices his reaction; it's nothing new. He knows that country boys don't like the rozzers. But he strolls round the car; it looks a bit rough.

You seem to be missing your rear-view mirror. You realise that it is an offence to drive without a rear-view mirror?

I'm sorry, Officer. It came off in my hand when I was reversing in the carpark; I mean I was adjusting it before reversing.

Well, can you fix it back now?

I don't know.

Here, can I help?

No, no. I'll try. He dives into the car, retrieves the mirror from the floor of the back seat and studies the fixing on the front window. Jeff is frozen the other side of the car, staring at the Officer in a daze.

Your old man there. He doesn't look too well.

Barney wiggles his way out of the car, stands looking at Grandpa. We've just taken him to the seaside. I think it's tired him out. We are taking him home.

Well, I think you should be on your way. He doesn't look too good at all.

He's only asleep, but yes Officer, that would be a good idea.

And get your rear-view mirror fixed, won't you?

The Officer leans back against his car while Barney reverses and drives off.

What do we do now? Jeff is bleating again.

Not much. We are at work in half an hour.

But... you mean... he just stays in the car?

You have a better idea? Barney knows that the policeman will have taken their number; he doesn't mention it to Jeff.

They drive into the evening. The light is fading fast. It is starting to rain.

THE DAY THE WIND CAME TO
THE VILLAGE

This is the Weather Forecast. There is a deep low over the Irish Sea moving rapidly East. Storm force winds are forecast, including the possibility of damage to trees and buildings.

The pub. A usual evening? But men are crowded in. Shut the door, shut the door! They huddle around the bar. Cor, that wind is fierce! I don't fancy working up a roof tomorrow. What do you mean Jack? I reckon you'll have more roof work than you can handle in a month of Sundays. Bert hiccups, turns. Well, I must be getting back to the missus. Tightens the scarf around his neck, buttons up tight, looks around the other ol boys. Reckon I'll be on my way, then. He pauses, until the barman at least sees him, wishes him a good evening; Bert glances at the huddled backs and slips out the door. There is a pantile, been loose for ages; nobody thought to do anything about it. It was high up on the roof, a bugger to get to, it was left. And now it leaves; the wind lifts it, as though inviting it to dance, and it floats down the roof, skimming daintily over pantile and gutter, to glide groundwards. Bert knows nothing when struck on the back of his head and spreads his length on the pavement with a halo of red clay pantile particles. And Bert's missus knows nothing as she waits the night through, fretful, not daring to leave the safety of the home.

Light is vanquished. It is long after sunset and the few street lights have given up the ghost. The electricity cables blew sideways in exaggerated loops before tearing themselves free to lash the poles, the hedgerows, the roads in a frenzy of despair. Telephone cables failed soon after, whipping like streamers over the roofs. Darkness creeps around the streets, invading unlit homes, shops and bus shelter, where a few young people have gathered to enjoy the thrill. Until the roof disappears on its own voyage, not to be seen for a month or more, lodged in a copse a mile distant. Trees struggle to stand, shedding limbs and leaves. But it is a useless opposition and great trunks collapse onto roads and roofs, to lie inert until reached by chain-saws.

And the noise. A moan at tea-time has grown to a shriek, a demon that winds its way around every corner, through old windows, under thresholds, down chimneys. A momentary lull is filled with the shriek of horses, stabled and desperate, panicking, beyond reason or control. And nearby a baby cries on and on, resisting the comfort of a mother's arms, a call that wrenches at any parent's heart.

The air is solid, blasts that weigh more than a person can stand, and filled with rubbish, the content of bins and waste that clatters along the roads, fills up narrow alleys, winds itself around the war memorial, which stands indomitable to the end. The Church looks down on the village as it has done for a thousand years; it is confident that it has seen worse but slates fly from the Chancel and the East window hastens its overdue repair by collapsing entirely. And the bells clang unharmoniously, rocking without control; the Tower captain struggles alone to still their discord.

And what of the people of this small village? There is no person to be seen abroad. The shop-keeper has retired to bed early; he doesn't want to think of his roof and chimney overhead. His wife has clung to him and now they are joined by the two weeping children who climb under the covers, cling to the only safety they know. The noise around them increases but it will not be until morning that they see that the roof is stripped bare, their loft a mound of tiles, branches, litter and dead birds. In her own little house, Emily has remained downstairs. She has been blind since young, a workplace accident, and she has learnt to recognise sounds. She hears the falling tiles, the child crying, the shrieks of the horses, but she has never heard the wind speak as it does now. She covers her ears and sits very still; she shakes a little but will not call for help. Not that it would be heard.

Time moves on. The men have remained in the pub, slumped on benches, chairs and floor, not daring to open the door to the street. The shop-keeper and family are still in bed, and Emily remains sitting downstairs. But the strain of the wind is taking its toll. The legs of the ancient water tower buckle slowly, gracefully like a horse lying down, and tip the contents down the street, an uncalled-for flood that washes the litter away, gathers the remnants of the bus shelter and floods the houses in the main street, washing through parlour and kitchen to seep under back doors, floating furniture and shoes in an ungainly dance.

The strain is taking its toll. The shrieking wind finds young Jack, a difficult birth and a difficult child. He has resisted efforts of his patient mother to be calm, to sit and eat. He is unnerved by the darkness, pierced only by a small torch. He stands in a corner and mouths words unknown and begins to scream; the wind and he make an awful chorus. Make it go away, make it go away! He cannot contain himself; he must conquer this demon that has insinuated itself through door and window and winds itself inside his head; he twists and turns, folds himself up in knots. Grabs the bread knife, waves it at the ceiling; his mother cries out, reaches for it, feels it enter her chest, collapses on the floor, while Jack stands over her, screaming… screaming…

WHAT WE KNEW

They tell it orl wrong.

Leastways thats the way ut seem lookin at ut orl these months later now. The dust as settled n water passed under the bridge n any case most people ave forgot ut n moved onter next thing, Charley's three-legged dawg. But that's no part o this story.

Tho yer niver knew the way things appen in this village, one thing followin onter tother, no connection, n then ut orl blew up n things like some woife leavin er man fer the milkman or builder or whatever are loike a ripple in the pool o village history reflectin so many things that went afore. This one goo a whole lot deeper. So deep you don't ever see ut proper n no one but no one ever come up with the same tale, seein as how they orl see it different as you do when lookin inter deep water. Its orl distorted, aint it?

So Oi'll get ter ut.

Yer need ter under stand the way people are ere, how they git on n live, no upsettin the apple cart, not that its too easy to upset apple cart n it dont git upset more thn twice or once a year. Not that you ear these things without walkin out late n dawdlin by winders that might not be toight shut, n may leak a few ome secrets that arght to ave stayed indoors. But theres a place that's free to orl, exceptin o course young uns who are banned but special occasions n in any case are in bed... or meant ter be.

Whativer they doin is no business of ours, Oi would loike ter think.

The pub.

Oi were there one evenin, not late cos Oi don care ter be late Oi ave ter be up Farm seven oclock. Any case by then pub is busy n most talk is off beam distorted by good ale that pick up a mans mind n give ut a shake but don't set ut down the way ut were but off n the world take on different look kind o rosy tho on occasion can turn topsy-turvy with a quick fight in the rood, blooded noses findin the way ome a scoldin from house-wife whativer the roights of ut. So Oi were there early.

There aint more thn arf a dozen of us. Oi knew em orl. In any case, they... were sittin apart. Down opposite ends the bar.

Now... yer don't need me to tell yer who they is. Everbody know em, chat to em loike they a couple sittin together tho everbody knew she's married but er ol man don't care for the pub an e's married too we see is woman sometime she don't seem concerned, its orl juss chat n maybe a bit o flirtin n that's as far as it goo as far as we are concerned. Uts no big deal... they old friends goo way back... mebbe there were more to ut some long toime agoo but ut would be water long run under bridge n we orl grew a lot older n don't spend too much toime draggin up the past not loike the good ol bors sittin under the tree on Green dreamin o the last war when they were young n way out o ties o home n misbehaving with no recall. An orl the toime forgettin that most of their years ave bin spent in the village earnin a onest penny. Or otherwoise.

But they were sittin apart one either end o the bar, couldn't ave bin further apart – apart that is from not bein at the pub at orl. Which is unthinkable.

So there you ave ut, sumfin ad appened n there were words startin loike flames runnin through stubble when uts fired n

42

no one person seem ter know the truth of ut. Mebbe some say mebbe... he or she step art the bounds of their self-appointed decorum, their sittin at the pub juss friends avin a sociable drink n mixin loike everbody ter jaw n swop rumours. Mebbe. An we would niver know bottom of ut. Unless some person ear somefin, see somefin n could not keep it under their at. Somebody must ave seen or heard somefin, the village aint big enough ter keep such a thing quiet.

Mebbe, some ol bor did say, it weren't they at orl but a usband or wife which got the wrong idea n felt cuckolded orl of a sudden, goodness knows why – arter orl this toime – n knew or tharght they knew what people would say n ad words, words that would split any friends loike lightnin cleaving an oak. An what could anyone say to this usband an wife? That it weren't true, whativer it were? An there were nobody could say what ut were in any case, we was orl lost n it weren't roight but nuffin could bring em togither agin, so ut seemed.

So that's when we begin ter believe it were somebody else all togither who ad said somefin dirty, so foul ut polluted the air o the bar, left the two reelin, some bit o history real or pretend dragged up n we wonder why old Ted behind the bar don't know but he play deaf so much we orl believe he really cant hear wot is happenin, its not as if it's the busiest pub in the county. An that somebody must be out of the village, not one of us could ave soiled the friendly stale air of the bar that we orl look on as second ome.

An thats when we don't know wot ter do, where ter goo, how ter think even, those who loike ter think bout things n the talk dried loike the Mere in summer. Did one sit between or not was a particular difficult question we chewed over some wonderin head in air some gazin out of window us orl standin there though by rights by custom by everlasting abit we should ave bin sittin cos how could yer sink a few points n remain standin around loike a spare prick at a weddin. Now nobody not a single one would talk cos ter talk would seem ter talk bout ut even if yer didn't talk bout ut at orl would seem ter be avoidin ut n if yer did talk bout ut then ut would seem takin one side or tother or disapproving when orl the time that was familiar that was village. An evenin without talkin is impossible, worse thn a days work without seein a soul cos then yer ave the work ter git on with no excuse ter be standin around whether yer jawin or not. We boys stood bout eads hung, ardly drinkin mostly silent.

An wot of the couple? If yer call em a couple n that's pushin ut.

E sat wiv is ead down. There were a point in front o him not ardly touched n he seemed ter be examinin the beer mat so ard niver tharght e ad ut in him. Hard ter say if e were feelin good or bad or juss allowin toime ter pass, as e did often lettin petty storms break over him, thunder n lightin around is ead n e would smile n the sunshine would pierce the clouds orl would come ter nothin e was lucky that way.

An she? A dark one, she.

There were those wondered whoy she got married at orl, seein as how she didn't seem the housewife kind, no child n a usband who walks is own path. Always busy rarely seen in pub n worked away most o the toime. An she were a deep sort not the koind ter offer any information of her upbringin er family that sort o thing, n if anybody asked, usually a stranger or mebbe a bloke in is cups, she would stare n cough n turn away, we orl knew ut wasn't somefin ter talk bout. So she was oo she was n that's how it were with us n ut ad no call ter goo further.

Oi did wonder myself a quiet night when the pub would be mostly empty cept the two o them togither at the bar holdin court as they did buyin drinks n acceptin them too n always

44

an argument bout this n that, big topics n little, why Jerry ad painted is front door a new colour when you knew ut ad always but always goin back foriver bin the one colour so wot brarght ut on ter bring im ter a new colour n we couldn't believe that ut were the missus she don't ave no opinion that we ever eard cept if the flowers were roight up Church on Sunday n when I mean roight Oi couldn't tell yer wot she meant but she knew wot she meant even if ut made no sense ter the rest of us.

Yeah, they were a great couple fer holdin the pub in their ands makin sure orl of us were happy n drinkin together if you see wot Oi mean n lettin nobody not even Frank sit there in a mope as though the weight o the world was on is shoulders n not carin fer a word with the rest of us. E wouldn't be left ter mope, not Frank. Miserable ol bugger but it made no difference no call when ut came ter a night at pub, it were a question o buck up or bugger off not that ut applied orl the time, yer wouldn't want ter git the idea that we didn't care fer some bugger wot lost is dog, a wife or a prize cow whatever.

Door opened, with a bang.

It weren't as if the room went silent it were pretty quiet already us juss standin around not knowin where ter put our lookin. But that door weren't in the abit o bangin. It were an ol one pretty eavy n three good hinges too with a block ut stopped aginst n if ut ad any problems ut were you couldn't be sure it were shut toight on a windy noight, there would be a call from bar ter shut the door toight n damn quick bout ut too.

We wheeled bout. Seein as how we were all standin it weren't ard but ut made an impression more thn if we were juss turnin our eads n there was some shuflin n bargin ter see wot the bangin wos bout.

She wus standin there, the wife, is wife. But it don't look as if the floor can hold er down, more loike a stockpot comin

45

ter boil n everthin roises ter top, meat n bones n froth n yer wonder can it orl be contained. She were leanin forward n a sort of bubblin squeakin sound were coming out of her n her dressed in er housecoat n an old pair o shoes hair in curlers wot a soight. There weren't a single one of us dared ter say a word or offer a hand. There were a feelin among us orl Oi don't doubt that it were an invasion of our place, the second home, the place where we don't spect ter be auled over the coals or dragged omewards unless tother arf as bin summoned by Ted cos the culprit were incapable. An it were her temper we could see, a sudden summer thunderstorm cutting inter the quiet that hung over the bar. What with the trouble we ad ad that evening cos it were a trouble with them sittin apart quite apart from the trouble they moight be avin that we could only guess at, not aving the sloightest idea of where it orl started or why or what or when. An now this.

An then Frank went n cocked ut up silly ol bugger thinkin would be nice – nice I beg yer – if we made her welcome, sat er down gave er a drink n listen to er tale o woe n e gits as far as clearin a chair n table n callin on Ted ter git er vodka or Coca-Cola or whatever. But Ted has a mood on, or mebbe e was particler deaf that night n e juss stand there lookin surproised as if is ol mother as got up out er grave. E niver seen such a thing in pub.

An the next moment she wheel on Frank n give im a few tart words ard ter hear but somefin bout mindin is own bloody business n keepin is miserable scrawny neck out of ut n Frank look as if is coat ad swallow im up n e gave a sort o look at us huggin imself ter imself n slip out the door no cheery bye to us or Ted as were the way of ut.

But e ad put cat among the pigeons cos she look at each of us real slow one by one n it weren't no look that yer wanted ter git when you ad done a long days work n gone ter pub for a quiet time a little drink good company.

An then she open er mouth. At first a raspin gaspin sound follered by a flow o words loike a grain bin fillin slow at first n then a rush that wont stop but wait until orl is gone.

What ad we bin adoin not tellin er bout er man n she the last ter hear? An who did we think we were, called ourselves friends, villagers n left an ugly story ter reach er kitchen door loike the cat draggin itself in arter a dirty noight out. An that's ow we arght ter feel, a load o dirty ol cats that crawl through the night spreadin filth on honest doorstep. She pick us out, one by one, with a choice word or dozen n left no one of us feelin clean or clear of er spite. An we still don't ave a smidgin of idea wot it were orl bout but she weren't avin no questions nor talkin back she juss barrel over us orl leavin a kind o stunned silence when it were over.

Wa'al, we were stunned orl roight. An don't spect wot follered.

Her ol man ad sat there orl the time lookin a little sad but not too upset as tho e ad bin expectin ut fer some time tho we ad no warnin. E don't shift from is stool merely turnin round n gazin at er loike she were an unusual exhibit at the Show that weren't dangerous.

But the woman, is drinkin companion, she oo we orl admired n yet were not a little fearful cos er silences not that she don't join in orl the usual chat n laugh n stories, she stand up n goo up ter this poor woman n take er ands n we orl wait fer an explosion sure ter come n were amazed when she – that's the housewife – juss stop loike er lectricity cut orf n stare at she n collapse in tears but we cant tell whether they is tears of anger or fear or barrassment n she – our drinkin companion – take er by the arm n goo out the door.

47

Yer could ave eard a bar mat fall.

We look at each other n at first ut were orl silent no word no call fer drink. Until e, the one oo started it orl we reckoned but didn't know at orl, said that ut were getting late n did one want a drink n we orl goo no rush to the bar ter git orders in n Ted look appy or as appy as e ever look n we start chattin bout anything that come ter mind cept matters concernin is wife or she. An we were so relieved n appy ter be talkin agin we don't notice e slip out juss gorn not a word n it take us a while ter notice ut n there were a brief bit o quiet lookin round n avoidin each others eyes n then we goo back ter talkin n drinkin.

An that were the end of ut really. Cos the next noight or mebbe a few noights arter they were back at the bar together holdin court as always n we fell inter ol pattern n don't loike ter ask or pry but leave things as they were. Tho Oi bet there are some who, when uts quiet perhaps middle o night, do wonder the truth of ut.

THE PIANIST

A t night, when the hish of tyres on the Turnpike is absent and the dogs have ceased barking and the wind has dropped, the sound of a piano playing weaves a way through the village houses, faint but undeniable.

The boy walked the dog. It was late, dark with a clear sky, and he stayed within the village, up lane and down street. Back of the Church, he heard the piano, and stopped. From what quarter did the sound come? From which walls did he hear the notes? He turned his head each way, an auditory detector, without enlightenment. He walked on. It became louder; he knew it; a Chopin Prelude, played like a lament. He hummed the tune, a distant look in his eyes. And realised; not a Prelude, but a Nocturne, No.2, E flat major. He had heard it many times and wondered when he might play it.

At the corner of the road rose the piers of a gateway, brick inset with armorial devices and capped with griffins, leering at outsiders. He paused; the dog pulled him on. A gate stood part open, grounded on gravel. Slipping through, he stepped slowly over the drive. Ground ivy, weeds and dead leaves held the stones tight; no tell-tale warning crunch.

The house loomed up in the dark, buttresses, finials, turrets, churchlike windows. He crept up to the nearest and brushed the ivy tendrils aside. He could see a faint figure, moving to the music in darkness. He raised his arm and swept the glass; dead ivy leaves, cobwebs, dust and dirt. The glass cleared.

A chiascuro of a black concert grand, moonlight reflections on the top, raised to embellish the sound. Chips of light in an unlit chandelier. White ivories in the keyboard. Deep darkness all around, apart from a low lamp near the piano. At which sat a figure draped in black, long white hair falling to the waist. The music changed, a faster piece he did not know. And then a rag played at full speed, the rhythms racing round the room, bursting to escape. The boy was paralysed, his mouth dropped open. His hand rested on the glass, as though to push through it, to feel the beat. He stood there, staring, aware of his mind opening, a force thrust through that revolved and revealed unknown lands.

The church clock struck the hour. He turned, striking the glass, a minute ping. The music stopped. For a moment, he was held in the pianist's stare and then he turned and ran out of the gate, down the road, away, the dog dragging at his heels.

That was the first time.

The second time was little different.

The third time, a stormy night with a wind that excited the dog, rapped branches against windows and built up drifts of early leaves, he stood again at that window. A note propped within: COME IN. Large capitals, shaky black lines. He stepped back, stung by the immediacy; he was being spoken to, trusted by a stranger. And not seeing barriers put up, common with a boy, a protecting of private proprieties.

Thought for a moment. And went to the door. Pushing it open, he peered into the dark hall, sensed a tall space with black stained boards that disappeared into unknown depths. Doors, a large lampshade, a dado rail, an old-fashioned umbrella stand, full. A little light seeping through the door on the left, with a

50

trickle of notes, a disconnected rag, slow time. He stood in the doorway; the sound stopped.

There was a snort, and she, for it was a woman, started to play a nursery rhyme, Jack and Jill, single notes dropping into the dark, that increased in speed, developed harmony, a beating base, a treble that broke into syncopation, variation upon variation that wound around the room, ribbons of smoke, invisible in the dark but as powerful as electrical currents. Wound around the boy, tickling his ears, astounding his mind. His mouth dropped open, a gasp. Even the dog stood still in awe.

A laugh. 'Are you coming in, boy?' A low husky voice, all gin and cigarettes.

He could say nothing, his throat grabbed him tight, his heart beat a sudden sforzando.

'Come and sit here.'

The boy looped the dog lead over the door handle, and was pulled to the voice at the piano. As he approached the curve in the grand, she turned to look towards the window. He stopped mid step.

The left side of her face was a morass of ridges, pits, bulges, and glowing orbs that pulled the eye down in a cruel distortion. The boy fled, taking the dog, through the door, a crunching rush to the gateway, gone.

For sometime in his young life, perhaps less than a week, he walked different roads and alleys and though he heard the siren's call, he turned away, seeking peace. Seeking to eviscerate the image of an ogre from his mind. He spoke to his mother, gave no details but asked about wounds, natural deformities, and the failings of old age; his grandparents did not look like ogres.

He found his way back. Without the dog. Stood at the window until she looked at him, raised a hand in welcome. He did not hesitate at the curve of the grand but stood beside her, looking down at the right side of her face, the keyboard, the music strewn over the stand, and smiled.

'Do you play?' The same husky voice.

He was silent; did he play as she did? Could he claim to be a pianist? What if she asked him to play? It was a dreadful mistake, he should not be here. He turned away from her.

'What brought you here? Something attracted you, nobody else has been here.' She was quiet, patient, a sad voice.

'The music,' he found his voice. 'I hear it, and I know it. Some of it. And I have to…'

'Sit here, next to me.' A simple command, no space for anything else.

He obeyed, and was aware of the warmth of her body, the rub of her silken gown, a slight musky scent. And her proximity; he had never sat next to a strange woman before, not even in Chapel. Not even with his school teacher or a relative.

'You knew some of the pieces?'

'Yes. There was a Chopin Nocturne, and then… I don't know the names, but I have heard them.'

'And do you play at all?'

How could he tell her of his father instructing him at the upright at home, hymns and carols, Chapel music, also the odd nursery rhyme? In his room, he would listen to his radio, BBC 3, concerts of music that he never heard before. She was waiting.

'I… er… a little. But only church music.'

'Like Bach?'

'No… er… just hymns and things.'

'And you would like to play more things, perhaps?' She was smiling at him. 'Where shall we start? I know.'

'At home, we always start with scales and arpeggios. Major keys first.'

'So boring! But necessary. I think you need a little light refreshment.' She tapped out Jack and Jill. 'Now you.'

He paused. 'What key?'

'Whatever you like.'

He chose C major, the easiest, and started on the tune. She came in with a harmonising bass, chords and a continuo at the same time. The second verse he played faster, with confidence, until suddenly she changed key, a minor key that threw him, for a second, before he continued, listening to what she was playing. She broke rhythm, syncopating, a jazz riff or two. All in the bass part of the piano.

'Wow. Where do you get that from?' He laughed, amazed, staring at the keys as though they could tell tales, reveal the magic that she had wound around his simple tune.

'Now,' she said. 'I'll play the tune.' And she started in a totally unfamiliar key, a minor key with strange harmonics.

He froze.

'Cat got your tongue?'

'What key is that? I don't know that key.'

'D flat minor. Play the scale and arpeggios.'

He started, a fumbling run full of mistakes.

'Stop. You're hurting my ears. Hum it to me.' And she played the key note; without difficulty, he sang the scale, picked out the arpeggios. And played them. She started again, single notes dropping into the air; he listened for half a verse, and dropped chords into the tune, pushing his experience beyond anything he had ever done. Broke the timing, pulled it back, stared at his hands as though they did not belong to him. He had never heard jazz, didn't understand what she had done, but it sounded right. Just right.

After another nursery rhyme, she pulled a piece of Bach from the stand. 'You read music, right?'

'Some.'

'Then let's pick at this. Key?'

He told her, and started to play, careful chords linked with sighs and grunts as he reformed his hands over the keyboard.

'What hard work you make of it! Now, forget the base line, play the top.'

She played the bass line, as he struggled through the top, emerging at the end with a grin.

'Again, and to time.'

Again, and almost to time, a hesitation when a note was unexpected. And then he started to put in the bass line.

'It's all timing. Or mathematics, the spacing and key changes.'

Time passed, and he felt weary. Exhausted from his experiences, so much to learn. He slid off the stool, thanked her, and started for the door.

'Shall I see you again?'

He spun round. 'Yes… er… yes please.'

'Perhaps we shall make a pianist of you. Listen to music; listen as much as you can. Absorb it, analyse it, break down the chords, note the key changes. And, above all, listen to the mood, the emotion; what is the composer saying? Bye bye.' And she turned back to the keyboard, a rapid hard piece. He did not know it.

He did not tell his parents. There was something about his secret that was golden and it would tarnish with exposure. And his father, the Minister at the Chapel, would be shocked, even hurt; haven't I taught you all these years, he would say. What do you want another teacher for? And he might even have hard things to say about the woman, her house and her dark seclusion. But the boy returned to her, almost on a daily basis, sometimes with the dog, sometimes without.

For years.

She refused to be called a teacher; she told him that she wanted to introduce him to things to explore, she wanted to take him by the hand and give him the confidence to go to new places; the piano will never punish you, she told him. It will help you to live; the only punishment comes from within you. And she suggested composers and musicians to listen to, modern and old, classical and jazz. And, but rarely, pop music.

One day, he was emerging from the gateway on a bright afternoon when a man from the village was passing.

'Ah, bor, so… 'ave you discovered the secret?'

He frowned. What secret? She was a pianist. What else?

'Heh, heh! You don't know what you be getting inter there, do yer?'

He looked away at the Church; it was all nonsense, she was his teacher, even if she would not accept the title.

'Yer never wondered why 'er face got all burned up, then?'

'No.' He had wondered, but would ask her nothing; it was her secret.

'Arr, it was a sad thing. She had a partner, yer see, a singer, and they was famous, singing all over the world, people said. But 'e was a difficult cuss, and used ter drink. Cor, I remember 'im down the pub, 'e was a riot. Got thrown out so many times I reckon Jem only let 'im in 'cos 'e had money.' He paused, looked down. 'Reckon 'e was afraid ter lose 'is voice or summat.'

'She was an accompanist?'

'If that what yer call it. Anyroad, by all accounts, and I was only told meself, they had a fight, a stinking rowdy fight that could be heard all over the village. Not that I heard it meself.'

'Where is he now?'

'Oo, e's gone. Long since. And I'm not surprised. They say

the police couldn't find 'im, but I reckon she let 'im go and didn't tell 'em.'

'But her face?'

'Arr, yes. What I heard, 'e picked up this oil lamp, and threw it at 'er. Broke all over 'er, 'er dress caught fire, 'er face caught it. And they say 'e didn't wait to help 'er, didn't wait to call the fire brigade. Just disappeared, like that. Reckon she's bin there ever since. Waal, must be gettin' along.' And he wandered off up the road, humming a tune, kicking at clods of mud.

The boy stopped still. It was dreadful, her face, her past. It rolled over him like a horror story, partly unbelievable and partly too true. What did it mean? What should he do? What could he do?

Nothing; nothing that entered his mind, still shocked by adult behaviour that had been beyond any experience. His own parents were always polite to each other; he had once found his mother weeping in the kitchen, but she said she had something in her eye. He thought of never returning, lest he show some sympathy that would curdle their relationship.

And what was that relationship? She is teaching me so much; how do I pay for that? Perhaps, this is what she wants, to teach me, as she cannot go out there, play for audiences. But, how do I go on?

He returned, but his playing tripped over the slightest difficulty, the timing was erratic, the tone flat.

'Do you want to tell me? What is interfering with your music? Why you can't play today?'

He stared at her; tears started to form, to run freely, dropping on the keyboard; he bent his head, mouthing unspoken words.

'Has you father told you not to come here? And stop ruining the keys like that, will you.' She was abrupt. Oh God, she thought, was this the time to get rid of the boy? Not such a boy I suppose; how old is he? Eighteen? He'll be leaving home anyway, I suppose, and that will be that. Anyway, he's being tiresome.

'No, no… it's not that. Not that at all. I can't say, but –'

'Some girl, I assume. You've been jilted! Get over it; it happens to everybody.'

'To you too?' He was shouting, out of control.

'Of course to me… oh, oh, I see now. You've been listening to tales.'

He screwed up his face, looked away.

She sighed, looked away. 'You'd better go. We'll do nothing useful today. Go on, get out.'

He stood, clutching his music case. 'Is it true?'

She gazed out of the window, showing her ravaged face. Do I have to tell him, she thought. Do I have to go through that again? Perhaps I should tease him.

'What do you think of it?'

'It's awful. Can't you do something about it?'

'Perhaps I don't want to do anything about it. But that's none of your business.'

He walked to the door.

'Shall I see you tomorrow?' she called.

He turned. 'How can I pay you? All these years and I have never paid you.'

'And did you think I wanted pay?' She spat with force. My God, after all this time, and all he can mention is money. She saw him reel. How could she talk to him except as a naughty boy? But then what happened? A look came over his face, he changed, stood up; something had come over him after all.

He walked back to the piano. 'Where are we going, then?'

She stood, walked to the window, gazing out at the afternoon sun. This was a change; the sun was shining after an ugly storm. A fresh beginning. 'That is up to you.'

'But… I don't know what I can do.' The boy again. Time he grew up.

She looked at him, her eyes adjusting to a thought that she could take him there, there where she had been, summing him up. What was she doing? Was he worth it? That would be a matter of time, but it looked promising.

'You're leaving school soon?'

'Yes.'

'And then what?'

'I… I haven't decided. My schoolwork is not very good; they say… oh I dunno, something about concentration, or—'

'Why not continue here?'

He stared at her. What would his father say? What would he do for a job?

His father found him a job working at a local bank; long hours in which he waited impatiently for the end of the day, the chance to return to the piano. His parents had accepted his devotion to the instrument, while not understanding the demands and time needed to progress.

Every weekend and almost every evening he returned to the house. There was no possibility of putting in practice at home, and all his playing was at the grand piano, the notes swelling and filling the room. In daylight, he saw that the room was bare, apart from the piano, the stool and the little light. An excellent sounding board.

For years they worked. It was rare for her to share the stool with him; she demanded that he own the whole keyboard, use the full range of eighty notes. She had brought in a chair that she set to one side, occasionally at his elbow, more often the other side of the room. But she could rise and stand behind him, handling his back, his arms, his neck.

'You must play with your body. No… no, don't sway around

like a puppet. But feel the emotion; what is the composer saying, and then what are you saying—'

'Me?'

'Yes, you. Here we have a pattern of marks on paper, a language that we use to produce music. But what interpretation are you making of these marks? Have you not listened to different pianists and their different playing of familiar pieces? Who is the artist, at the concert? The composer or the performer?'

'We have directions on the music, forte and so on—'

'Aah! Come on. You have heard more than that; listen and learn. Come with me.'

She took him into another room. A sittingroom; it looked scarcely used. There were two large speakers, and amplifier, record deck. She took out two records, dusted them carefully, and played the second Nocturne twice, different pianists.

'Now you hear it.'

He smiled at the new knowledge, a knowledge that he had been hearing the varied interpretations without noticing, focusing on the notes alone.

He worked. He achieved all the Bach Well Tempered Clavier pieces, Chopin, Mazurski, Scott Joplin, a wide range of piano pieces, a wide cultural field. And concertos, accompanying records. She sent him to piano competitions; some he won, some he did not. She sent him to concerts, occasionally in London, paying his way, with instructions to listen, make notes, but above all, to listen; the keys, the themes, the way that the piece interweaved the themes round changing keys, what the players had to say. On his holidays, she sent him to other teachers, to learn techniques that she could not supply. She seemed to know pianists all over the country, who was a good teacher, who was a good performer. She sent him to play at concerts, to get experience at being on stage; at first, he was terrified, almost shaking, his hands cramped. But he went on, and played. And received invitations to play elsewhere. His father never came, though his mother did, a few times; she said she did not understand it. His teacher never came, and he never saw her leave her house.

The day came when a major piano competition was announced, a national event, in London.

'I'm not ready. What will they ask for?'

'Scales, arpeggios, sight-reading, a prepared piece. Or two.'

'The sight reading. I don't know; it's so much.'

'But no more than you have done all these years. You are feeling the notes now. It's not just a question of technique; they will be expecting that of everyone. But it's the heart and the head, to float and feel the notes before you play them, translate from your head to the audience. You must give them what they want. And then a bit more.'

It was in London, the Wigmore Hall; he had been there for concerts. He sat at the piano on the platform, sure that he could go nowhere, that his head and his hands were not communicating. And then he looked along the piano, and saw his teacher, sitting in her usual chair the other side of the room, her room, a slight smile, her hands resting on her legs, her burnt face in the sunlight. He played to her, forgetting the examiners, the audience, the competition. At the end, an examiner broke into applause, quickly silenced by the chairman.

He sat in a side room with the other pianists, all silent, surreptitious glances at each other. A lady came in, summoned him; he stood before the examiners, hardly noticing the audience, or the heat of the stage lights, or the trickle of perspiration.

A brief announcement, some comments on his playing, and then applause; he could not be sure what was said, his ears rang, a discordant chord. The chairman came to the stage, shook his hand, presented him with a sheet.

He had won.

Life changed. He returned to the village, but he soon had a manager, that she had chosen, and a string of concerts around the country, and then abroad. Recordings followed. And he was more often not in the village, but staying in a flat in London, close to the action. He made friends, stayed at country houses for weekends, bought a car, talked of working more abroad.

Of course, he returned to the house in the village as often as he could. His parents had retired, and moved away. He would drop in, take her a bottle of wine or flowers, tell her what he had been doing; occasionally, she would ask about a particular concert. She showed him newspaper reviews. They never played together. And he rarely played for her. They would sit around the piano, a disjointed conversation, until she sent him away. He would sigh with relief; the past was the past.

There was a space of time. He could not say how long it had been, one month or three. He returned to the house.

It was locked, closed up. He went to the pub, asked anyone; did they know what had happened, where the lady was. Nobody seemed to know. Until he went to the shop.

'So there you are,' she said.

He frowned. 'What do you mean?'

'We've been looking for you.'

'What has happened?'

'You didn't hear then?'

'How could I? I was—'

'It's a real pity.'

He waited.

'She's gone.'

61

'Where?'

She looked at him, a long moment. 'The cemetery.'

He took a moment to take it in. Stared at her. 'What happened?'

'She left this for you. Now, where did I put it?' She searched the shelves behind her, disappeared back into her house and after several minutes, came back with an envelope. By that time, there was a queue of customers, some of whom knew him, asked after his parents, when was he coming home. He wondered what they meant, coming home; his parents had left, years before. He stood, a little embarrassed, forgetting their names while they all knew his. When she was free, the customers had left wishing him well, looking forward to seeing more of him, she closed the shop early, and took him into her parlour.

'She made me executor of her will. Don't reckon she knew many people, at least, not here. But she was a good customer. She left you the house, and what money was left.'

He sat down suddenly.

'There are conditions.'

'How did she die?' he asked.

She gave him an old-fashioned look, like the schoolteacher used to when he spoke out of turn. 'Did you not see the obituaries? In the papers?'

He had seen nothing; he may have been out of the country, or anyhow busy.

'She committed suicide. Read this letter; it's addressed to you.'

Committed suicide? He froze, and a feeling of guilt crept up his body, a tingling in his ears. He should have... why didn't he... Oh God, what had he done? He said nothing. A stiff envelope, good paper, the wavy pen that he had seen so many years ago, and occasionally since. His name on the envelope; the letter started without preamble.

"I can teach you no more. You have achieved all, through hard work. Well done. My time is over. Now it is yours.

You may have the house, on one condition. You will select a pupil, and teach him or her as I taught you. The piano awaits you. You will spend at least one day a month at the house.

Should the conditions not be acceptable, my solicitor and executor will sell the house, and put the money into a charity for poor musicians.

I wish you well. I regret that a farewell was not possible; it would have been too hard for me.

Yours..." and a scrawl followed. Indecipherable.

He stayed at the house, ran summer music schools there, piano, trios, quartets. But never singers. And brought out a series of pupils, some local, many from afar. Always, her ghost hovered at his elbow as he played and taught. With her wealth, he retired early. He never married, and kept to the house more and more, often playing in the dark, except for a low lamp near the keyboard, the whisper of ivy on the window a susurrating accompaniment.

THE CUPBOARD

She's a dear old lady, my Gran. I drop in as often as I can, but my work is a bit demanding, and so it's not as often as I would like. Embarrassing really, as she has told me that I will inherit her house and some plants. It's a pretty little house, two up two down they used to describe them, but of course it's a bit bigger than that; there's a kitchen out back and a bathroom over it. She is a dear, very easy to talk to, always generous with a freshly baked cake and sandwiches.

It was a Friday afternoon and I reckoned that I had done enough work that week. Instead of going home, I thought I would drop in on Gran, see how she was and spend a little time with her. She had been unwell recently and I was concerned whether she was looking after herself properly and not doing too much. Because she was a great one for doing too much, getting involved with the WI, the Church, and, no doubt, elderly friends who needed a helping hand. And it wasn't as if she was young herself.

She answered the door, looking as spry as ever, and told me that she was feeling fine, just fine, and I wasn't to worry about her. And would I like a cup of tea and a biscuit; she was sorry that she didn't have any cake at present and why didn't I give her some warning and she would have baked. It was always a pleasure to bake for me because, she said, I appreciated the cake so much. I chaffed her, told her I could do with less cake, patted my stomach, pointed out that Christmas was approaching and I would get enough cake to see me through the year. We sat before her fire, one of those with pretend flames and one bar on, and I asked her if she was keeping warm. And, of course, she said she was fine, just fine, and I didn't need to worry. In fact, the room was not cold, and I admired her flower arrangements and her pictures. Would I like to see the garden, she asked; there are a few new plants I wouldn't have seen, and she would love to show me.

But first, she said, she must show me the indoor plants. We went around the house and everything looked very tidy as usual, though the stairs creaked a bit; she told me that it had always creaked. I admired her pots plants; they were everywhere, even in the bathroom. I don't know much about plants, but she was keen to tell me all the names: cyclamen, aloe, mother-in-law's tongue, spider plant and so many others; I couldn't remember them. However, she said, there was one she just didn't know it's name. And that's not often I don't know the name of my plants, she said.

She took me to the cupboard under the stairs and opened the door; at once a peculiar rich musty smell came out. She switched on the light, and I fell back with amazement and shock.

Hanging from the underside of the stairs was a large white bulbous body, with reddish parts to it. And spreading out from it were long white tendrils, spreading all over the floor and climbing up the underside of the staircase and the wall. Indeed, there was hardly a bit of floor, wall, or underside of staircase that was not covered with tendrils, spreading out as if they were taking possession, devouring everything in their path. It looked like a scene from a sci-fi movie, where alien creatures invade the Earth and take over. The smell was intense and sections of the staircase were crumbling, like an over-baked cake.

I gasped; I knew what it was, but I had never seen a growth as large as the one before my eyes.

It's wonderful, isn't it, said Gran. Look at that red in the white bit; isn't it beautiful. And it's growing so well.

But Gran, I gasped, you… it's…

You know, she said, when the gasman came to read the meter, he stared, said he'd never seen anything like it, and that I should mind to take care of it. So I give it a little water every day and it's has grown splendidly. It is beautiful, isn't it?

How could I tell her what she was feeding, that it was eating the house bit by bit and that she would already need a new staircase? She smiled with pride, switched off the light and closed the door. Now, she said, come and look at the garden.

When we were sitting down for a second cup of tea, and another biscuit, I broke the news to her, and told her that it would have to be killed and that there would have to be repairs. She gasped; not killed, she asked. Could I move it, put it in the garden? I told her it wouldn't survive and that it was dangerous; it would eat all the wood it could. It needed to be burnt, along with all the wood that was affected.

Burnt? She said, and stared at me in horror. I think she thought more of the dry rot outbreak than she did her house. I told her I would take care of everything, but she would probably have to go away for a few days.

No, no, she said. I couldn't do that. Who would look after my plants?

THE CARD

Your feet sank into the carpet. No problem with noise. Parents' bedroom of course, not the thin matting of your own room. Had a look around, and examined your gob-stopper; the colour had changed to pink; tasted better. You wiped your fingers on your handkerchief and used it to open the drawer so as not to leave fingerprints. It was a bit sticky, but not very.

And stopped still. Procedure, learnt from Bulldog Drummond. Listen, observe, action.

The house was quiet.

In the drawer, a mass of strange strangled clothes, of the sort that you had seen on the drying line. Other boys had boasted knowledge of them, had seen their mothers wearing them and compared them to film stars. But it was an unknown world to you and when you tried to talk about it at school, you were quickly found out and bullied. A smell crept up your nose at first familiar and then unpleasantly intimate, threatening with adult overtones. You wanted to sneeze. You closed your nose, breathing through your mouth like going to the bogs at school and slid your hands beneath the tangle, ignoring the catch of hooks and buttons, searching for her spare packet of cigarettes. Nothing. Damn.

Forbidden, she'd said. You're too young to smoke; it'll stunt your growth. But Mother, they smoke in films and you smoke.

One of her croaky laughs; I'm so old that it doesn't matter. Just do as you are told and don't argue. And she turned away, ignored you as usual. You knew it wasn't as bad as swearing and masturbation, but bad enough. You had wondered what masturbation was, but she wouldn't tell you. The older chaps in the dorm said they knew all about it and told you some unlikely tale that you had forgotten.

Anyway, she was out. A bridge game or a tea dance, somewhere in the village; you couldn't remember where. She was out most afternoons. She would be out for an hour or two and you were alone.

Your fingers had almost reached the other side, sliding over the drawer paper furtively like a fugitive, Hannay in the Thirty-Nine Steps, or something. Still no cigarettes.

Something was there, something that wouldn't lie flat on the bottom. Too thin to be one of those rubber things in its case, though what that was you had no idea.

You managed to slide the thing back towards you, listening out for sounds in the house, a spy stealing secret papers. There was the distant murmur of music in the kitchen; Cook was washing up lunch and then she would leave. And it would be hours before Father came home from work.

A lorry went past. Then silence.

It was a card. A photograph of a town with fishing boats and things; it looked foreign; mountains rose up behind the town, covered with fir trees. Surely, there was nowhere like that in England. You turned the card over. Bergen. Some foreign place.

It was like the cards you had seen at the Post Office with a line down the middle. But the hand-writing went right across. It was your mother's writing; you recognised it from the notes you took to your House-master at the beginning of term.

You sat down on the bed to read it.

"Darling, here we are on this ghastly boat, chuntering up the coast of Norway."

That was strange. You didn't know she had been on a boat in Norway, and anyway, why was she writing to Father if she was with him?

"Here we are, cooped up with a ghastly crowd who all smoke like chimneys and drink like fish. Honestly, you should hear their conversation. Not a single intelligent one, you know, one who you can really talk to."

Why did she go?

"Today, we all went ashore to look at a fish smokery. Something to do with the bank. The smell!!! Appalling. I made excuses, slipped away by myself. And then he got ratty because they couldn't find me to go back to the ship. God, he is a bore. When will I see you? I long for your hands on me. Can you get away when we get back? How about Wednesday at two? I miss you."

And there it ended. No name or address. You turned it over and looked at the picture; it must be rather exciting to go on a ship in foreign waters; coastal bombardments, invasions like Gallipoli and things.

You could ask Mother where they went. No. She would guess that you had been in their bedroom. Forbidden territory. What if you asked Father? You were always encouraged to learn about foreign countries, particularly if they were in the Empire. You didn't think this one could be; it didn't look hot enough.

But who was she writing to calling Darling? You heard her calling Father darling sometimes, but not often. Who was she missing, and why did she want hands on her? It didn't sound like she was writing to a doctor. And the card was at the bottom of the drawer.

You slipped it back under the clothes without disturbing them. Closed the drawer slowly. Smoothed down the eiderdown where you had been sitting and opened the door a crack. All quiet. You slipped off your sandals, wiped the door knob, and tip-toed back to your room.

Halfway back, the kitchen door opened.

'Jamie, is that you?'

You froze. Had she heard you? After a minute, she said, 'Well, I'm just off now. Be a good boy. Your mother will be back soon.' And went back in the kitchen.

Sitting on the bed, a forbidden activity, you settled down to think about the discovery; it was a bit like things found in an old trunk, or discovering a dead cat. Worthy of investigation. Damn, you hadn't checked the date on the card; perhaps there hadn't been one.

"Darling". "God, he is a bore". "Hands". "I miss you." What did it all mean?

One of the chaps in the dorm had stolen a letter belonging to his big sister. He said it was a "love letter" and read out bits at night and some boys started groaning and saying 'Ooh' and 'Aah' and things like that. You couldn't remember much of it, but it did have Darling and "I miss you", and lots of other "loving" stuff. Perhaps the card was a love letter.

From Mother to another man.

Why was thinking about it so difficult? At school, you got into trouble for thinking slowly and other boys laughed when you gave the answer long after them. Father had said it was all right; there wasn't much need for fast thinking unless you were an army commander or a submarine captain. You didn't know why he didn't mention a pilot; you'd had a talk at school from a fighter pilot. It was thrilling. He had said they were going to need a lot of pilots in the war that was coming and the Nazis had some very good 'planes. Mother said it was all nonsense, there wasn't going to be a war.

Anyway, Father said that at the bank it was always better to think slowly and balance the odds; he didn't explain what the odds were or how you balanced them, but it was comforting. Mother just got impatient and always wanted the answer before she'd even finished the question; she said the teachers knew better than Father and you had better pull up your socks.

You'd heard it all before. Still.

What would happen if you told Father about the card? He would probably refuse to believe you and tell you to go away; or tick you off for lying. Mother would get angry and punish you for looking in her drawer and shout at Father until he shut himself in the study with the whisky. Or perhaps Mother would say that it was a joke, and that of course it was written to Father. And the card would disappear and there would be no evidence.

Or Father would go away like the fathers of a few boys at school and you wouldn't see him for a long time, perhaps years, and have to spend all your time with Mother because they would not be able to afford to send you away to school; which could be quite nice, because you were sure that the teachers at the local school would be all right and you would have friends of your own who lived near you. But it wouldn't be so good with Mother alone; she was always so strict when she noticed you and she never wanted to do things with you. It would be much nicer to spend time with Father. Cook was your only friend but you couldn't ask her about important things like when to change your pants and what did it mean when they said prostitute and things. Recently, Mother had told you it wasn't good for you to spend so much time with Cook; when you asked why; she told you not to be impertinent.

71

Suddenly, there seemed to be so much you didn't understand about your parents. You wished you had friends to visit in the hols like other boys. It didn't look as if you could tell Mother or Father about the card. You could always do nothing.

It didn't seem right. And perhaps things wouldn't stay the same anyway; they never did in books when a discovery had been made. People always started to do things differently. You were getting tired of thinking and went outside to bounce a ball against the scullery wall.

Mother appeared round the corner and stood looking at you. Her make-up was smeared and her hat wasn't straight. She was sneering as though she was asking why, why did she have to be lumbered with you; she had too much to do without worrying about a boy.

'What are you doing there? Sitting on the ground in your smart shorts, getting all mucky.' In other words, God, I wish it were term-time; they would know how to deal with you. She swayed a bit, put out a hand to the wall; stared, hiccupped and disappeared.

You looked at your sandals. Shouldn't be wearing those outside. Against the rules. How you hated Mother; she always spoilt things, made everything horrible. You wished she was at the bottom of the sea; no, the ocean, much deeper. You imagined ways in which she might die, little accidents, but you knew you could never do those things.

Upstairs in your room, sitting on the bed, scuffing your sandals against each other, you thought about poisons. Perhaps the gardener had some in the shed; you had never explored it properly. He always left it locked. Bloody nuisance, you said, imitating Father. Were there poisons in the house? You remembered her pills by the bed. Would she notice if you tipped the whole bottle into her glass? That would make her sick; that would show her. But she would see the empty bottle.

Have to think of something else. What did Commandos do, when they set an ambush? You rummaged about in your tuckbox; there might be something there. Old conkers, useful lengths of string, gobstoppers, of course, and... ah, that might work.

You took off your sandals and tip-toed out onto the landing. How easy would it be? It would be interesting to see, to experiment. You tied a thick fishing line from one side of the stairs to the other, about four inches above the top step; was this how they did it? You were just considering it, how invisible it became, when her bedroom door opened.

She leant against the doorframe looking at you. What was she thinking now? You froze; you felt as though she didn't know you at all. As though you were a stranger from some other country; one of those refugee children from Germany. She looked ill. You stared at her. Were you frightened, or guilty? According to her, you were always guilty of something. You saw a flash of something strange in her eyes, perhaps warmth, followed by a brief look of disgust. She made for the stairs, muttering tea, yes tea.

You raised your hand, opened your mouth, a squeak. She swept past.

They stood by the grave. Solemn words, things happening. A small crowd, some cousins, neighbours. A sort of goodbye, Father had said.

The rain had stopped. It was becoming brighter. The fall on the stairs; it had seemed impossible; there was nothing there to cause it, no loose runner or hole in the carpet. The doctor had declared it an accidental death. You wondered what Father was thinking; how had it happened? Was she dizzy or something?

Would he miss her? You didn't want to think about it, the 'accident'.

He looked down at you. His expression seemed confused, as though he was wondering what to do with you. Did he know what you liked? He had never asked you. You did as you were told, didn't you? You were only upset for a short time and you stayed close to him. Didn't he realise that she had never had time for you? Had he forgotten the arguments that woke you at night? You heard them all – 'God, how do you think we can afford to live like that? As it is, you get through your allowance fast enough…'. Perhaps she had hoped for a different life with him, holidays cruises, and the South of France, all that sort of thing. Without a boy.

Later, when you were alone with him, after all those other people had left, and there were plates of half-eaten sausage rolls and things lying around, you asked if you had to go back to boarding school. You could stay with him, keep him company, play cricket on the lawn, and Snap in the evening; that sort of thing.

You went back though; Father had a little talk with you. Explained how things were going to be different. You would have to spend more time with him in the holidays and he hoped it wouldn't be boring. You could go on holidays and days out together. And he would hire a young house-keeper to keep you company; you were a bit old for a nanny now, weren't you? He didn't seem very sure.

Things were different at school, for a while. Housemaster had a little talk with you, told you 'Not to be afraid to come and have a little chat, whenever you feel like it'. Of course, you never would.

At first, the boys, your so-called chums, left a little distance around you, as though you had a disease. But things fell back into the normal routine before long. Sometimes you wondered; did you miss her? Would she have been nicer when you were older? And then your thoughts turned to other things; the House cricket match, and going away with Father at Christmas.

THE SHOPKEEPER

– 1 –

The red arc over the Norfolk horizon signals sunrise, and releases a cacophony of bird chorus, the sign for a renewal of friendships and enmities. A lark rises high over The Common, a trill in the morning air until it dives to the ground at the appearance of a soaring buzzard. The rabbits cease their games and dive also, into the ground. Except for a little one, playing far from home, snatched from the ground; it experiences a very different rabbit experience as it heads to the heavens, bleating for help to the parents safe in a deep burrow. They nod wise heads, When will they learn?

The sun rises further; the buzzard is seen off by a clamour of rooks, whose territory extends far beyond village and rookery; they take turns to dive-bomb the intruder without a care for themselves. Warming rays cast over cattle who, having left their bedroom under sheltering branches, are already wading through thistles, thorn and grasses on The Common as they chew the morning cud; it is hours until they will stray onto the road and disrupt the traffic, enthusiastic volunteers causing more confusion among the beasts. The rays reach the little village, home to no more than five hundred souls and one hundred dogs. Hovering above ancient roofs, they light upon the Green, a single ray passing over an early dog-walker and illuminating the front of the shop as the blinds are pulled, dazzling the shop-keeper. It is a small village shop only, but we know that it is of the greatest importance to all the villagers; where else would they be able, with a short walk, to buy Lottery tickets and daily newspapers, brew some tasty gossip to enliven the day; and do some shopping.

The paint, once a tasteful green of a moss hue, is peeling, exposed as it is to the southerly sun, and the display stands before the windows have surely seen better days, but does that matter? We know that it is not a pretentious village. Before long, the newspaper van and the greengrocer will be here, chucking their packets onto the pavement. Jac, the shop-keeper, will drag the papers and boxes inside, unpack, mark and allot, and retire for tea and toast.

An hour or two later, Donald trips on the cobbles outside, 'harrumph', instructs his dog – a patient Labrador bitch – to stay, leans against the shop door and enters, shuddering as he always does at the harsh clang of the bell over his head. He pauses, looking around, sighs as usual with delight at the display of order and cleanliness to which he has become accustomed, and yet every time assaults his sensibilities. And halts, a look of dismay on his fine features; Mrs. Jones is ahead of him, already firmly moulded to the front of the counter; short, round, stained raincoat adorned with chicken feathers, galoshes on a fine morning, black hat jammed onto her head, grey hair that escapes in long tendrils like an unclipped thorn hedge.

She is in a tiresome mood. 'Now, them eggs were no good.'

'No good, Mrs. Jones?' Jac is sharp; she has run the gauntlet of patience with Mrs. Jones before. Donald wonders whether her hands are gripped beneath the counter; if he had more imagination, he might have imagined her punching Mrs. Jones in her feather bedded chest. Donald has no great imagination.

'No, them were no good.'

77

There is a tone of abruptness, of warning in Jac's voice, alarm bells. 'What you mean, Mrs. Jones?'

'There was a bad un.'

'Sorry to hear that.' And is she sorry? Most unlikely. Now, if it was Donald, or one of her more generous spenders, she probably would have been sorry …

Mrs. Jones is not in the least discomposed. 'An what are you goin to do bout it?' She shakes her head; a few chicken feathers drift to the counter to be brushed impatiently aside by Jac.

'Well, Mrs. Jones, you bring it in shop, I—'

'What you talkin about? I'll not be walkin about with a bad egg. Gets one a bad name. What would people say? I mean, if you want people to know that you sell bad eggs…' Mrs. Jones is beginning to show some signs of weakening; she twists her hands together, shuffles her feet. More feathers fall on the counter.

Jac sounds impatient, but reserving her gunpowder; Donald who knows her better, is waiting for a discharge. He stands back.

'I want to see bad egg.'

'Pity you couldn't see it before.'

And now Jac explodes, her foreign accent swamping her acquired English. 'And how I see it before?'

Mrs. Jones bleats. 'Well, it were bad, weren't it?'

'Mrs. Jones, you see it bad before?'

'Before what?'

'Before you use it.'

'Now, how could I have seen it before?'

Jac sighs; she realises that nothing is to be gained, and stands down the gunners. 'Ah, Mrs. Jones, you keep chickens. You have good eggs?'

'Arr but I sell them for more than I pay you for yours. Haha.' She grins toothlessly at Donald with an "I told you so" expression. A few feathers drift to the floor.

'Here, Mrs. Jones, take egg. If not good, bring back.' She turns to Donald. 'Now, there is nothing else—'

'I aven't finished. Butter and flour; an I don't want any of that cheap powder you sell as flour. I want the proper stuff.' Mrs. Jones knows her rights; she recovers at speed, standing stiffly upright. If upright it is; she is so wrapped in coats and scarves, and of such a reduced height that it would be fair to say that she is as broad as tall, and therefore 'upright' is a relative term.

Jac serves her with some haste, raising a storm of draught as she sweeps the bag of flour off the appropriate shelf, slaps the butter down on the counter; she manages all this without looking at her customer, who has fallen into a profound silence, an unaccustomed state with her; do we think she is feeling outflanked by Jac? Donald wonders at Jac's behaviour; what is she thinking? Is it hell and damnation? Or is she possibly, just possibly, looking forward to serving him and keen to rid the shop of Mrs. Jones and her chicken feathers? He straightens himself self-consciously, adopts an understanding patient gaze, flicks a morsel of dust off his trousers with his cane. Jac waits while Mrs. Jones finds her purse at the bottom of her wheelie shopper, waits while she extracts coins one or two at a time, spreading them over the counter top complete with old bus tickets, pellets of dust, out-of-date bus time-tables, and a few more chicken feathers. Waits while she stows her shopping, one item at a time, in her trolley; is there now a slight hint of a hum emanating from behind the counter, the hum that we associate with high power electricity lines? Waits while Mrs. Jones thrusts her purse into her raincoat, pulls her hat down over her ears, gives Donald a hard look, eyes screwed up, and makes for the door, her wheelie basket bouncing off the newspaper stand, the snack display, the potato sack and the charity box; to pause beside the last and select a single egg from her shopping and

79

place it on top of a box of out-of-date cornflakes with a comment that she wouldn't have used one of her own eggs.

At the door, Mrs. Jones stalls and gives a loud sigh, more chicken feathers detaching from her coat and drifting to the floor as she looks round in silence. The shop is still, a state of stasis as the occupants recover, Jac standing with folded arms, Donald caught in a brown study; he is not fast to adopt to new situations but understands at last. A loud 'harrumph'; he comes to attention with a stamp, performs an about-turn and advances, undertaking a detour around Mrs. Jones, her coat, her shopper and her look that threatens to provoke, and pulls the door open. The bell clangs.

A pause. Then, 'An I thought there was a genleman in the place. It's wicked, that it is, the way some men are.' She sways out of the door. It closes, a loud clang again.

Returning to the counter, Donald says, 'Surprised you don't show her the door,' biting back the temptation to call Jac "old girl", a term of affection that he has used freely on all from his dog to the post lady. Where he came from, it was an accepted form of greeting, one used on all of the opposite sex. But there have been murmurs that have been brought to his ears by his daily that all is not well with the use of "old girl"; he can't understand it. How can it cause offence? A few words of appreciation can't be amiss, can they?

'How I do that? I will lose customers.' Jac shrugs. 'And how the village feel about her, that man of hers? Barred from the pub last night; again. Now Donald, do I do for you?'

Briefly, he thinks there is so much she has done and could do for him, but with an effort, he limits his thoughts to food needs, which are simple. Or so we think, but Donald has travelled widely, in an earlier life. These modern supermarkets where you have to do all the work yourself don't suit him; indeed, he feels that the owners are taking liberties, expecting their customers to do all the work; he has written letters to that effect, but received no replies. Harrumph. He places his list on the counter, written in large capitals with a Biro, steps back and stands at ease, feet apart, hands behind a straight back, gazing at her, an expression of deepest affection that he trusts won't be misconstrued. But hopes it might be all the same.

She smiles in return, a brief flash before she travels around the shop gathering the items, humming a vague song that weaves around his head, and displays them on the counter for his approval. He ticks off the list, pausing to read the label on an unfamiliar packet. Wonders whether to question it; why can't these… manufacturers keep to the same packets? It would save a great deal of worry… He would join in the hum but doesn't know the tune; perhaps it comes from her old country; he has not served in that part of the world. Wherever it is. At his brisk nod, she puts the items into his shopping bag, the eggs on top after she has checked for cracks and passes him an envelope. 'Could you put in postbox for me? Too busy this morning, with Mrs. Jones, and—'

'My dear, don't mention it.' He bestows a warm smile on Jac, brushing his moustache with his first finger; another brief flash of smile in return. He resists a salute; might be misconstrued. And passes over cash, notes and small change to the exact amount. He wonders about asking for a receipt, but believes that he can trust Jac.

Jac and Donald: they don't have history as villagers would say; which is to say that we know that they do have a history but there has been no more to their friendship beyond a few nights in the pub and a few evenings over a good meal. Usually at his place. She has been good to him ever since his wife died, found him his daily, Beryl, and has been a source of company when others kept their distance out of reserve; not knowing what to say and in any case, not knowing him. After all, he is quite new to the village and will not be recognised as a local for the next fifteen years. He has never considered why she has been so good to him; it seems perfectly natural that some good soul should rally round. He is fortunate that she has been the support; in fact, few have shown any sign of wanting to know him. It has not occurred to him that she might be feeling the same sense of isolation, excluded from village life by her accent and recent arrival, though the shop is used by necessity and custom.

The sun has risen further as he emerges from the shop, heralded on his way by yet another loud clang; he blinks in the brightness. 'Harrumph'. It would be as well if we give some description of him, now that he has emerged into full light. In appearance, he is the epitome of the retired army officer: he is of above average height and stands very upright, almost to the extent of appearing to fall over backwards, with a greying moustache on a bronzed face, a pair of sharp eyes set a little close beneath bushy eyebrows over an aquiline nose. His lips are thin but mobile, often revealing a poor misshapen set of stained teeth; his chin is resolutely square. His garments are equally standard; a tweed cap, the peak pulled down low, tweed hacking jacket, though he does not ride, Newmarket shirt, regimental tie, crisply-coutured corduroy trousers, highly polished brogues. Anyone might have thought that he has just stepped off a parade-ground or out of an officers' mess. In spite of his age, he marches rather than walks, a strong confident pace, arms swing at his sides, head held high generally looking straight ahead, swinging a slim cane; we have the impression that he misses his swagger stick. Some village people are scared of him; he appears to represent an authority that they are damned that they will recognise, a resentment that has run through their genes since

Lord Kitchener beckoned their ancestors. Or possibly long before, back through lords of the manor and droit de seigneur, to Anglo-Saxon kings.

As he emerges from the shop, two men appear out of the shadows on the other side of the road. Donald gives them a quick inspection, a habit developed over years of processing squaddies. He sees men of limited stature, black suits, narrow black ties, white shirts; all they need, he thinks, are chauffeur caps. Harrumph. He decides to ignore them, slips the envelope into the box, summons the bitch and establishes a route for home.

The men, with a tacit exchange, adjust their strategy and redistribute their forces to set up a blocking tactic across his path. Without a change in pace, Donald performs a neat diversionary move, passing to the lee of the men. The dog passes between them, ignoring both. Donald notes to one side a black car, a vehicle that would be not worth the slightest notice, apart from the fact that there are a couple of long whip aerials on the roof. Ah. 'Harrumph'.

'Oy, you!' An estuarine accent, resembling more a rook's coarse croak.

A blackbird, scenting danger, emits an alarm and flaps away in haste. Followed by his mate, and a thrush. Donald continues on his path; he has not been addressed in a proper manner and he is accustomed to communicating only with those who share his admittedly elevated methods of communication.

'Excuse me, sir!' The words drawn out in a primitive howl as though the speaker has been summarily brought up before the beak.

Ah. That perhaps calls for some response. He comes to a halt, makes a sharp about turn, clicks his heels together and surveys the two men. Aged in their thirties, short cropped hair; army

83

written all over them. Not tall enough to have been admitted to his regiment. They don't look like officers, more like squaddies. Boots in a disgraceful state. The one who has spoken is a little older than he has thought at first, probably in his forties. Eyes like gimlets under skinny eyebrows, a small scar above his left jaw and it is possible that his nose has been broken at some time. A man used to violence and getting his own way; well, Donald is sure that he is not going to get his own way today. He can find little to recommend them; they appear to be the product of the lowest ranks of an unimportant regiment. He says nothing.

'Can we see in your shopping bag?… Please?' The last word spoken pleadingly after a substantial pause.

This is going too far, totally unacceptable. His nostrils flare, he looks down his leg, the crisply-coutured corduroy, to the immaculately polished brogue. He taps his stick against the side of his leg. How on earth does one deal with the lower ranks these days? It is years since he stood on a parade ground but old habits die hard. Donald comes to attention. 'Ten-shun!'

The two men jerk upright like marionettes, the younger instinctively at full attention, hands lined at his sides. The older, on the way to attention, frowns, shakes himself at his reaction and puts his hands in his pockets.

'Now sir, if it not too much trouble—'

'Sergeant,… if you ever succeeded to that rank, which I am beginning to doubt, you do not address me in that familiar tone. Did I instruct you to stand easy? Remove your hands from your pockets at once.' The man reluctantly withdraws his hands; with a scowl. 'Who is your commanding officer and what regiment are you disgracing?'

'Now sir,' a pathetic wheedling tone. 'We're not army—'

'You expect me to believe that? You are a disgrace to any unit you represent and you obstructed my path. Your manners require mending and your boots are in an appalling state.' He beckons with his stick. 'I am astonished that you are allowed to leave barracks in that state. Stand down and repair there immediately. Carry on! Harrumph!'

And with that, Donald performs a crisp about-turn and continues on his way, the stick tucked under his arm, army style. A passing cat, if there had been one, would have noticed a distinctly hostile atmosphere. It will have seen a brief conference between the two men in black suits, heard a few unseemly words and observed them regroup.

And then it would have fled. There is a roaring sound offstage, accompanied by a loud musical chant delivered at such volume that robins, attempting to settle their young to sleep half a mile away, are shaken into disciplinary parental duties. Even the dog hesitates before aligning herself with her master. The roaring bellows out of an approaching cloud of dust such as might not have been a disgrace in the film "Lawrence of Arabia". The dust cloud comes to a halt next to Donald and as it settles there can be seen a vehicle.

A pick-up truck of some description. It is not in its first youth. Indeed, we can see that its first youth is long past and its mature years are signalled by peeling rust, slabs of alien colour and a random chugging that indicates that whatever is under the bonnet no longer runs to a regular and true rhythm but rather struggles for life, the sounds varying from optimistic phrases of a beating heart to periods of seizure and coughing. It dies.

'Donald, mate!' The speaker leans against the driver's door, which opens with a grating sound and hangs from one hinge, and steps out. A big man in overalls and boots; the overalls snag on the door. He tugs them clear with a rending sound; they appear to match the pick-up, long past their pristine youth with the appropriate signs of misuse. Beneath an oversized New York

Yankees cap, there is a cheeky grin in a young face that has not seen a razer, or a wash, in recent days. 'How are yer doin, mate?'

Donald has stopped at this appearance. He seems a little non-plussed, looks down his trouser leg once more, flicks a morsel of dust off a brogue and unbends; to a degree. He does not welcome being addressed as "mate"; after all, there is nobody in the village who has ever worked with him, and it's familiar in an unseemly way. However, he has come to learn that there are some in the village who have no knowledge of an alternative term of address, and represses his natural instinct to turn away and ignore the speaker. And Kevin has become more than just a neighbour. 'Ah, Kevin.'

'How yer doin?'

Before he can reply, he sees that Kevin's attention has been drawn to the two men in black. They have followed Donald at a short distance but come to a halt at the arrival of the dust cloud and stand staring at the new arrival. Who is, after all, considerably taller than the two of them, and obviously fit for manual work; they don't fancy their chances. The younger of the two coughs in the dust and is rewarded with a scowl from the older.

'Who are these two then, Donald? You going to introduce me?'

Donald harrumphs, stamps, 'Bounders! Charlatans! Ought not to have been deployed from their barracks. Disgrace to the Army.'

Kevin looks the two men up and down slowly, a mild questioning look on his face. He gives a quick laugh, a humourless chirrup. 'Need any… er… help, see what I mean, Donald?'

'Thank you, Kevin. But why don't you come down to the old place and I'll fix us a snorter?'

'Sounds good. And I'll take that,' he says, lifting the shopping bag out of Donald's hand. 'Not from around here, are they?' Kevin is loud, showing no signs of embarrassment. Strangers always needed keeping an eye on; they didn't belong.

There is no call for a Neighbourhood Watch scheme in the village; strangers are noted before they have emerged from their cars, a brief description passed to the shop, a log kept, complete with hour of arrival, description, car registration plate and hour of departure. The police have been full of admiration; until an officer pursued a village girl only to find his amorous activities reported to the whole village. The girl's comments were unrepeatable.

A pigeon flaps lazily overhead, drops a large smear of white birdshit on the black car. Kevin laughs. Giving the men a final slow look up and down and leaving the truck where it stands, door gaping, they turn their backs on the two men and walk off down the road, Kevin galloping to match his step to Donald's pace. They turn down a narrow lane. Donald lives in a small single storey house in the centre of the village. Some might call it 'bijou'; this word is not in Donald's vocabulary. Most villagers call it a bungalow, not that he will ever countenance that description. Bungalows belong in India; he lived in one. He describes it as a convenient bivouac, no more than he needs, less than might be inconvenient.

The morning sounds return: calls of sparrows in the hedges, blackbirds competing for territory, a tractor chugging by on the main road, two helicopters passing over at moderate height, a couple of girls laughing at a boy, a neighbour emptying his bin with force. A hedge cutter sets up a buzz nearby, followed a lawnmower. And another one. The village is proud of its well-trimmed lawns.

'Quiet, ain't it?' Kevin grins, a happy innocent grin.

Donald harrumphs.

'So, if you'll spare the nosey, what was that all about, Don old mate?'

Donald unbends sufficiently to give his friend a brief look. 'Damned if I know. Assume it was common assault. Sort of thing you read about, never heard of such a thing here. Glad you came along; might have been tempted to take measures to suppress the oiks.'

'Right.' Kevin keeps a straight face. 'They weren't from around here, rough types, in spite of the suits. Look like gangsters, don't they? I'll take a look at them when I go back. You going to call the police? Now, are you all right?'

'Good gracious, Kevin, faced worst things in the Army.'

'Tell me sometime.'

'Well, I don't know. Wouldn't want to be bragging.'

Actually, there are times when Donald would like to unbend, and tell a few tales of army life. We would like to hear some of them, but Donald is not in that mood today.

At home, he pours two stiff whiskies and they sit side by side with the front door open, enjoying the morning sun. Donald can't help comparing their respective footwear; Kevin's boots peel at the toe and are a colour that is impossible to find on any colour chart, but he can't find it in himself to regard them in the same light as those worn by the two oiks. Kevin is certainly not the product of any regiment and therefore to be excused. He is not really sure what Kevin does to fill his time, and it is not a matter of concern; Kevin has been instrumental in obtaining posts for the garden, and carrying out the heavier jobs that are occasionally necessary, like sawing down trees, moving furniture and so on. Donald likes a clear area around the house, as was common with Norman castles; gives one time to prepare ordnance. He has also had installed those lights that come on with movement; however, a hedgehog has been causing him some distress, putting the lights on late at night, and causing outrage from near neighbours. Unfortunately, Donald cannot understand what the problem is; barracks were always well lit.

A pair of blue tits argue over a piece of bread while a cat spies on them. His dog is stretched out asleep on the ground, oblivious to the birds, oblivious to the cat.

'You like cats, Kevin?'

'Not much.'

'Can't stand the perishers. If they take out those tits, I'll be out with my shotgun.'

'Don't think it's the season for cat shooting, mate.'

Donald harrumphs. 'Bugger that.'

Kevin laughs. 'Yeah, bugger that.'

– 2 –

Ah, the shopping. He gets up from the chair that he has slumped into and starts to put the shopping away. Bread and cheese and butter in the fridge, vegetables in their basket, though some go into the fridge; which ones are they? Where is the larder of old where everything went, the butter on a marble slab, the pheasants hung until they dropped off their legs; Mother liked them ripe. A bone for the dog.

One of those things Daphne did well, putting away. He misses her, still. It is a few years since he bid farewell to his College at Cambridge, where he had gone after leaving the Army. He had ceased his tutoring of students in Medieval Warfare and moved with his wife Daphne from their large Shelford family home to the village; down-sizing with a vengeance, his sons said. His wife died rather earlier than expected of the virus; she was apologetic, scarcely able to forgive herself for dying before him. After all, she had promised on their wedding bed to outlive him. Persuaded him to adopt a dog, for company; he has but only to honour her memory, an old bitch who might not, with luck, outlive himself. He has escaped his own illness, cancer of the prostate, and can see no good reason why except he takes it as a punishment of some sort. He feels good for another twenty years. Or so. Not quite good enough to return to active service but good enough to live a little and complete a book on Medieval Warfare; a little trouble with the publishers who, thinking of their profits, want a gaudily illustrated volume for children, while he is aiming for those with rather more education. Really, were the publishers only interested in profits? Sadly, the University Publishers are not interested. They took it amiss when he confronted the head of publishing with a medieval weapon, that he had believed would convince them of his historical correctness. The Publishers were persuaded to drop the charges.

He watches two ladies walked their dogs up the lane; one of the dogs squats on his grass.

'Harrumph!'

The ladies flee; don't even pause to remove the offending faeces. Good gracious, he wouldn't allow his dog to behave like that.

And at last, he can get back to his battle, laid out on a board in his livingroom; Jac has seen it but showed no interest beyond a comment about toy soldiers that Donald found deeply offensive. He has a large collection of model soldiers, buildings, field equipment and so on; his interest is in replaying the battles to see whether there might have been another outcome. The battles are often Medieval battles, usually English, Wars of the Roses, that sort of thing. His present battle was the biggest and bloodiest battle on English soil; Towton. The Yorkists were outnumbered by the Lancastrians but defeated them after a drawn-out battle with 50,000 soldiers fighting on Palm Sunday 1461. He understood that 30,000 men were killed and the rivers ran red for days. He is not sure how to model the rivers running red nor can he field more than a couple of hundred men representing the armies. He has prepared the Yorkist archers who started the battle and hoped that Kevin might join him, operate the Lancastrian side. Would the Lancastrians have won? He is intrigued. Kevin has shown no great enthusiasm for the role; damned shame. Can't think of anyone else who he could approach.

Later in the afternoon, he walks up the lane to post a letter, his dog at his heel; no squatting permitted. He is still replying to letters of condolence; it seems that everyone has stories to tell about his wife; very odd, they seemed to know a person he didn't recognise at all. Dashed awkward; what does he say? He is restless to set all that behind him, and get back to writing and warring without interruption. And living, whatever that involves.

– 3 –

The car has gone; there is a small pool of oil where it stood. He stands, staring at the ground, recalling regiment days, the dog patiently at his side; it makes to step into the puddle, and he gives a quick jerk on the lead. Typical, he thinks; poor regiment, poor maintenance, and what a mess. Nobody to clear it up. State of the country, soldiers running around bespoiling innocent villages. They ought... He wonders who they were; wonders what their commanding officer will have to say about them. All very well pretending not to be Services; they had it written all over them. One army man can always recognise another. He could have named a couple of regiments of no great repute that probably spawned them. 'Harrumph'. That little threat diplomatically evaded; he wasn't really looking for action, but he felt that some action was called for. He sighs, and walks on.

The shop is closed.

Damned odd; she never closes early. She will even open up late in the evening if there is call for it. And she is always open at seven in the morning until seven in the evening. The blinds are pulled down. The windows stare back at him; no sign of life, apart from the usual brash notices, times of opening, advertisements for tobacco no longer available, icecream and packet cereals from thirty years before. 'Harrumph'. He peers around the edge of the door blind. The dog squats against the bin on the corner. Oh damn; he produces a doggy bag, picks up the offending faeces and drops the bag into the bin. That's the way to do it. Harrumph.

He peers around the blind again.

One should appreciate that Donald is used to a sense of order; his past was a culture of order and orders. That was how the army worked, and for the most part, he believed he fitted in, was part of the family of the regiment. Now and then, there was a little disturbance to the smooth running of his career; usually smoothed over by an understanding Colonel. And the College? He had the staff well trained, and his students compliant. His home is well ordered, everything in its place and a place for everything; no need to waste time and effort in locating anything. Even the glasses stand in ordered ranks, each on its own spot, spic and span; wonders where that term came from. He would use the term "ship-shape" but that belongs to the Senior Service and he is Army. The tea-spoons are stacked, the number noted each time he washes up, which is in the morning after breakfast. The table cleared, sinktop polished, cutlery and crockery stored in drawers. And so on. He appreciates Jac's similar sense of order. She knows how to keep a shop, everything in its place. He knows where everything in the shop is shelved, even if he does allow Jac to locate the items and fill his shopping bag. How else could a shop be?

But the place is a mess; the floor covered with boxes and packets, the shelves mostly stripped, the counter piled with a detritus of wrappers, small packets and odd vegetables. It has been turned over by some thugs who didn't care about the goods, flung them here and there. Shocking! Unbelievable! Donald feels a thump in his heart, a sweat break out on his forehead. He steps back, panting a little, passes an immaculate handkerchief over his brow. It's not the sort of thing that happens here in this village; it makes him feel a little shaky; he's getting too old for trouble.

There is no sign of Jac. He goes round to the back, as he has never done before, and rings the house bell. No answer. The police; he should call the police. Damn, he has forgotten to report the men he saw this morning. He hurries back home, the dog slightly reluctant as both its morning walk and afternoon walk have been terminated, and after sitting to recover his breath and allow his heart to slow down, calls the police station.

At first, they take his details, his description of the shop, the absence of Jac and then ask him why it is his concern. What? What happened to neighbourly concern, that Neighbour Watch thing? That brings him up all standing – oh dear, a maritime term. What? What? 'Harrumph!' Are they not interested in a robbery at the shop? There were two rough men near the shop in the morning, describes them and says how he is worried for Jac. They tell him they know all about the shop and Jac and he does not need to worry any more. Nonsense! How can he? He worries more. But they tell him no more, ring off before he can even obtain the name of the officer in charge. Kicks himself;

always go to the man at the top. Slipped up there. Perhaps there is some underhand operation that has carried his friend away on false premises; and they would be false; how could a shop-keeper be involved with "an underhand operation"? But what can he do? He curses the police, just refrains from kicking the dog who has settled for an extensive snooze, eats a small meal, no more than iron rations, and settles himself for bed early in an unhappy state. No quiet time with a whisky snorter looking at the peace of his garden, no happy reading of medieval doings. One day and the village has become a bog; all green and peaceful on top and underneath… what turbulent stirrings?

$$- 4 -$$

The next morning, he feels that some action is called for, the police obviously incapable of investigating the burglary, and he bustles out before breakfast, before walking the dog, who is unhappy at being left at home – he is early to the shop – it is open and all is in order, Jac present behind the counter.

He stands in the middle of the shop, looking round; Jac ignores him, which is a bit disconcerting. Everything is in its place; shelves clean, no sign of the mayhem. Even the floor looks as if it has been washed; he could swear that there is a little dampness in a further corner.

Donald is confounded. 'What the… I say, old girl… No, sorry, didn't say that… But… well, one was concerned…'

She attempts a smile, but looks frayed, brushing a wisp of hair back constantly, restless, her eyes darting around. This is not the Jac he knows, the friendly hard-working woman who has done so much for him; where is the smile that lights up his day? He is astonished and worried. What has happened to her?

She looks at him, and says 'Taken away in the night, interrogation… like being back home. What is it? What is England?'

Hmm. Donald does not like the sound of it, does not know how to answer. England is the cradle of civilization, of peaceful democracy; night-time interrogation is not part of it. He always breathed a huge sigh of relief when the regiment returned to home grounds. 'What did they want?'

She is sharp, spluttering. 'Oh, they talk about shop, goods, the customers, and I run another business… how I have time for another business! Is madness, is not England I know.'

'Did they look after you?'

'You joke, Donald. They don't let me sleep, they search me… oh! Disgusting! And one cup of coffee; disgusting.'

'Who were they?'

'Two rough men, in black clothes. They don't listen, just questions, questions. They very rough men, they threaten me. And then, in the morning… I feel really sick and so tired… this old man come in, all nice like a priest I think at first, and ask if I can help him. And he will help me, he say. Very gentle but he does not let me sleep. I don't like him.'

Donald thought back to the time spent abroad, in the Army. The 'quiet' men, they were always spies, or 'intelligence gatherers.' Not a nice sort of person, one could never know them or trust them. 'What… what happened to you? I mean, it's not right. I should talk to someone, someone high up. Or something.'

He mutters threats, claps his hands together. Would his Colonel be able to do anything? She looks away and mutters that she will tell him sometime about 'home'. Refuses help though he offers to come round after closing. And then she rallies, very upright, staring at Donald and proposes that they have a chat at the pub. One evening soon. Would that be good? Oh yes, he says, that would be very good. But remains confused, why it would be so good when it might not be something good at all. Poor Donald, why has the world become so complicated?

The two 'rough' men; he could guess who they were. The trouble-makers, oiks. It really was time that were seen off, dismissed.

He goes home, a fog of confusion, the Jac he has known transformed into... what, he can't say. Something needs to be done; what is it? Who can he contact? Ah, the days in the Army; always someone to sort out little problems then. He tries the number for the regiment; not available. Damn. Another restless night.

$$- 5 -$$

He doesn't see her for a couple of days, absorbed in processing paperwork, old clothes, books, jewelry. Moving on. It takes time and a lot of it is very boring. All duty, of course. Occasionally, he wishes that she had kept her word, survived him, and that brings on a type of loneliness which he dispels as quickly as he can, by thinking of battles. But you can't stand still in life; best way to get shot by the other side; whoever they might be. Not that Donald is paranoid. Keep moving. He is spurred on by the energy of life outside, the birds mainly who wake him early in the morning, compete over the food he puts out for them, build nests in his hedges and leave unattractive droppings on his car. The hedgehog visits occasionally and wakes him in the dark with bleats of loud mating and one day an injured muntjac hid in the corner of the garden, to disappear before the RSPCA arrive to cure its cuts. And he thought village life would be peaceful.

There is always dog walking, a daily stroll up to the cricket ground, exchange the odd word with a neighbour – a term used for anyone he recognises as a villager – ignore the visitors, walkers and the like; there are too many of them. Return home for breakfast and so on.

He has been shopping. It is a wonderful day, white puffy clouds in a blue sky, larks trilling, the sharp smell of fresh cut grass. The local town: the bank in order to sort out the manager, and a few minutes dawdling in a bookshop and a bookmakers; sometimes gets the two confused. Kevin has given him a tip; he has rarely betted on horses though he received a good grounding in Cambridge from the Porters. There was a flutter on a horse at Newmarket that filled his pocket with notes; an unaccustomed feeling. A cup of coffee in a friendly café, to sit down and enjoy a new book; the revelations of a retired General, fascinating stuff. Sorted out the Far East war, single-handed. Nobody he knew there; he surveyed the crowd of chattering people without resentment. He drove back in a mood of contentment, all well with the world, harrumph. We see the complications vanish from his mind; for now.

He is still full of the joys of the day, contemplating whether battles occur without warning, a surprise as it were, rather than armies coming to battle, which is what he has learnt, though there were always the scouting sallies that he recalls from the Middle East, but they were hardly battles… as he parks the car in his drive, three inches from the hedge as usual. Picks up his shopping, locks the car, checks it once. Twice. 'Harrumph'. Notes the tits enjoying the nuts, sunshine, must cut the grass sometime.

His front door is ajar, a few inches.

He stops, dropping his shopping bags. Did he leave it open? It takes a few moments to convince himself that could not have

97

been possible. He is stunned. How dare they, whoever they are? And what could he have that they might want? There is a high hissing sound in his head, the blasted tinnitus, drowning out the background. His heart is dancing a rumba; he leans against the doorframe, panting.

One of those odd things; it was never to happen to him. Heard about break-ins on friends and neighbours in Cambridge; sympathised, offered help, usual sort of thing. But it never happened to them and it was never to happen to him. Didn't have anything anyone would want for goodness sake; a ten year old television, ordinary crockery and silver and a mass of books, a few old weapons that would be easily traced. And what are they worth? And now there is the police, the insurers, builders, decorators. Oh goodness. He stands back, breathing easier; is there still anybody inside? He listens but can hear no more than the blackbirds in the garden behind him and the hissing in his ears. Can it be Beryl? But it's not her cleaning day and she usually has the radio on to keep her company. Wonders if it's the same bounders who did the shop over.

He pushes the door gently.

A murmur, something is dropped on a floor.

What next? Retreat and call the police? From a fog of indecision rises a flame of determination; dammit, it ain't right. What would the Regiment say? Take the fight to the aggressor, don't wait to be overcome.

He steps silently into the kitchen. Nobody there. It's a mess, cupboards emptied onto the floor, crockery spilled out of drawers, cutlery spread over the table. Looking for silver no doubt. Bastards. Looks just like the shop the other day. Now, what to do? He thinks; if he doesn't have a weapon, he will be in trouble.

The door to the sittingroom is open. Nobody in sight, but they're in there, down the other end he reckons, rooting through his books and things; what on earth for? Have they disturbed the battle? It took hours to set up; he would have them in chains, replacing the figures, one by one; might teach them a bit of history.

On the wall on the right within easy reach resting on a single hook, we can see a glaive. It must have been an unpleasant weapon in medieval times, probably deadly; it consists of a long pole, with a single edged blade on one end, at least a foot long, a hook at the working end, and a nasty spike on the back of the blade. Probably used in a scything action by men who were used to scything, but with a vicious backswing. He keeps it clean; it shines with malevolent purpose. He grins with equal malevolent purpose and plans his next move.

In a single stride, he is in the room, glaive in hand, blade down, his face set in a rigid glare. He is prepared; bugger the harm, he will tackle these miscreants.

A moment of confusion.

Two men stare back, completely surprised. Donald grits his teeth; the same two men in black suits who obstructed him. Oiks, men of the lowest calibre. Well, if they get hurt, they only have themselves to blame. Donald has returned to fighting action; we feel his anger and his belief that any action is justified. To be honest, we hope that he doesn't go too far; we are afraid that he has lost his natural restraint and his sense of living in a modern society.

'Down on the floor. Now!'

The men do not seem to be obliged to follow his orders but glance at each other, looking ready to pounce. Damned fools.

'Down, I said.'

They charge; a stupid move. The blade scythes through the air, narrowly missing both men but unfortunately becoming embedded in the sofa. While he retrieves his weapon, with little difficulty as the blade is so sharp, the older man slips behind him and is out of the front door, gone. But Donald has the younger man at his mercy; he dithers, eventually putting his hands up and kneeling on the floor.

'Please boss.' His voice quavers hopelessly. 'You wouldn't?'

Donald smiles a nasty smile, waving the weapon over the man's head. He feels on top of the situation, the absence of the older man not troubling him at all. 'I don't much care for people who invade my home, without invitation. And I don't recall issuing an invitation to you; do you?'

'Er… You don't know who we are.'

These are words are like a red rag to a bull, that call for a good parade ground volume. 'What?!'

Birds leave the garden, frustrated at leaving the ripe redcurrants. A cat unwinds itself and slips away through the hedge. Even a buzzard, hovering high over the village, elects to soar elsewhere. 'What?! You think you are entitled to raid a man's home? A mere squaddie? Perhaps you could tell me which of those words you are not acquainted with? Invitation? And as to who you are, I believe that an Englishman's home is his castle and not to be invaded by anybody. Without notice. And I believe that I am entitled to carry out any action necessary to subdue invaders.'

'Er…' The young man shakes his head, stunned by the volume of sound.

'Stay there, or I might be tempted to act and I'm sure you would not wish me to act rashly. Would you? Your… mate has deserted you.'

The man shakes his head, again.

'Name, rank, number.'

'Er… we're not meant to give our names.'

Donald manages a foul smile; it has been many years

since he has exercised such control over a man, but he feels full justification in carrying out any manoeuvre that might be demanded by the situation. He waves the glaive over the man's head, thinking mildly that it would not take much to behead him. Oh well, reasonable force in dealing with a thief. 'Would you prefer me to extract it from your unconscious body?'

'Oh… please, sir.'

'Name, rank, number. Now. Quick!'

'Er… well… it's a standing instruction.'

'Standing instruction?' Donald sneers.

'I have a number.'

'Unit?'

'Unit?'

'Your Regiment, you idiot!'

'But… we're not army.'

'So you are some illegal gang?'

'Oh, we're police.'

'Really? A likely story.'

'Er… yes, a special squad.' The words do not seem to give the young man any confidence; indeed, he is shaking and sweating.

'Who specialise in robbing homes.'

'Well, not really. We're meant to tackle big crimes.'

'Then what the hell are you doing here?'

'I'm not at liberty to say.'

'Not at liberty to… You certainly are the one "not at liberty". What on earth do you think you are doing?' Donald attempts a sneer of superiority.

'Please sir, could you just call the police?'

The glaive waves erratically over the man's head.

'P… Please.'

His eye passes, at last, over the battle. It looks in order. But… 'You've moved a troop of horse.'

'No… no, honest, didn't touch a thing.'

'Didn't touch a thing?!' Donald looks around, his books and CDs cast around, cupboards open, cushions pulled off chairs, pictures awry. 'What can you possibly mean by that?' Back up to parade ground volume.

'Well, we were just looking for something.'

'And what might that be?'

'Well… I can't tell you that—'

'You demolish my home and can't tell me why you are doing it?'

'Well… er… I—' The young men is almost curled up on the floor, as though he can no longer bear the sight of the weapon that moves lazily to and fro over his head.

'I'm waiting, though why I don't just put you out of action, I can't think. Actually, it would make things much simpler—'

'I mean… oh, please call the police, sir. The battle, it's terrific, sir, but we didn't move a thing.'

'Then who chose to reposition this Yorkist troop of horse?'

'I… I dunno, sir.'

'You miserable little oik. You ought to be put in the guard room for a week.' Donald reaches for the phone, dials 999. Which service? Police, burglary in process. The police act promptly. Astonishingly promptly. Sirens are echoing through the narrow streets and lanes only shortly after he has replaced the phone and cars screech to a halt below his house, men running to the door. Donald withdraws from the sittingroom, glaive in hand, and welcomes them.

'I regret that one has escaped. Here is the other. You already have descriptions of both; I phoned the station only the other day, when the shop was ransacked.'

'Thankyou, sir. Would you oblige us by lowering your weapon?'

Donald hangs up the glaive and smiles as the police haul the man to his feet; his heart beat is retreating to a lower level. There is a muttered conversation between police and man; Donald is somewhat aggravated to see two policemen walk off with him, the man unshackled, walking easily behind them. Like a well-trained animal. Must be a regular offender, he thinks, well known to the police force. Perhaps jail this time.

– 6 –

The dog; where is the dog? He searches the house, and finds her shut in the bedroom. Irritatingly, the bitch has found the bed a sensible place to retire to and was not in the least disconcerted to be placed there by two strangers. So much for a guard dog. She reluctantly leaves the bedroom at her master's stern eye.

'Now sir,' says the remaining officer. 'Is anything missing?'

Donald promptly suffers a minor seizure; his home has been broken into, his belongings scattered far and wide, he has had to confront the burglars, the man has been led away like a… well he isn't sure what it resembled but it was rather like a young bullock that has strayed from its field. We can sympathise with him, can't we? It has all been too much for an old soldier, who should be taking things easy. 'What the… I mean… how could you… dare to—'

'Now sir, I'm sure it's very distressing but why don't you sit down and I'll make us a cup of tea.'

Donald has had enough. 'I've had enough. Please leave me to clear up this mess and I'll look forward to receiving your report in due course.' His heart is taking a beating.

'I must oblige you for a statement.'

Donald stares at the man. Was he out of his mind? 'Very well. Here it is.'

'One moment, sir.' The words are drawn out as he extracts a notebook from a pocket and licks a pencil. 'Yes, sir. Proceed.'

'I was returning home—'

'From where, may I enquire?'

'Does it make the blamed bit of difference?'

'I'd be obliged if you would watch your language, sir.'

'I cannot recall the word 'blamed' ever being accused of being a word of insult, abuse, or swearing. But I can check it in my dictionary—'

'No sir. That won't be necessary.'

'The door was open.'

'And which door would that be, sir?'

Donald grits his teeth, stares out of the window; stupid man; why does he have to put up with him? A few seconds pass. 'Harrumph! The front door. It's the only access to the property. I had considered adding another front door, but—'

'The front door was open, sir?'

'I believe I said that.'

'And how open was it?'

Donald stares at the man, who looks back calmly, his pencil hovering over his notebook. 'About that much,' he says, holding his hand up.

'That would be about two inches then.'

'I would say so.'

'Except, if you'll excuse me sir, we are not allowed to use Imperial measurements anymore and therefore would it be possible for you to give me the metric equivalent?' The officer looks not in the least embarrassed at his question.

Donald sits down heavily. 'I had thought that they would have educated you in the conversion from imperial to metric. Now, let's start at the beginning; one hundred and two millimetres is close to four inches. Therefore, one inch is equivalent to twenty-five point four millimetres. I prefer millimetres as centimetres become confused with inches but as you can see an inch would be two point five four centimetres. Our naval guns remained sensibly in inches; the Hood had fifteen inch guns, I believe. But in the Royal Artillery centimetres are used for gun barrel diameters and shell sizes. The Germans used a similar system in the Second World War, though they were happy to use millimetres, like the – can't remember the field gun, was it the eighty-eight? Perhaps that was centimetres. No, can't have been. Of course, there are different systems, like the old twenty-five pounder; do you remember that one? Hero of the desert war. The twenty-five pounds referred to shell weight, I believe. No, that can't be right; damn, I can't remember. Now, I can look it up.' Donald rises. 'Anyway, is that clear?'

The officer struggles to keep up with the conversion; and the conversation. He gasps slightly. 'Would you mind, sir, could I have a glass of water?'

Donald obliges and sits again.

'So, sir, your two inches would be—'

'Fifty millimetres, close enough.'

'And what would that be in centimetres?'

'Officer, there are ten millimetres in one centimetre.'

'You know sir, I was never very good at sums at school. I'm going to write down two inches and the station sergeant can translate it for me.'

Donald stands as though to usher the officer out of the door. 'Is this going to take long, officer?'

'No sir. No, of course not. You must have a lot to do,' he says, looking round.

'I made a recce of the kitchen and—'

'How do you spell that, sir?'

'K... I...'

'No sir. That Recky thing.'

Donald is getting tired of the constant questions. He starts to speak faster. 'I made a recce of the kitchen. I heard two men in the sittingroom, lifted the glaive off the wall and confronted them.'

'Excuse me sir. How do you spell that Gave word?'

'One man evaded my sally but I held the other at bay until you arrived. With commendable speed I may say.'

'Ah… yes sir. In the area, sir.' The officer is avoiding his eye. 'Were you by any chance in the Army, sir? Only I have observed a number of things—'

Donald harrumphs. 'If there is anything else, officer?'

The officer stands. 'Thankyou, sir, you've been most helpful. There is one other matter that I have to attend to; that weapon you were holding when we came in. It must be illegal, a blade over four inches in length.'

'It is an historic artifact that I have owned for many years. I believe it is exempt from the law that applies to flick-knives and the such. Nor do I carry it; what about these Scottish castles with huge arrays of swords, cutlasses and so on?'

The officer makes a note in his book. 'I'll check on that, sir. May I take it into custody for the present?'

'I'd rather you didn't.'

'And I'd rather you did, sir.'

The officer leaves not long after, carrying the glaive, a self-satisfied look on his face. With a look of loathing, Donald watches him go down the path, and starts putting his house to rights.

– 7 –

It is one of those times in life when we are confounded by the behaviour of fellow citizens. It does us no good to ruminate on such matters, when we have been broken into by those who claim to be policemen, watched a criminal – and that is not too strong a term – walking off calmly with the policemen and then had to educate another police officer in metric conversion. We can appreciate that it tries the patience of anybody; it certainly tries an exhausted soul. And when the burglars have been those who accosted you on a public road, we would be forgiven for putting Donald on the sick list, taking a long bath, and sitting in deep shade in the garden with a long drink, preferably of the alcoholic type, and considering moving to another country, preferably in the Commonwealth. Had some experience of the Commonwealth when he was in the Army. Jolly friendly chaps.

However, Donald is made of a different fibre. No time for meditating on the ills of the police force or even feeling sorry for himself. He rights a chair, pushes it up to the table. Piles dishes and places them on the kitchen counter. Stares at the chaos; it reminds him slightly of the mess that was left after the last dinner in the regiment; what a long time ago that was. And then one could call on the corporals, do this, do that. Oh bugger. What is missing? Goes through and checks on the places where he has concealed his passport, driver's license and other essential papers. All present. Then he looks into drawers and finds that none of his wife's jewellery has gone and neither has the television, an old small screen, or the music player. Or apparently any of the CDs though they are scattered around his desk. What were they looking for? The bounders; what a mess.

The sun continues to shine but it has become to him a hostile glare like an interrogator's lamp. It holds no pleasure for Donald; he pulls down a blind, shuts it out. Buzzards are setting up an unbearable keening. The dog looks up for a walk, realises that it hopes in vain and slumps into its basket.

Ever since the shopping trip and the two oiks, he feels an aura of threat. The birds no longer give a friendly call but screech at every moment and why does barking sound like the hounds of hell? He feels drained. He doesn't bother to call the police back but makes tea and retires to bed, so early that he was sure that he would rise before midnight. He sleeps and sleeps until four o'clock when he rises with the sun and starts again to set things to rights. After walking the dog, which is reluctant to be disturbed from a long dream about two nice men who gave her the master's bed.

It is about nine o'clock in the morning. A knock on the door.

Donald is weary already, brushing and washing, cleaning all the books before replacing them, the saucepans and the dishes to be put back... he hasn't finished, there is a mess of cutlery and plates around him. He hasn't thought of contacting Beryl, wishing to put everything ship-shape before she can return; can't have her see a scene like that. Wouldn't be right. Not his standard. Hasn't even walked the dog up the cricket field. Harrumph.

He opens the door, two inches, and wonders whether he should open it fifty millimetres. Metric measurements; why? What was wrong with feet and inches, pounds and ounces, cables and fathoms? Perhaps they still use fathoms. What language is used for timber and flour and...

His rambling thoughts are disturbed. There is a man. Not young, a raincoat on a warm morning, hat and a tie. A face that looks well-travelled, the eyes deepset, sharp. Jehovah's Witness.

'Good morning, sir.'

'Oh, is it? No, sorry and all that but can't talk now. Good day.' He starts to close the door. Now, what was it that he was doing when he was interrupted? Ah yes, the crockery –

'Please wait. I believe you have had some trouble, a break-in.'

What the devil. 'Who are you?'

The man shows an identity card, briefly. Donald identifies nothing; some damned insurance man or something. Soon have him out of here.

'Could I come in? I won't be long.'

'Why?'

The man blinks and says that he really will be no trouble and has come to offer help. He looks harmless, too old to be trouble.

'Help? I don't need help. I need to be left alone and hopefully the police will lock up those two miscreants, ruffians, oiks and bounders, and throw away the key.'

'It is about those two men that I called.' A mild voice rather like a chaplain.

Donald sighs, opens the door and dusts a chair. 'I have had a break-in... dust everywhere... oh, you know that.' Old habits of hospitality assert themselves in spite of his frustration. 'Harrumph. Can I get you anything?'

'If you have tea in the pot...'

Damn, shouldn't have been so polite; of course he doesn't have tea in the pot; the very idea. Donald is not one of those who have an eternal brew; he likes clean pots, fresh brews, and puts everything away when finished and washed. Donald makes tea, puts mugs, pot and milk on the table, pours, sits. The other man has taken his hat and raincoat off and apparently settled in for a long stay. Donald feels a wave of fatigue wash over him. Confound the man; reminded him of the Colonel visiting the Mess. Walked in when he felt like it; no damned peace. We see him square his shoulders, shake himself. Rally the troops!

'My name is Smith. I came about your break-in. The police told me that you had not reported anything missing. That is surprising, is it not?'

'I don't know. I've never had a break-in before.'

'It's awful, isn't it? Quite a shock.'

'Who are you?'

'I've come from the police station.'

An ambiguous answer; sounds like a politician, sort of chap who never answers a question straight.

'I don't understand it. Meaningless. Nothing stolen, just a hell of a mess.'

'It's possibly that they could not find what they were looking for.'

'What on earth could that be?'

'Could it be something from the shop?'

Donald frowns; what on earth has the shop to do with anything? He is tiring of his visitor and his endless questions. He should be giving answers, not questions. Now, what questions should he ask of someone who has come from the police station? But he looks too old to be a police-man; perhaps he's a detective inspector, or something.

There is a knock at the door. Without thinking, Donald goes to the door, opens it halfway and stops. There is a lady standing there; tweed suit, lisle stockings, good leather shoes with a slight heel, well controlled hair. Looks like the Colonel's wife. She wears a hat with a silk flower, and a penetrating look as though she will be refused nothing, the kind to leave policemen apologising for having spoken. Rather like the Colonel's wife.

'Good morning. It's Donald isn't it?' A gracious smile that reminds him exactly of the Colonel's wife; this is getting a little unnerving. 'Now, I hope we can become acquainted. My name is Mrs. Fortesque; I live in the village over on Mount Street and

I chair the village fete committee. Now what I was wondering was whether we could have a chat. You know, most people in the village contribute in some way and we have a very successful fete. On the Green you know. Held it there for years. Well—'

For some time Donald, already lost in the conversation with Mr. Smith, had been holding up his hand to halt the flow; without effect. The dog has sniffed the lady's legs in detail, become bored and returned to its basket. Donald does not feel obliged to apologise for its behaviour.

Over her shoulder, a blackbird sets up a loud alarm before flying away.

'Oh.' She peers over his shoulder, though she is not a tall woman. 'You have company.' Stated as though it is a nuisance. 'I'm so sorry.' But she doesn't sound it. 'Could we have a friendly chat sometime, earliest would be best? I'll come round later; four o'clock suit you?'

Donald stares at her. Who the devil is she? 'Today is not convenient. I must go.' He closes the door as he hears her saying, Well, really. Returns to his chair.

Mr. Smith continues. 'As I said, could it be something from the shop?'

Donald stares; what the devil is he talking about? He pours more tea, looks around the room. Who the devil is this man? Why can't he bugger off? He is wasting my time. 'They broke the photograph of my wife.'

'I am sorry. Perhaps I can help you,' says Mr. Smith, round shoulders in a tweed jacket, a striped shirt, a tie from some organisation, a kind smile, a slight stoop of the balding head, sipping his tea.

'Help me?' He was assuming that he must be CID, a plainclothes man investigating the break-in. But he is having doubts; there is something else here. 'I can manage without help, thank you.' An old Army man can do without some random unit butting in; we feel for him.

'Well, we think that you might have taken something from the shop without being aware of it, something quite small. You know, picked up from the counter as you picked up your shopping.' A mild tone, almost avuncular but allowing for no opposition.

The shop again.

Donald notes that now there is a "we". 'Would you like to see my shopping?' A sharp tone; it's too much. He rises with a lurch, starts opening drawers and cupboards, the fridge, spreading bread, butter, cheese and the vegetables among the mess of cutlery and plates and saucepans. His movements become erratic, his hands shaking, knocking over things. A mug goes flying to the floor with a smash. He stops, pulling himself up. A parade ground 'ten-shun'. Eyes closed. Poor Donald.

A plane passes over at speed, low, the sound blasting through the village like a flood surge.

'My dear fellow.' Mr. Smith has risen, taken Donald by the arm. 'Here, sit down. I didn't mean to distress you. I'll send someone in to help you restore everything and, if you allow me, I'll have your wife's picture restored.'

'I don't know what you are talking about, something picked up at the shop.'

'Well, I wonder… if I help you, do you think you could help us?'

Donald stands, looking around. He is becoming more settled, giving himself time to think, to assess the man before him. How can he have thought that it was a Jehovah's Witness? There is something much harder here, something that burrows beneath the skin that doesn't give up. Like a parasite; remembered those from hot countries. Took a hot poker to them.

He looks down at the little man; wondered what he would say with a hot poker up his… 'You refer to "we". And who is "we"?'

'I wonder… of course, we know of your work, the Army and then the College and so forth. And were you not approached by the Secret Service after your Army career with a view to enrolling you? I've seen the file. You didn't think you were suitable though you were interested.'

Donald sits, gazing down. Join the Secret Service? I should think not. Funny lot, never know when they are coming or going. Couldn't understand them. And as for saying that I didn't think I was suitable, they didn't find me suitable. What is going on here? But what is it that he has not picked up from the shop that is so important?

'So… you have probably guessed; I'm in MI5. I'm sure you know what we do, who we are. And I must apologise for the mess,' he sweeps his arm around the room. 'It was not intended but the Special Branch boys can be a bit blunt, always in a hurry.'

Donald is silent. Was that what he is saying? Those oiks were Special Branch? He never came across them in the Army; they belong to the Police in some manner. But dammit they're not above the law.

'Do you mean… are you saying, that those two miserable little squaddies, who by the way accosted me on the road outside the shop, are you saying… ' Donald is running out of air. Slow down, Donald.

Mr. Smith starts to speak. Summoning his best parade ground face, Donald gives him a fierce look, holds up his hand to arrest any interruption. Speaks slower. 'Are you saying… that you are responsible for this… this illegal break-in?'

Mr. Smith bows his head, shakes it a little and looks up, full of regret, hands clasped before him. 'As I said, I would be happy to get someone to come in and help you restore things. I am very sorry that it has been necessary to proceed in this manner; as I said, Special Branch are a very blunt chisel. But I would be grateful if you could do something for me.'

'You break into my house, breaking and entering I believe it's called, create mayhem, encourage a couple of unprincipled squaddies to threaten citizens on the public road and now… now you want me to do something for you. Harrumph!'

'It's not a lot of work.'

'What on earth could I do for you? What should I do for you?' Donald is tiring; he is finding that this man does not bend to his onslaught. He becomes wary; reminds him of those odd men from Army Intelligence; they couldn't polish their shoes either.

'Oh, I don't think it would be too hard for you. We would like you to watch the shop-keeper.'

Donald gulps. 'Watch? You mean… spy… spy on… what can you mean?' His heart has started a quick march to an unfamiliar tune.

'I wish I could tell you. But there are good reasons why we think something is going on at the shop. And I would be very grateful for your help. For the country.'

Donald stands up, shaking himself mentally, looking out of the window, at the mess in the kitchen, at the gap in the wall where his wife's photograph had hung. It was a low blow, "the country". He has served his country faithfully in his regiment; he knew about serving the country. But spying on the shop cannot be serving the country. It is stupid, a fantasy by some damned Whitehall mandarin. Well, they can go to hell.

'You don't live in a village, do you?' he says, a tone only two decibels beneath a parade ground sergeant major but increasing in volume as he makes his point. 'You talk about spying on the shop-keeper; it would be like spying on your wife. Or near enough. We all know each other well, our blessings and our faults. And you are a stranger, an outsider. You cannot understand; you can have no idea of how what you ask is impossible. Totally unacceptable. Not on. Harrumph!'

A sparrow, munching peacefully on a berry outside, takes off in a panic, loud warnings to family and friends who broadcast the alarm until the garden is a discordant deafening chorus.

'Oh… I'm sure I didn't mean—'

'Well what did you mean? It just isn't cricket. What did you expect? And don't talk to me about serving the country; I don't recall seeing you in North Ireland… or Iraq or…' He has run out of breath, again. He subsides into a chair, a crash. His heart is doing double time, like a platoon on the parade ground.

The garden is empty of birds and even a local cat has chosen to threaten the wildlife elsewhere.

Mr. Smith is unhappy, a little flustered, looks this way and that, his hands restless on the table. 'I apologise. I have not handled this very well. I'm sorry. I didn't mean to… well, we have a problem.'

Donald is silent. Dust, usually floating in friendly motes, starts to settle.

'There's not much I can tell you. But would it be possible for you to tell me about any strangers that you see around? Near the shop? Going in or around the back?'

Donald speaks slowly, spelling out the words as though speaking to a new very green recruit. 'I don't spend my time hanging around like the youth of this village. You would be better recruiting them… no, perhaps not. Their parents would never forgive them. And as to strangers hanging around, I believe you were responsible for the last two.'

'Well,' Mr. Smith has risen, 'if there is anything that you

would like to know, or tell us, will you call this number?' He lays a card carefully on the table, next to the teapot. Puts on his raincoat slowly.

Donald opens the door. 'I should imagine that we will not meet again. Good day.' And good riddance.

Mr. Smith walks out, a sharp look at Donald as he passes. Donald closes the door firmly and collapses into a chair at once. In time, the sparrows return to happy family bickering, and Donald's heart resumes a more familiar pattern.

– 8 –

Donald is lost; we know he is doing more thinking than is good for him, but what can we do? His tinnitus is bad, his heart is arythmic, his digestion is starting to cease activity. What is he to feel, when he has been visited by MI5? What would we feel if MI5 came knocking on our doors? What is he suspected of? And how could they demand that he spy for them? Within the village? It is disgraceful. Working for the country, indeed! Poor Donald.

He reaches down and scratches the dog's back. The dog doesn't receive much attention and arches her back gratefully. And then Donald moves on. He thinks of the spy catchers of the Second World War, of Walsingham, Queen Elizabeth's Spymaster, and of earlier periods. Who did Henry III use? There must have been somebody, a man who investigated the threats against the King and Country, who divided the faithful barons from those who usurped. Or took sides with the Scots. Or the French. Traitors.

Is he, Donald, really a threat to Queen and Country? But to be conceived as not helping MI5 puts one out of kilter, out of the safe hearth of Englishmen. What would the regiment say?

'Harrumph.' Could imagine being drummed out of the barracks on Feast nights. Wouldn't do. Feast nights provide a chance to meet the fellows, and have a damn good meal. Confound it.

What is it about the shop? Who is Jac? He has never explored her past, as she has never explored his own. Is her slight accent a clue? What is Jac short for? He assumes that she has been an immigrant at some time, perhaps second generation. She has mentioned the North; how far North? Never very clear where the North becomes the North. You take the old Great North Road, and somewhere North of Lincolnshire, you…

All these questions leave him feeling dizzy. Not good for the heart. Or the head. Too much to consider at one time. Must break it down. Order of combat. First, coffee. Then a bit of exercise; dog-walking.

A man comes, the day after Mr. Smith left, offers his help. The dog growls at him. Donald sends him away at the door, tells him not to come again. Not going to have yet another person rummaging through his house; good gracious, thought he'd made that clear to that thingummy man, Mr. Smith. If that is his name, which he doubts. And if the dog growled, then he wasn't right. Useful animals, dogs; no side, good instincts.

He doesn't want anybody else in his home; he cancels Beryl's next visit, asks her to come in a week's time. The weather turns, and he burrows down in his bivouac, lights a fire, reads deeply, carries out research and returns to his book. Nothing like a bit of peace, bedding down, running silent like a submarine in a war film he has seen. Time passes, interrupted by the post deliveries, the barking of local dogs, the morning chorus and the baaing of sheep, down in the river meadow. And all the other village sounds; the grass must be growing at a furious pace, according to the activity of mowers, here and there.

And then Mrs. Fortesque calls again. He has mellowed; a

little. He looks her up and down, pauses a minute to establish his command of the situation, and lets her in. Can't remember her damned name; oh well. The dog repeats its inspection of her legs and her shoes and returns to its basket; visitor to be trusted. Donald notes the way she looks around the room, gives a little sigh, but what can she mean? She produces a tissue and dusts the chair offered but noting Donald's expression apologises immediately. It is clear that she feels that she has not made a good start and produces a terrifying smile. Donald chooses to ignore her for a while, busies himself with making tea, goes outside to feed the birds and is tempted to brush the floor but feels that that might be taking it a bit too far. He senses a woman who is used to exercising a measure of power. He has little experience of women in power; his own wife was a dutiful officer's wife, carrying out officer's wife type duties; pretty much everything to do with home; come to think of it, she actually found the home and furnished it, did the shopping and meals, supplied the off-spring and, in time, saw them off to their own homes. All the while servicing a base for him. Nature of it. He always avoided the Colonel's wife, as much as he could; there was a battleaxe of the old school, poorly educated, brought up no doubt in a cold house with numerous siblings over which she maintained an iron fist. Limited private education. What else could he say about her; except that she was to be avoided. He had seen young lieutenants fall under her eagle eye and end up running pointless errands and escorting her bony daughters to dances. God knows how she got them married off, the girls. And the young men.

'I've come about the fete.'

Ah, Mrs. Fortesque, that was it. Donald is rescued from memories that haunt him. Her accent, Home Counties, exaggerated, haughty, protecting her self-esteem. 'I am the chair this year you know.'

Donald didn't; he has not read the Village News for a while, finding that there is little to interest him though he would be offended if a copy did not fall on his door-mat regularly. He says nothing, pouring tea, pushing a cup on a saucer over the table followed by milk and sugar. No biscuits for this lady.

It is a symptom of villages that there is nobody in charge or prominent, in the way that towns and cities have Lord Mayors and Councillors. Some villages we know retain their feudal chiefs, a hangover from the Norman knights, who own most of the land and a good number of houses as well. These chiefs occasionally serve in the most beneficial way to their settlements, acting as chairman of the Parochial Church Council, head of charities and so on and disbursing contributions from their own wealth to maintain the church and the village hall; indeed, in many cases, the village hall is named after their family. But they rarely take civil appointments such as chair of the parish council. A good healthy village will have a great number of chairpersons, to the parish council, the parochial church council, the cricket club, the football club, the gardening club, the Green trust, the Common trust, the Village trust, the village society, the Am Dram society, the Hall committee, the reading group, the old peoples group, and any number of charitable trusts. They all operate individually without reference to each other, except occasionally agreeing a timetable so that there isn't a clash in potential audiences and income. And now here is the chair to the fete committee. He sighs.

She has fallen silent; she seems thrown from her customary position of dominance by Donald's quiet contemplation of his cup, the table, her hands and her hat that has remained firmly in position. It's the same hat, with a silk flower. She slides off her gloves and conceals her hands below the table; Donald notices that they are bony and a little large. Jac has lovely hands; as did his wife. Surprising really, the amount of hard work she, the wife, did; but her hands were always lovely and she made good use of them. He dreams of the past again, intimate loving thoughts. He misses her, from time to time; he remembers… oh well, perhaps not the time.

After a good pause, while Mrs. Fortesque sips and stares at him, Donald drags himself back. 'The village fete?'

'We have had a fete here for some thirty years you know. And a jolly good one too. People come from miles away; a nightmare of parking.' A quick laugh, like the clash of a sabre. 'Oh well.'

'There is a fete this year?'

'We thought that it was time to stir the stumps, to get ourselves moving you know. Nothing for the last two years as you would expect. Got to have a good one this year. And we wondered if you would like to contribute.'

There is a pause as Donald pours more tea. He sits back and looks at her. A slow smile of relief.

'My dear lady, of course. I should be delighted. How much did you have in mind?'

She sits up, a hand across her mouth; she looks like a startled fawn. There is a burst of laughter, an unmelodic clatter.

'Oh no, Mr.… er… sir. That's not what I meant at all you know. Oh no.' Another rattle of laughter. Donald wonders whether she was a giggler at school, one of those tiresome girls that would never shut up. There were those dances organised with the nearest girls' school; hordes of girls bussed in to bring a slight sense of civilisation to the senior boys. Things got out of hand on occasion… the girls were frighteningly mature, compared with the boys. School didn't seem to mean the same thing to them; they appeared to enjoy it. And hunting boys. He remembers the fear, and hiding in the Gym; and the relief of getting into the Army, a largely male environment. Surprising that he ever got married, in retrospect. Or was it? Taken in hand…

'Perhaps you would be so good as to enlighten me.' Donald is tiring of this woman already. He gazes out of the window and considers the next move at Towton; would it be the cavalry charge? Sometimes, he has a certain difficulty; it is difficult not to have a favourite side, in this case the Yorkists. And that would prejudice an objective exploration of how the outcome of the battle might have materialised. Damn tricky. Harrumph.

Outside, the sun is creeping behind a cloud and the light palls; birds hush their young as though it is bedtime.

'The fete is about people, the village people you know. We never think of the financial gain. Though we have done quite well in former years; thousands distributed to village charities you know. No, no. The fete is about our people.'

Our people? Does she mean village people? Or is there some other meaning here? Some business that she is involved in? If it is village people, she makes it sound as if she is lady of the manor. Donald's mind goes back to feudal days, the power exercised by the local lords, the villeins and merchants. What was it like, the way the lords exercised power? Did they really practice droit de seigneur? Perhaps to improve the blood stock. And there was archery practice, mandatory… oh well. He is limiting his efforts with Mrs. Fortesque, stifling a yawn.

'I see.' He doesn't see at all. How long will this wretched woman carry on?

'No, no. I wondered, you know, whether you might contribute with your particular skills.'

'My dear woman, you must be mistaken. I have no particular skills and I am not in the bloom of youth.'

She rallies, a sniff, her hands appear in a gesture. 'I have heard, been told that you lectured in Medieval warfare. We were wondering if you could organise a re-enactment you know. That would be marvellous, quite marvellous.'

Where the devil did she heard that? He didn't think he had spouted and boasted about his past; he has looked for a quiet life, one without others placing expectations on him. And how long is she going to assume that he knows; he doesn't know and he doesn't want to know. This "you know" is getting him down. And who is this "we"? 'Oh, I think I'm too old for that sort of thing.'

'We would find lots of help for you, you know. You need expend little energy on it, just tell us what to do.' A pause. 'And I hope you would join in.' Another burst of machine-gun laughter.

Donald gives her a parade ground look, no humour at all. 'Have you lived here long?'

She smiles, apparently completely untouched by his attitude. 'Years and years. We moved here when my husband retired from the bank, you know. He passed away two years ago. I understand that your wife went at much the same time. My sincerest commiserations.' The hat bobs in sympathy.

'Where did you live before?'

'Well, I married into the Fortesques of Derbyshire, you know. My husband did not inherit; he has... had an older brother. Old family, money in mines but great farming family in former centuries. Honoured in Victorian times you know. Not that we pretend to anything like that nowadays; of course.' She gave a tight smile, clasped her hands together.

'I would have to think about it.'

'Perhaps a little procession and a small battle, you know. And if you could put up a small display and tell visitors about the weapons and...' She tails off as Donald has risen and is standing by the door.

'Good day, Mrs. Fortesque.'

'Oh. Yes. Thankyou for the tea. Yes indeed. You will think about it?' She stands, gathers her handbag and silk scarf, looks around once more and turns for the door. Does she have a look of regret?

'Good day.' He closes the door firmly behind her and returns as rapidly as he can to his earlier state of deep peace, putting the village fete entirely out of mind.

– 9 –

Donald has a predicament; he must avoid the shop, afraid that if he is to be left with Jac alone he might slip up and blurt out about his visitor and the Special Branch and the MI5 and their request to spy on her. Which he is jolly well not going to do. She knows him too well; she will tell if there is something amiss and he can't tell her about Mr. Smith. It would scare her, send her into a panic possibly; create all sorts of problems. It does not cross his mind that if he told Jac, and if she is unwittingly involved in some crime, that he might be warning the criminals. Jac can't be a criminal; the very thought…

But it's damn inconvenient. He is obliged to patronise a supermarket at the local town. He can't find anything, and calls upon the assistants for help. The first two times they smiled and took him to where he could see what he wanted, but after that, he noted a distinct coolness and found that he was deserted in aisles where he recognised none of the products and he became deeply frustrated, tempted to leave his trolley, walk away, return to peaceful isolation. Until the memory of an empty refrigerator and the problem with avoiding the local shop drove him to wheel his purchases to a kiosk and pay cash; if he lacked anything, he would have to manage without. Harrumph.

He passes a week working, keeping to his home, welcomes Beryl back to her duties, does a little gardening. It is not something he enjoys much; it is nice to sit in a hole cleared from the wilderness under a parasol, reading but he has no interest in clearing the garden beyond his nest. When he feels it is becoming a wilderness, he hires a local boy to trim the hedges and lower the growth but that is all. Now and then, he gets the idea that his neighbours think he is 'untidy'; but doesn't he live in a village in the country? Damn suburban ideas.

One day, as he is dozing, a book on his chest, the dog asleep at his feet, a ball crashes through the branches of the apple tree behind him, and lands in his lap. He surfaces with a groan. What the…

He stands, looks around. The birds are still singing, bees hovering over the blossom, the dog has scarcely moved and he is standing with some uncouth ball, presumably used for recreational purposes, in his hands. 'Harrumph!'

He negotiates the apple tree, approaches the boundary fence and throws the ball over.

There is the loud and unmistakeable sound of breaking glass.

'Oy!' The voice is unmistakeably angry. 'What the – do you think you are – doing?'

Donald does not approve of other people swearing at him, and stands up straight, addressing the unseen man as though he was the fence.

'I do not like balls being thrown at me, particularly when I am taking my ease in my own garden.'

'I don't know anything about a – ball and you've just broken my greenhouse.'

'You don't know anything about the ball?' Donald is beginning to have doubts, feel that he has moved into an incorrect but not unfamiliar scenario. We have seen that exercise when he was at Army College; gave the young soldiers a set of coordinates and was surprised by a very angry farmer who telephoned to say that he had had his ewes disturbed at lambing time. Called for a personal apology; the Colonel insisted on that, and there was a process of remuneration to be followed by the Army. Donald's name was mud with the Colonel for a time. And there was the time with the nudist colony…

'Well, I am very sorry but the ball did come from your direction.'

There was a pause. Then he heard the man's voice again. 'Ere, Jonny, you playin with that ball again?' A muffled reply.

The man's voice again, raised. 'Well, you had no right breaking my greenhouse.'

'And you had no right disturbing my peace.'

'I'll be round to disturb your peace if you don't pay for my greenhouse.'

Donald feels the powers of right deserting him and agrees that he will supply glass for the greenhouse, on condition that no more balls come crashing into his garden. He goes indoors; somehow, it is no longer peaceful in the garden.

He telephones a son. An odd echo on the line. Rum. He asks his son, why do 'phones develop an odd echo, a bit like when one is 'phoning America? The son goes quiet and doesn't talk about anything useful except to suggest he looks at the underneath of the 'phone. The underneath? What the… but the son has rung off. He looks at the telephone; two screws showed scratches. It has been opened recently; how dare they? Is this what they mean by being bugged? If only he had known before Mr. Smith came, he would have made him remove it himself. He groans and feels less secure; it's as if there is a spy in the room, spying on him, spying on what he does, who he talks to, what he buys, where he goes. What had he done to deserve it? He considers ringing the Mr. Smith number and taking him to task. Yes, he will do it but not just now.

He feels tempted to call the regiment; like calling on your family. Speak with the Colonel. But he comes up against that MI5 thing, not supporting "the country", and discards the idea with regret. As to his own sons, well they're always busy.

He feels an insect worming away at his conscience; he knows that he will have to confront Jac. He rings, ignoring the bug; she is delighted to hear from him, asks how he is, why hasn't she seen him for a while; she leaps at the chance to meet at the pub.

A midweek evening; the pub is quiet. A few looks from the men at the bar, a titter; Donald ignores them. It is curious, he thinks to himself, how some men have little else to do than generate gossip. Why, any gossip in the mess room stayed in the mess room. If only it was the same for the pub.

They sit. Small talk, how had he been, she had heard about the break-in, it must have been awful, and how is the shop, have you been busy, and then…

'Where do you come from, Jac?'

She sits up, stares at him. 'Why this question, Donald?'

He gulps, smiles. Can't tell her about Mr. Smith; it would scare her. 'Well, you know, I realised that I didn't even know where my friend came from, except I suspected it was not from England. Well, not the North of England.'

'Aye, I do. Brought up in Gateshead. Parents immigrants; are immigrants. They live there. Not a bad country, you know. Interesting history; you must go. There're all sorts of museums, on—' She was rambling. He has to interrupt.

'And where did your parents come from?'

'Oh, you mean to label me? Oh Donald, am I not worthy English girl?'

'When one has been brought up in rural Norfolk and live in it now, your accent is as rare as the call of a… well, some rare bird. I was interested in your accent; didn't recognise it.'

'My parents come from Georgia. It makes me laugh; people wonder why I don't have an American voice.'

'Never been to America. Full of Americans. Harrumph.' He has, but has strong views about Americans.

Jac laughs. 'What a surprise. You don't like Americans?'

Donald ignores this question; he has had some trouble in the Army with Americans when he was sent on a joint conference in the States; all over a caddy of tea, that the American servant had disposed of with the best of intentions, suspecting that the English visiting officer was harbouring drugs. He had words with the American colonel, the echo of which rebounded across the Atlantic. And earned him his Colonel's reprimand. He drags himself back to the present.

'Your parents; they escaped?'

'Yes.'

Donald looks at her. She seems to be someone he has not known before. He sees her sitting bolt upright, proud.

'They were teachers, good teachers, but here they qualify for menial jobs only. They were so proud when I went to university; I could live the full English life; they feel they are not English yet.'

'Do you remember Georgia?'

'Oh yes.' Her eyes sparkle. 'It is a beautiful country and proud. Georgians proud. And they drink, not like a pint here. Happy drunks, I remember. We always speak Georgian at home; I have always speak our language. I was the first to learn English, at primary school. It was easy.'

Donald notices that her English language has improved, and the Georgian accent receded. He has never heard the English language described as easy to learn; perhaps if you are a child... 'So you escaped with them?'

'Mm. I was on school exchange; they arranged for me to defect, a child. I was eight.'

'It is interesting, Jac. Thank you.'

'And you, Donald. What of your life?'

And he tells her briefly of his past, school, Army, University, marriage and family. She asks what the Norfolk life was like in his youth; had he lived in a small village like this one? Where did his friends live? What did his father do? He responds, but briefly; he doesn't find his own past interesting, and what can he say about his father?

Must address the MI5 problem.

'Jac, can you tell me about the envelope you gave me?'

'What envelope was that?'

Is she concealing something? He rummages in his mind for a way forward. Harrumph. 'Oh, the day your shop was turned over; did you lose anything?'

She frowns. 'Not one thing. It is very strange. I remember, you post envelope for me. Mrs. Jones come in talk about a bad egg; wasn't it awful?'

'What was in the envelope, Jac?'

'In it? That's a funny question, Donald. I don't talk about your letters.'

'I've been asked what I took away from the shop and I didn't take anything. Well, obviously my shopping. And your envelope.'

'You've been asked? I was taken away, all night, interrogated... it was like back in the East; I have no idea what it is all about.'

'What did they want?'

'Oh, they talk about the shop, where I get my goods, what I sell, is there other business in the shop… it goes on and on.'

'Did they look after you?'

'You joke; it go on all night. One cup of coffee; disgusting!'

'Who were they?'

'Two rough men who don't listen to what I say; it was being recorded, like in Georgia. Threatening me. Crude men. And then, early morning… I was very tired and sick… this old man come in, all friendly like a priest and asked if I can help him. And he help me. Very gentle but always asking. I don't trust him.'

Ah, Mr. Smith. 'Could the envelope have anything to do with it?'

'No.'

'Really?'

'You must know, Donald, just some poems that my beautiful lover in Norwich send me. You have never read such letters, so beautiful, so full of love… I love him, he so busy, he doesn't have time off to see me.'

'What does he do?'

'He is at university.'

'A student?'

'Oh, much cleverer. He is working for a Doctorate, doing research.'

'Clever lad. What's his subject?'

'I don't know.'

'Really?'

'I know nothing about it.'

Donald fills their glasses, sits back. Damned odd; you would expect her to know something of his work; maybe he is concealing something from her? Or maybe it's all nonsense; the MI5 people have got the wrong idea. He remembers a time when they were sent on a sortie in Iraq and it turned out to be a local wedding; damned intel was up the creek.

Time passes. There is a loud laugh from the bar; Donald sees heads turned away, sniggers over pint glasses. A man comes in, swaying, and is ejected by the publican.

'Jac, I don't understand. Why do you post the poems away when he has sent them to you?'

Jac gives him a long look. 'I don't know why they are important to you.… he is having them bound in special book, a special present for me. Isn't that wonderful?'

'What a marvellous present. I don't know much about you young people but he sounds like an honourable man.'

' 'Honourable'? What is that?' Jac laughs.

'Jac, I haven't told them about the envelope. I forgot about it, and then…'

So that's it. Mr. Smith is barking up the wrong tree. They talk of little things, a little of Georgia and her background, and leave together in peace. Donald believes that she is telling the truth, and he wonders about how Mr.Smith would treat her; better to keep them apart for now.

– 10 –

We suspect that it's all nonsense and it will go away when the powers that be realise what a stupid mistake they are making. Pestering Jac and himself; it shouldn't be allowed, but how can he do anything? A bit like school bullying; difficult to report. Even the masters didn't like to hear of it. The Regiment? Damn, that damned MI5 thing.

He resists the temptation to kick the dog but walks it, ignores the friendly enquiries from other dog owners, returns to his home and burrows down, avoiding any contact.

He presses on with his book, planning a journey that will take in important cathedrals and castles, Pevsner in hand. He reads history, learns of the kings who ensured their longevity by the repetition of their armed image, in stained glass, parchment, painting and tapestry. He plans chapters, headings, themes, illustrations, and becomes absorbed, meals an interruption, nights passed from need alone; ah, this is the life, everything else is just a distraction. The fete and its re-enactment troubles him not at all; he doesn't think of it at all. Actually, he has forgotten it completely.

One morning, he has just started work when there is a knock on the door. He ignores it; work is more important. A few minutes later, another knock, louder and then another, his name is called. Damn it, he strides to the door, determined to send this intrusion away. Isn't a man entitled to his bit of peace, particularly when he is retired?

It's Mr. Smith.

He stares. 'I'm working, I'm busy, and I believe that we had nothing further to discuss. What do you want?' Good gracious, couldn't these men ever take a hint? He is quite prepared to be rude when the occasion calls; it doesn't come easily not after a career in the Army but a bit of bluntness worked well at Cambridge. Though he did regret the time that he sent a student away in tears. A misunderstanding, he was sure.

Mr. Smith smiled, his hat in his hands. 'There has been a development; I feel you should know of it. But I can come back later, if it suits you.'

'Yes... er, no, blast it. But don't be long.' And he turns, the door open behind him. When a man has been tested as he has, he doesn't feel obliged to pursue good manners, particularly with the agent of his break-in, his obstruction on the road and questioning. He is entitled to his freedom, freedom from questions and obstructions. And break-ins. And, history has shown it clear enough, the right to freedom prevails in this world more often than not. He feels weary, the need to preserve his independence.

Mr. Smith follows, taking off his raincoat. Hangs it over a chair, places his hat on the table and sits without being invited. Donald stares at his audacity, says nothing but sits facing him, his hands clasped in front of him; he is not going to offer drinks, he is not going to waste time. His vein of hospitality has run dry. He gazes out of the window; at least he has nothing to fear from this old man, whoever he represents.

A blackbird is perched on a branch of the fruit tree, gazing in the window. It's saying something; Donald wishes he could understand. Maybe blackbirds could be used for spying in the future; they are so intelligent and friendly. What would it be like to –

'Your work; I'm sorry to disturb. Is it related to your teaching?'

Donald drags himself back to the man in front of him. 'In a manner of speaking.' More questions.

'You are still tutoring or mentoring?'

'You know, you have it quite wrong.' Donald examines him; he sees a man who sits meekly in his chair, his hands folded in front of him, his eyes deep as ever but downcast, no interrogation. 'You have something you must tell me though I am not interested in the matter that you have to convey. In fact, I see your presence here as a further intrusion on my privacy.'

Mr. Smith sighs very quietly; he does not appear in the least discomposed by Donald's words but sits at the table, his hands clasped in front of him, a benign expression. 'Your work, it must be interesting, considering your vocation.'

Vocation? Donald has never thought of his life in the Army and College in that light. Vocations are for priests, aren't they? His life; one thing led to another: school, college, the Army, a Lecturer in Medieval Studies at a Cambridge College, a pastime in coaching the Third Eight on the river. The odd visit to the College pub, the occasional dinner in Hall, celebrations and the work; not an unpleasant life, competitive to an unexpected degree but charmed with meeting pleasing young people who became victims in his enactments without complaint and dons with a range of interests far beyond their teaching lives; horse racing, illicit stills, breeding pigeons, cooking raised pies and setting up speed records for the drive to London. Not a whiff of the Army but a similar shared feeling of belonging, chaps you knew and could depend upon for the loan of a tenner, undergraduates who would babysit at short notice; as long as you concealed the whisky.

'What is it now? I don't have much time.' His mind is a blur. Damn tricky; he likes to finish a job properly before going on to tackle anything fresh. He has been working on his book and now Mr. Smith wants him to learn something else. A long way from medieval warfare. It's just too much for his mind to jump; six hundred years, apart from anything else. Basically, just a damned nuisance.

'I wondered whether you had had any success in observing strangers in the village.'

Donald reels; is this all it's about? 'I thought I told you... I don't hang about the street corners. You have not selected an appropriate person for your task; I rarely leave my home, except for a bit of shopping. If that is really all you want –'

'No... no, I do understand that. But you are friends with Jac, the shopkeeper and you even go for a drink with her. I should imagine. From time to time.'

Of course. He must know that they met at the pub; the bug. Spying on him. He hadn't spotted any "spy", some unwanted person hanging about in the dark and he doubted that it was the men at the bar. Perhaps of which, could it have been the barman? 'Talking of which, might I see the license that you obtained for putting a bug in my 'phone? Without any cause, I may say.'

'Oh, I'm sure we can arrange that. And as to any cause, we do have a cause. But to return to the shop-keeper, she might have given you some clue, some dropped reference to the… er… problem.'

Donald feels a spark of anger. 'I'm surprised that you haven't bugged the pub. As well. And when am I to learn of the "cause" that you hold against me?'

Mr. Smith shakes his head, a slight smile. 'It is unfortunate that we have to do these things. You know, the public really have no idea of the troubles that we have to contend with. You speak of two rough men who, you say, threatened you on the way back from the shop. And yet, we deal with problems of such scale that you couldn't imagine. So, I must beg that you don't dismiss me as you dismissed me last time.' Spoken apologetically.

Donald is reminded of the occasion when the headmaster of his prep school 'carpeted' him over a matter of correcting his form master over the dates of kings. He was accused of cheek; he knew he had been right on the dates. He didn't do it on one occasion but a number and it made him unpopular with the staff; and his form colleagues. He remains silent, a slow burn of anger concealed behind a rigid face.

A pair of American F15 fighters roar overhead, lower than usual. Mr. Smith pauses, looking up.

'Do you often get this noise? Ah, Americans. Not unrelated to our work I suppose. Anyway, where was I? Strictly speaking I should not be giving you this information. But I have resolved to trust you. In effect, I am trusting you to the degree that you would have been if you had signed the Official Secrets Act. So please take notice that any departure from those standards will mean that you have breached those conditions. Do I make myself clear?'

Donald blinks, sits up. 'I am not aware of the latitude that you are giving me and I do not accept your limitations. I do not wish to be involved in your work; I do not accept that I am under the conditions of the Official Secrets Act. While I am sure that it is important, I cannot think that a retired man in his mid 70s would be much use to you. You are welcome to make use of the door.' What is wrong with the man? Can't he get a simple idea into his brain?

Mr. Smith ignores him. 'I am talking about a breach in national security, of a research project and of a village shop.'

'It sounds a most unlikely connection. Neither Jac nor I are aware of any breach that you refer to. I was appalled to hear that she was kidnapped and interrogated, overnight I may say, and no charges were forthcoming. What do you think you are up to?'

'And yet we have sound evidence that all three are linked.'

'What do you mean?'

'Help me with information.' Mr. Smith's eyes bore into Donald, seeking, demanding, persuading.

'Again, you ask me to spy on my friend? With no sign of any wrong-doing?'

'Let us say that you must act as if there is no problem at the shop. You may continue to see your friends, including Jac, and talk of normal things, things that do not intrude on the shop. And let us know of anything that seems illegal.'

'How the devil am I to recognise something illegal?'

'Oh... oh, I'm sure that a man of your experience would recognise something.'

Donald is silent. What was he taught as a boy? Silence is golden, but he feels severely tested.

'What I am going to tell you now is strictly secret and I am telling you so that you can appreciate that our concern is not fickle, or related to a minor indiscretion.'

'Don't tell me. I don't want to know.'

Mr. Smith continues as though he hasn't heard. 'There is some secret research related to the defence industry being carried out at the local university; it does not matter what field it is in, that is irrelevant in this case. But it appears that there is a leak; someone in the research team is sending out important and secret information to the shop here in this village. It is an odd situation; normally, there are letter drops, couriers, dead-drops, all the normal transmission devices for the espionage business.'

Donald is amazed. Nothing like the openness of regiment life. It sounds so far from village life, so far from anything that he could imagine that would involve Jac. He sits in silence and wonders whether Mr. Smith is going gaga. The village shop and national security; what nonsense. Poor chap, it must hard keeping track of everything and having to deal with little problems like this one. Now, if it had been in another country…

'However, as I said, the use of the shop is highly unusual. We believe that Jac is encrypting the material and transmitting it by email.'

'Then it must be very easy to terminate the connection. You know, the server thing.'

'And what would we have but a link from a chain, when we would like to see where the chain goes.'

'Can't you look at the emails? I thought you chaps could look into everything. Why don't you arrest the leak?'

'I wish we could. But we don't know who it is and the last thing we can do is interrupt the work.'

'Surely, it must be possible to catch the leak and put up with a delay.'

'There is another complication that I was not going to tell you. We assume that since Jac is a Georgian immigrant that she is a sleeper, now active, sending product back to Georgia. The last thing that Whitehall wants is to be seen slacking, slowing up the research. We discovered the leak but not the leaker; it is embarrassing enough and we do not know how it was established. Now we fear that Whitehall will act heavy-handily and take out the shop with Special Branch. They have no legal right to do so but it doesn't always stop them.'

Donald wonders what 'take-out' meant in these circumstances; it sounds rather violent. They have already acted in a heavy-handed manner in his own home. He guesses that the shop would close forever; Jac will be taken and convicted of treason, a spell in the Tower. No, no; getting carried away. They don't do that anymore. 'Have you spoken to Jac?'

'Of course. She is not admitting anything. Won't give us any name, denies any connection, says she's just a shopkeeper and so on. Now, we could remove her under suspicion of treason; we have the powers. But it would not help; we need to catch the leak, hold him or her in position while the work proceeds and close off the transit to… to wherever. Which brings us back to you.'

'Me?'

'I'm afraid so.' A look of deep regret.

'Why?'

'Why what exactly?'

'Oh for goodness sake, man, why does it come back to me?'

'Oh, I thought I'd explained that.'

'No. No, you have given no reason, no evidence, no… blast it, why can't you leave me alone?'

Mr. Smith looks down; minutes passed. A blackbird sets up a long call of alarm; Mr. Smith looks up, out of the window, a light in his eyes. 'There, you see. There.'

Donald looks out of the window, sees nothing, stares at Mr. Smith. Yes, the man is going gaga; saw it in the Regiment after a long spell in North Ireland. Men who couldn't take the strain. Not surprising really, the troubles he must be involved with. 'Look old chap, I don't know what you are seeing, but perhaps you should take a break, go on leave, that sort of thing, to cool the brain. Seen it before, you know, in North Ireland.'

Mr. Smith gives him an icy look. 'I was referring to the alarm set by that bird. Don't know the bird—'

'Blackbird. Always panicking about something, going off the deep end. In humans, we call it paranoia, don't we?'

'Then how are we to announce an alarm without lay people such as yourself calling it paranoia?'

Donald gave him a cool look. 'Where do you suspect the leak is going?'

'Oh, without doubt to Georgia. Who probably sell the product to Russia and plenty of other places. Secrets command a high price.'

'What if you terminated the research? Turned off the tap?'

'Politics, politics. Whitehall is telling us that it is important.'

'So you carry on with a leaky operation, Whitehall baying at your ankles, and some Eastern power taking the bread home, laughing all the way. My goodness, you are in a mess.' Hold on, Donald, you are getting drawn into the fantasy, this make-belief world that Mr. Smith occupies. All stuff and nonsense. Now, when he was in the Army, they dealt with real problems, nothing that is just rumours and heresay. Give me strength.

Mr. Smith sits in silence, gazing at the floor.

Donald rises, makes tea.

– 11 –

There is a pause.

Mr. Smith is looking at Donald; Donald is gazing out of the window. A pair of blue tits are feeding from the nutfeeder, always a pleasure to see. No cat in sight. He doesn't feel inclined to say anything.

'I don't know whether you have anything from the shop; you say you have not but it is a twisted picture involving friends and loyalties and I don't feel inclined to apply the thumb screws just yet. There is no doubt that Jac is involved in treason. Passing secrets to the enemy. It sounds like good old-fashioned stuff, doesn't it? Well, we have to get on top of it, find the leaker and the end of the chain. Piece by piece. And then we act.' Mr. Smith doesn't say how far their suspicions go, where the end of the chain is, who might be the leaker. He stops. Donald pours tea, offers biscuits, says nothing.

Mr. Smith sighs. 'I know, you are reluctant to be drawn into this mess and I can't blame you. Now, I have choices: I can arrest Jac, which we believe will disrupt one link in the chain though the leaker could use another method of transmitting secrets. It doesn't help us find the person leaking secrets, a traitor in old-fashioned terms. We need to capture the whole chain in one operation; eliminate the leak, prevent interruption to the research and keep Whitehall happy. They will not allow us to stop the research to find the leak.

'I can arrest you on suspicion of aiding and abetting Jac in the process of espionage. But I fear that it would prove nothing and apart from an uncomfortable stay in a safe house, followed of course by an apology when it is all over, I don't believe it would be productive.'

Donald watches Mr. Smith. Don't say anything; leave it to

him to come out with it. He doesn't feel scared that he will be shut up, though the sight of a 'safe' house would be interesting. He wonders what to cook for supper; will there be time to go to the butcher in the next village? It's not a 'fish' day, he is sure. At least, fairly sure. What is in the freezer? Maybe a steak…

'So… 'Mr. Smith looks at Donald, a slight smile, a look of commiseration rather than accusation, 'I would like you to help me. Do you think you could persuade Jac to help us, to reveal the leak quietly so that we can disrupt the research as little as possible, cease her activities, submit to a period of confinement, not long if she helps us and bring it all to a happy conclusion?'

'A happy conclusion?' Donald is cynical, a grim look, shaking his head. He thinks of Jac's boyfriend who sends her love letters and poems; it can't be him, they would have found out about him.

'That way, we can keep her out of the hands of Whitehall, out of harm, pretty much, and hopefully she will return to the shop.'

'Do you think I could persuade her?'

'There is another thing; the Georgians, or whoever, might execute Jac if they find her unreliable. I'm sure you wouldn't want that to happen.' The same quiet smile.

Donald's heart takes a leap; this is blackmail. He has to extract the truth from Jac, preferably an admission of guilt, or he will see her being killed by fellow Georgians who no doubt would stop at nothing. 'You must deal with a lot of big problems.'

Mr. Smith looks at him, raised eyebrows, a quizzical expression.

'I mean, it must be a heavy load.'

Mr. Smith says nothing.

Donald groans. 'Well, there must be some paranoia around. You know, in your business.'

'Paranoia?'

'Seeing ghosts under the bed.'

'Ghosts?'

'Spies who evaporate with the sun rising. Problems that are not really there.'

Mr Smith smiles, slightly. A cold smile that never reaches his eyes. 'How do you tell whether a problem is there or not until you investigate?'

Donald stares at him. 'Well, for goodness sake, something happens, doesn't it?'

'Quite so. Something happens. And a little voice told us that there is a leak in the research unit. A reliable little voice. We listen, we check. But there is no more, except that one of the team is sending out material that reaches where the little voice is located. There, I've told you more than I should.'

Donald is wavering; part of his mind lodges with the thought that it was all stuff and nonsense. But the threat of the Georgians acting; that is something else. And blackmail by Mr. Smith. 'Do you think I will succeed?'

'I don't know, I hope so. But is your heart in it?'

'I hear all that you say, I read the newspapers, hear the news. But Jac; that is something else. Perhaps it should not be me.'

'We have tried. Who else?'

Shortly afterwards, Mr. Smith left. Donald found it impossible to return to work; his mind was in turmoil. Why should Jac even listen to him? What was their relationship? She had been caring towards him, a good friend but he had done little for her, he realised. And might now to be putting their friendship at risk… no, he would destroy it, whatever happened.

And yet.

He telephoned; bugger the bug. Mr. Smith would be glad

to hear their conversation. He invited her to supper, the two of them, a cosy evening; she said she would bring wine.

$$- 12 -$$

The evening is beautiful, the sun setting over a warm and contented land, the sounds of lambs and swifts. The haunting smell of honeysuckle and cut grass. Low voices and noises around, a light murmur only.

They dawdle in the garden, a crisp white wine, bread sticks, nuts, speaking of everything and nothing; a companionable time. Birds chirrup, the smell of barbecues wafts over the hedge, cats creep through the gloaming. Bats flit, unseen. All is well with the world. Even the sounds, children shouting, lawnmowing, tractors and overflying aircraft are muted as though falling asleep. Jac says that she has never been in the garden before; it's wonderful, a wild paradise; she says she feels as innocent as Eve in the Garden of Eden. She trips around the mown paths, through wild flowers, long grasses and beneath the apple trees. Donald harrumphs, says that he is no Adam and there's no snake to offer her an apple. And considers that she seems well, even happy, the break-in set behind her. When the light has drawn in and a chill enters the air, they find themselves indoors, Donald serving up a cold supper, Jac drawing the cork on a fresh bottle of wine.

Donald feels a kind of paralysis growing, becoming breathless, unsure of what to say, to start; reminds him of the lull before going into action. That's what it is, really; tricky business. It was Jac who saw his difficulty.

'You have something, don't you, Donald? Can I help?' She leans over and presses his hand. 'What is it? What's the matter? Let me help you.'

An early owl swoops over the garden, scouting the long grass.

He sipped his wine, staring at the table. Dammit, why has he been given this mission? 'I don't know... don't know where to start. Damned tricky. Harrumph.'

'What start, Donald?'

'You know, the whole damned thing.'

'What "whole damned thing", Donald?' She enunciates the words with care, as though they might explode.

'Where do I start?'

'Tell something. Start.'

'Look, Jac old girl.'

Jac frowns; she did not like to be called old.

'Look,' he said. 'A couple of ex-Army oiks challenged me on the road—'

'I didn't know that.'

'My house is broken into, turned over. Nothing stolen. Turns out it's the same two oiks. And I'm visited by a man who says he's MI5.'

'I say, Donald, what an exciting life.' She laughs, silenced hastily as Donald glares at her. 'What do MI5 want? What is MI5?' She says this in a comical tone, and laughs again, again silenced when she observes Donald, who stares at her, a dark serious look.

Donald explains briefly the role of MI5, of state security, of suspected spies.

'Oh Donald, you danger to country? Or spy?' a quiet serious tone. 'A joke, yes?'

'What?'

'What I say.'

'What bit of what you said?'

'Um... danger to country... spy...' She is frowning,

controlling a chortle that breaks out, hastily stifled. 'I don't believe a word. Come on.'

Donald stares at her. What does she mean? He is mastering his thoughts as best he can; but he seems to have been thrown a googly. Jac thinks all this trouble is his fault, that he is guilty of… what Mr. Smith called treason. A bit stiff, going too far. He gulps his drink, chokes; Jac pats his back.

'Look, old girl—'

'I am not old girl. Don't say that.' She looks affronted.

'Oh, what did I say? Old girl… oh, sorry. Bad habit.' Plucks at his moustache.

'You must not say that to anyone. Even if they are old.'

'Really? I didn't know.' He thought it was just an expression of familiarity, like the French calling everyone "mon vieux".

Jac sits in silence, sips her drink.

How shall he start, gets things onto the right footing? 'Tell me Jac, did the men who turned over your shop wear black suits?'

'Funny you say that. Is true; black ties.'

'Black ties?'

'Black ties.'

'Like a funeral?'

'Yes, like funeral.'

'Did they identify themselves?'

'No.'

'I bet they were the same two who broke into my house.'

'Oh Donald!'

'And did they take anything from the shop?'

'Nothing… no, nothing, just me.'

'You?'

'Yes, I tell you. Interrogate all night.'

'Bastards!'

144

'Yes, bastards.'

'Why did they take you… I mean, did they say?'

'No.'

Donald havered; was this the time to tell her Mr. Smith's story? No use putting it off. 'Now, look old, girl… oh, woops, there I go again, many apologies. Look Jac, I have a story to tell you. Don't know how much is true, how much is just propaganda.'

'Propaganda? What you mean?'

'Maybe the wrong word. Sorry. I mean, just some story that people want us to believe that maybe not be the truth. If you see what I mean.'

'Do you mean "propaganda"?' Again, a careful enunciation.

'Well, actually, maybe. That might be just it. Yes.' Donald strokes his chin, meditating on the meaning of words, lost to thought. What is it when you are sold some story to make you feel guilty, or persuaded that it might mean something…

There is silence for a while; Jac drinks, Donald continues to be lost in thought. It is all so improbable, that Jac should be part of… of whatever it is, as the MI5 man described. The industrial espionage, the university, the chain…

'Er… Donald, I think you tell me story, which may be "propaganda". But is trouble for you. Yes?'

'It was this man from MI5. A quiet man, you would have thought a meek little man. But you would be wrong; he was like a… a… one of those fishes that grab you underwater and don't let go.'

'An octopus?'

'Is that a fish? Well, not quite what I had in mind. Perhaps a leech.'

'But they not fish. And small.'

'No, quite right. I think you are right; an octopus. Or perhaps a crocodile.' Donald is lost again, wondering which

145

fish, or otherwise, drags you down underwater. Perhaps it was a crocodile.

'Donald, you tell story?' Jac is sharp; she is used to Donald's lapses in concentration, but it can get frustrating.

'Anyway, he, this MI5 man, is persistent, hangs in there like anything. Maybe the same man who talked to you.'

'What does he want?'

'He told me this story. I still don't know whether to believe it or not.'

'How does it go?'

'Do you know, I'm not really sure.'

'Can you tell me story? Is it secret?'

'I'll tell any damn story I like. Not going to have some popinjay telling me what I can or can't tell.'

'Well?'

'Well, it seems to have bits that connect. Firstly, there is the Government that he calls Whitehall. They are very demanding, require things to be just so. I don't know whether they run MI5 or not. Maybe…'

'Yes, Donald? And next?'

'There is a research establishment in the local university carrying out research for Whitehall. And there is a leak in the research unit; sending out secret material.'

'Send it out?'

'Industrial espionage.'

'Industrial?'

'Yes, you know. Some process that is meant to be secret.'

'I ask you, what research?'

'I don't know. He wouldn't tell me. But Whitehall is very concerned that it continues in spite of the leak and MI5 has a damn tricky job of exploring the leak and finding out where the 'material' – that's the word they use – goes. So they can stop it going without stopping the research.'

'Like spy film.'

'Well.' Donald paused; now the tricky bit. 'The leaked material is being posted to your shop.'

I don't think we need to concern ourselves with how MI5 knew that. Perhaps an inside source, or a defector, or… Nevertheless, Donald and the MI5 man, "Mr. Smith" – like Donald, we don't really believe that that is his name – are working with that piece of "info".

There was a long silence. Jac stared, mouth open; Donald felt sick, a rush of blood to his face. He coughed; Jac poured him a glass of water.

Jac recovered first. 'What you talk about? I run village shop, food, papers, usual things…' She faded, staring into space. 'The men in black suits; they ask me same thing, information coming to shop.'

An expression of confusion passes over Donald. 'Harrumph. Probably all just stuff and nonsense.' It better be.

'The letters that I receive are from parents and my lover and I tell you, his letters are full of love. Private, nobody see them. Bills of course. And my parents are North, not to do with university.'

Donald sits up, a smile, slaps the table. A wave of relief pours over him. 'It's all nonsense, then. Harrumph! You're not transmitting secrets to another country, I'm not transmitting secrets to another country… I don't know what they can be talking about. And there's nothing else that you get from him, your lover?'

'Only poems; I read and post them to Cambridge, to be bound.'

'Poems?'

'All love poems, beautiful, I love them. I tell you; he binds them for me.'

'Doesn't sound as if they are spy material.'

'No, no. Tomas do not spy on England. We stay here for ever. He not naturalised; it come soon.'

Donald sits for a while, pours more wine, chews over the facts in his mind. This whole business is annoying him; it has nothing to do with Jac and himself; Mr. Smith should trot off and deal with the miscreants. There is just a thought…

'Jac… Jac, I have to ask. Damn rude, I know, but I must know.'

'Go on, Donald.' A weary tone.

'All right. Are you emailing anything to Cambridge? Like when to expect the next poems, or to hold back on one particular poem, or… or… oh, I don't know.'

'Well, now I think… no, goodness sake, Donald, no, no. I never email Cambridge. I email Tomas; he so busy, I see him not often. We email, often at night, like a conversation. I love him so…' Head down, a few tears drip onto the table.

Donald is deeply embarrassed; tackling women's tears has never been a strong point. He offers a white handkerchief, plucked from his blazer's top pocket. He mutters, dash it, shouldn't come to this. And he sits, letting time pass, letting the tears dry. His mind revolves slowly over the events of the past few days, over Mr. Smith's revelations, the Special Branch activities; is there anything that he has missed, that he has forgotten? Wouldn't be surprised, things have a way of slipping. Why, the other day, he made breakfast and wondered why the toast was dry; forgot the butter. And then… No, this wouldn't do. Must pull up his braces… that didn't sound right; garters? Whatever. Must pull everything up.

'I say, Jac, old… Jac, is there anything that I should know?'

'What?'

'Oh, I don't know. Guess I wouldn't be asking if I knew.' A quick laugh, more of a choke.

'I think I tell you every thing.'

'Right. Good-oh. We must plan what we do about it.'

'Do? There is nothing to do.'

'I say, there isn't the faintest chance that your man works in this research unit?'

'I don't know; he not allowed to talk what he does. Tells me it will give competitors too much if it is talked about; I say, you can't tell me? And he say, well it's boring, you do not understand; so I won't tell you. And then you won't be at risk.'

'At risk?'

'That's what he say.'

'What from? What risk?'

'I don't know. He just say it. Maybe it's competitors.'

Competitors. Perhaps he is the leak, extracting information from the research, whatever it is, and sending it to... oh, I don't know, it's all so complicated. At that moment, he remembers Mr. Smith's warning, that the Georgians might want to take out Jac; was it just part of his blackmail? If the whole tale is true, then it is possible. And hang on a moment; it occurs to him for the first time. Why did Mr. Smith say "the Georgians"? Are they the recipients of the leaked material? Or was it simply because Jac was a Georgian, once, and he was jumping to conclusions. Does he suspect Tomas already, purely by nationality? Oh, more confusion.

Donald wishes that he could return to his battle, withdraw from the world, just... retire. We feel for him; it has all gone on too long.

And then... why would Mr. Smith and Special Branch expend so much energy and time if it were not true. He wonders how he can test the situation, see how much of it is true; a deployment by himself, not putting Jac at risk. One thing; he will not tell Jac of the warning that the Georgians might take her out; it sounds fatal. Tomas has already mentioned a "risk". What should he do? He can't investigate the research unit; he doesn't know where it is and he wouldn't get very far in the University. They would probably call in the guards, whatever they are called. Perhaps they have porters, like at… Careful, wandering again. But he could investigate the Cambridge end.

'I say, Jac, what sort of place are you sending your poems to? Publishers, book binders?'

'I don't know. Just an address. Here; what you think?'

Donald looks at a scrap of paper; an address scrawled in pencil. He knows Cambridge well and memorises the address. Or tries to; how on earth is he going to remember it? Ah. 'I've got a Cambridge mapbook somewhere. That should help us.'

'Why you want to know?'

Donald sits back. 'Oh, just interest. I used to know Cambridge well and I was just interested to know its whereabouts. No reason.'

Jac smiles. 'Research, yes?'

'What do you mean?'

'You want to know details, all the time. My background, my parents, the poems; you can't help it, can you?'

'I… I…'

'You, you can't help it. I guess it's in your blood.'

Donald doubted it; he had been brought up a few times in the Army for not asking questions and assessing a situation.

'Go on, Donald. Fetch mapbook. Let's look.'

Donald rises and before long he has a road map of Cambridge spread out in front of them. The address; it appears to be behind a language school up an alley off Jesus Lane. He thought it was all residential, college rooms and so on; who else would want to live there? A pub and school nearby. With school and pub, it must be noisy. But then printers, or binders, they will be noisy. Maybe he would go and take a look. Sometime. But he won't tell Jac; he wants to leave her thinking that it's all nonsense, that there is no information being leaked to Georgia.

And they eat, drink, and chat; Donald remembers the fete and tells her about the re-enactment and she encourages him, says she will help if she can though she is already busy on fete day doing teas. They part in good spirits; he offers to walk her home, the proper thing to do but she gently deflects him, points out how close her home is, how he should retire, get some rest. Donald bridles at this; nothing wrong with him. What does she think? That he is getting old? You have to be very old to be old in this village. Goes indoors, slumps into a chair, and then remembers the bug; but surely, it only works when one is using the telephone.

$$- 13 -$$

Poor Donald! He is in a pickle. There are times in life when all the training and experiences that one has gone through in life just don't serve; haven't we all experienced that? What would his wife have said? He didn't ask for this. What would the Colonel have said, or thought? What should he do? It is too tiring thinking about it all, and he can't think what would be the best way forward. He wonders who he can talk to, apart from Jac. Nobody. Quite apart from the Official Secrets Act, there is nobody to whom he can entrust personal secrets that relate to Jac and himself. A dark cloud has settled over his home, pierced with the odd shower. He forgets to eat until Beryl stands over him, reminds him of his responsibilities; harrumph, he does not have responsibilities but she says responsibilities to himself, who else? He cannot tell her of the problems with Jac and the fear that Jac might be taken out and he himself arrested for... for espionage. Oh God, what a lot of nonsense; harrumph.

But things have changed in the village, and we should worry for him. There is a distinct chill in the air whenever he meets a fellow villager. They won't talk to him, even to exchange comments about the weather, let alone a little gossip about the cricket-ground pavilion and who is going to paint it. He receives no notice of the Green Trust that he sits on, though he is sure that a meeting was programmed. Neighbours cross the road rather than meet him on the pavement and turn away in the shop and in the pub, the barman evades him by going to wash glasses. When he goes to the Church, the vicar is welcoming and full of questions but all the village people find that they had more pressing business or shut him out of conversations. Nobody will tell him why he was sent to Coventry and what has caused it; it's not pleasant being sent to Coventry. He finds himself halfway through a greeting, a warm enquiry about health or partner and shut off like a tap by a turned back or another person cutting in.

He asks Beryl. 'Beryl, old... harrumph, Beryl, can you tell me why I am a persona non-grata in the village?'

'Now Donald, what would that be? There you are using them long words again.'

'Nobody will talk to me. All of a sudden. Like I've trodden on someone's grave.'

'Trodden on a grave? Oh Donald, you didn't, did you?'

'No, of course I didn't.'

'People get very precious about the graves of their loved ones, you know. You only have to walk up the cemetery—'

'Beryl, I have not been to the cemetery.'

'An' it's the same in the churchyard—'

'And I haven't been to the churchyard.'

'Well, maybe that's why people are not talking to you, then.'

'Eh?' An unaccustomed response from Donald.

'Well, if you ain't goin to Church—'

'I am and that's not the problem.'

'Well, that's all right then.'

'But why—'

'Oh Donald, I'm sure you're imagining it. You know, as you get older, they say you become invisible and everyone gets so busy, rushing around...'

Donald does not find this conversation comforting. He considers applying to the whisky bottle for resuscitation but is worried that Beryl would spread the story "that Donald is going to the bottle."

All in all, it is hurtful, it is wrong. Considering the degree of warmth and welcome he has received, he feels it is damned rude. Eventually, he button-holes Kevin in the Square. Prevents his escape by standing in front of him.

'Kevin—'

'Don, old boy.' Kevin's eyes roam anywhere but at Donald.

'Please Kevin. Tell me.'

Kevin looked hurt, frowning. 'It's not me.'

'Well, I didn't think it was but what is it?'

'Well... er... doncha know?'

'No Kevin. But everybody seems to be against me. Treating me as though I had the virus.'

'Well, that's gone and good riddance.'

'And so say us all. But Kevin, what have I done?'

'I don't know. Really, I don't know.'

'Well, what is it—'

'They keep asking these questions.' Kevin is panicking, looking around, edging around Donald.

'Who? What questions?' Donald counteracts Kevin's movements, sideways, deployment of arms to block him.

'Those men in black suits. Hard men. You know, with the black car.'

'What? Those oiks? Who do they think they are, asking questions about me?'

'And they don't let up. Anything. Your missus, Beryl, what you drink… it goes on and on. Won't leave me alone.'

'Oh Kevin. I am sorry. I don't know what it is but I've obviously got mixed up in something. I am sorry for all the hassle, the questions.'

'S'all right, mate. Must be off.' He is gone.

Donald can't think whether to be furious, or sunk into the ground. There must be somebody who can stop this nonsense, that Mr. Smith perhaps. How dare they blacken his name in a village where he had hoped, and was settling into, a quiet retirement? We would feel the same.

– 14 –

There is a knock at the door.

Donald looks up from his breakfast, a late breakfast after an early dog walk on the Common, during which he saw nobody except for a fellow church-goer who put her dog on lead and dragged it in another direction. So much for the Christians here. He picked a book, P.G. Wodehouse, and read for an hour; it calms the mind, reassures him that his world is a good place, peaceful and rewarding. Birdsong became a harmonious morning chorus, there were no chain saws or hedge trimmers, and the buzzards with their haunting call had not arrived.

He rises, book in hand, and opens the door.

Perhaps it is the early hour, perhaps it is his absorption in his book. But before he has time to react, a short busy sort of person has walked in, straight past him, and deposited an umbrella on his table among his papers and plates, a bag on the floor and herself in front of him.

'Now, you are not looking after yourself. I can see.' A sharp voice, reminding him of matron at prep school. Matron was not the comfortable mother type; more of a dragon that the boys feared. Particularly when she said that they all needed dosing, and lined them up in their pyjamas...Donald sets Matron aside, and is racking his brains; this person is on the edge of his memory, a face he has seen before, a name that is quite beyond recovery.

'Er... hullo. Can I help you?'

The woman, short and busy, has a large number of layers of clothing that make her look like a stuffed doll, all topped with a coat, quite smart, a reddish woolly affair, all excessive in view of the weather, a pair of galoshes over old leather shoes and a hat squashed down onto her head. The tip of her nose turns up in a fashion that might have been provocative some sixty years earlier in her life and her eyes, deepset and surrounded by wrinkles, peer up into his face with some determination; and accustomed aggression. But her mouth; it is remarkable, wide and obviously highly mobile through much use.

'Now come on my boy. You know me; we chatted at the christening of your son.'

Donald searches his memory; which son, and how long ago was that? They are all grown up, a long time ago.

'Daphne always sent me a Christmas Card but I only heard of her death through Mabel. You know Mabel, my second cousin, your wife's third cousin, once removed I think...I expect it's a while since you saw any of them... you never told me and I have come to help. I would have come earlier but I was attending to your second cousin, by marriage of course, she has sciatica and was finding life very difficult. Needed a little discipline if you ask me and that is probably what you need, if you ask me. Now, do you have tea?'

Donald stares, immobile and shocked.

'Come on, my boy! I can see, you're going to need some attention. Well, here I am.'

And with that, she makes for the kitchen, brushing past Donald with a vigorous gesture that sends him to his chair.

'You just sit down. I'll find everything, I'll manage. You must tell me all about it.'

For the next ten minutes, Donald hears the kettle boiled four times, mutters of "well, you don't keep that there" and "I'm putting the tea with the sugar" and "now, that's just ridiculous. Who but a man would put herbs with the Worcester sauce?" and "you don't need that chili powder. Into the bin with it" and various other interjections as she reorganises his kitchen.

And he still doesn't know her name.

At last she is sitting across the table, apparently a few layers of covering less but the hat still firmly in place. 'Now, what have you been up to?'

Donald is beginning to feel invaded by a random species and wondering how to eradicate her; would poisoning do it, or a heavy hammer to the head? He remembers watching rats being killed, when he was young, and feels that a similar approach might be needed here. And then is forced to the realisation that it is a human, of the feminine variety; a difficult one by all appearances. Not that he has much experience of the other sex, as his wife used to console him frequently.

'Come, Donald, you must have a tongue in your mouth. Your dear wife Daphne used to say to me, Gertrude, you are a treasure, and I felt that the least I could do would be to see that her memory was preserved by seeing you right.' A long pause. 'If that is all right by you.'

That is the moment that Donald might have put his foot down, made moves to preserve his peace, extradite this so-called cousin and return to his quiet life. But the moment passes; he is still in shock, the memories of Daphne bouncing around his head, her connection with this cousin that he was completely unaware of, and some distant obligation that he felt to his dear wife weakens his resolve. And Donald is not a fast thinker, as we know. He gives in. 'Well, I live a quiet life, the dog and I,—'

'You have a dog! Nasty dirty things! Doesn't it live in a kennel outside?'

'No, my dog is my companion and—'

'Well, while I'm here, there must be a few changes.' She clasps her hands together on the table, gives a quick look around the room. Donald notices grey curls attempting to escape from her hat.

He sighs, drops his head, looks up and groans silently. 'What do you mean, while you are here? I don't really have accommodation for visitors.'

'But my dear. I have brought my case and booked a train ticket for a week's time. I assumed that you would have need of help and some company.'

Donald shakes. This is worse than being persona-non-grata in the village. How will he survive a week? It is like being in prison; at least his Cambridge College gave him a room of his own and he had progressed in the Army long beyond a barracks room shared with other soldiers. But his home has only the one bathroom, and the spare room isn't really spare. And he is going to have to reorganise the kitchen after she has left. 'I wouldn't want to put you to any trouble and I don't think it's convenient, I'm afraid—'

'My dear, no trouble at all. Now, where is your guest room?'

'I don't have a guest room, as such—'

'A spare room, perhaps.' A note of anger creeping in.

Donald feels out-manoeuvred; it is not the first time. He was out-manoeuvred in field exercises by cheeky lieutenants but at least that was in the Army and didn't involve second cousins or whoever she is. Meekly, he leads the way through to a small room, with the bed piled with Daphne's clothes.

'You see, it really is not convenient.'

'My dear, leave it to me.' And he is propelled to the door and the door shut firmly behind him. Oh well.

He returns to the kitchen, manages to make himself a mug of coffee after locating the necessary and replacing it where it lives. He sits and wonders how long it will be before he is summoned to respond, organise and essentially compromise his whole life. He considers going away but feels that that is too far beyond the pale, beyond acceptable behaviour. In any case, it is no better than running away and he has never been inclined to run away. Whatever the cost.

It is a matter of thirty minutes or so before she reappears. Thirty minutes during which he has not managed to read or write or do anything useful, such as washing his breakfast things. He sits among the dirty crockery, gazing out of the window. It is pleasantly sunny, a warm day with no rain forecast. He wonders what it would be like to wander up the Common; are the cowbells still in flower, is the farmer preparing the cattle to come onto the Common, as they do every summer?

'Now my dear.' She does not sit but an apron has appeared round her middle, a middle more generous on account of the quilted waistcoat that she has acquired. The hat is still in place. She notes his critical eye. 'You know, you country people are very careless. You could easily catch a chill, out here in the wilderness.'

Donald struggles to equate the local cultivated fields, even the Common, with the wilderness that he has seen and fought in in countries far away. But to remonstrate would obviously be a waste of time. Harrumph.

'What was that? You sit there and I'll see to these things.'

This is going too far. 'Thankyou, but I have my own system for washing-up; and organising the kitchen.' He rises; she obstructs the way to the sink, arms crossed.

'Now, we are not going to have a tiff about a little thing like that, are we?'

Never in his married life had he experienced such a conflict. Occasional arguments of course, some quite important in his view. But no simple obstruction in his own home.

There is a knock on the door. For a moment, Donald does not notice it. He is still in battle mode, wondering what action he can take with this interloper. She must leave, that is certain.

The knock is repeated.

He turns, goes to the door, opens it to find Mrs. Fortesque, complete with hat. What is it with women and hats?

'May I come in? I really need to talk some details with you, you know.'

Before he has stirred, she has walked past him and is putting papers down on the table, pushing his crockery aside as she surveys the room, as before.

There is a loud "humph". Gertrude has her hackles up and is advancing like a fighting cock on Mrs. Fortesque. Before the latter can say anything, she opens with a preliminary barrage.

'You can leave now. Donald is not well, in grief, and he needs to take life very calmly. And I can see that you are not a calm person.'

Donald stands back; there is nothing he can say, nothing that he can do but watch the conflict. We don't blame him; who would interpose themselves between them? Reminded him of certain postings, watching warring tribes face up to each other. He feels a certain disinterest in the proceedings, a face-off in preparation, and a sense of invisibility which would allow him to take the dog and disappear. That would be something; but that would be beyond the pale. Dammit, it is his home, his alone – sadly. And in any case, he is still hoping to rid his household of Gertrude.

Mrs. Fortesque looks Gertrude up and down; her face registers first disapproval, second a sour look of appraisal, and thirdly a firm dismissal. 'And who is this?' she says to the air as though Gertrude might be dismissed to the nursery.

'I think I made myself clear. Really Donald, is this how they've been treating you here? No respect,' Gertrude spits.

Mrs. Fortesque stares with venom at Gertrude. 'Well really, do you think you might wait your turn? I have some business to discuss with Donald and I don't think it is any of your business. Why don't you...'. And here Mrs. Fortesque fades, realising belatedly that she is not in her own home, that she does not wish to alienate Donald, and wanting to achieve a modicum of organisation for the fete. She is an organiser at heart, and cannot stand to have her organisation ignored, made little of and misinterpreted.

Donald can no longer stand on the sidelines; we know him too long to see that. There have been many times standing on a side-line, watching a rugger match at school, a boxing match in the Army, many times when he has stood on the sidelines. But none have been in his own home. He edges between the two; rather like between two fighting dogs; he does not feel safe. It is rather like when he had to place his unit between two warring tribes in the Middle East with the fear that they would to fight it out over his unit, ignoring his presence. However, it is his home and he feels a certain obligation to good manners. 'Er, Mrs. Fortesque, this is Gertrude, an old... er, a cousin who has come to... er... has come. She is staying here.'

'Well, in that case, I'm sure that she can spare us a few minutes to go through these details. Can't you?' She says with a hard stare at Gertrude.

Who stares back as if she might overcome her with a look; experience has taught that her that it works most of the time, though almost always she must admit with men. It is apparent that Mrs. Fortesque is quite accustomed to such confrontations and will not be overcome; she takes up a position at the table, sliding into a chair, pushing Donald's breakfast dishes to one side and opening files. Gertrude is confused; she is not accustomed to others getting the better of her. She looks up at Donald, who shrugs. Turns and disappears into the bedroom, slamming the door behind her.

'Well really, you do have some odd friends.'

How many of my friends have you met, Donald wonders. He suspects that he would not like her friends; they would all be the organising type, office workers, captains of small industries. She starts to talk, of the fete programming, his part, insurance, the amount of space he will have to work within, the police and minor details. She carries on. And on.

'Your armies; they will have to change at home, you know. We don't have changing-rooms or anything like that. In fact, there are not even toilets. It's a matter that has been distressing me; it does not seem correct that a function of this sort has no toilet provision. And what do the men coming out of the beer tent do? Well, I wouldn't like to tell you, it's not decent, I can tell you.'

It washes over Donald. When she asks if he is happy with the arrangements, he smiles, nods and sees her on her way. He can remember not a thing of her "arrangements", not a single obligation that she has placed him under, not a single detail. He brushes her visit aside, out of mind, and returns to the present with a sigh.

– 15 –

When she has left, Gertrude comes back into the room. 'One of the village ladies, I assume. Are they all as demanding? Really, Donald, you must take it easier. A strict diet; and milk and bread for supper.'

He tries to ignore her too. The business of the shop and MI5 reasserts itself in Donald's mind, a worm devouring his concentration. The matter of the villagers' behaviour is uppermost; he wonders whether to confide in his "carer". She will notice the reaction in the village before long; she will wonder why the villagers are so unwelcoming, to her as well as Donald. 'I… I have a little problem.'

'Oh my dear. Have you seen the doctor?'

Donald stares at her; stupid woman, can't she see that problems don't always involve the human body? 'No, no. It is a matter of er… er…' How the devil does one explain without telling her anything? 'I… er… the shop is… there is a problem with the shop that seems to have involved me, and the police have—'

'Police?!' A shriek, as though she is being attacked by gulls.

'I haven't done anything. It is an impossible situation, being accused of—'

'Accused?!'

'Of being involved with something at the shop. Which doesn't exist in any case.'

'What? The shop?'

Donald frowns. 'The shop?'

'The shop doesn't exist?'

Donald stares; stupid woman, it's getting too much. He speaks very slowly and clearly, as he used to, to new recruits. 'The shop exists. The situation in which the police are involved does not exist. But the villagers have got it into their heads that I am non grata here.'

There is a long pause.

Gertrude sighs loudly. 'You poor boy. I can see that you have become overwrought with grief and now you are talking nonsense.'

'Nonsense?' Donald's tone approaches parade-yard level.

'Don't shout at me, my boy. I will not have it. Why, if it wasn't for dear Mary and your sad situation, I would consider leaving you.'

A brief flash of relief courses through Donald; if only... He stares at the ceiling. The dog looks up, sensing an escape from the horrible discipline that he senses approaching. Dogs are not the stupid canines that some believe; it is true that they do not always behave as their owners would wish, and can have urges that humans do not understand, but they rate high in empathy, and the dog has noticed his owner's reaction to this intruder. He is almost tempted to raise a leg against her coat, or place a stick in her bedroom.

'However,' she says. 'I cannot desert my obligations. I shall remain, in spite of the unpleasantness that I must endure.'

Another long pause.

'Now,' says Gertrude. 'I don't know whether to be surprised at you, getting mixed up in—'

'Harrumph! As though I was looking to get mixed up.' Donald is furious.

'But if the police are on to something, it is obviously something that needs tackling. And I'm here, now.'

Donald's heart sinks; he is being taken over. He considers taking the dog for the afternoon walk; will that be "allowed"?

There is a sharp knocking at the door, a summons that can't be ignored. Donald rises but Gertude is at the door before him and opens it a crack.

A village voice. 'What's the matter with you, then? I've got something for that Donald.'

Gertrude allows Mrs. Jones to cross the threshold but no further than the doormat.

'Ere, who's this woman? Donald, you should be more careful, having women like this in the house.' She peers at Gertrude from under her hat, a grimace on her face.

It is an interesting confrontation. Both are of similar height, and as Donald observes, similar age. They both wrap their stout bodies in numerous coverings, a coat to the external world, and God knows what beneath. They prefer thick stockings and flat-bottomed shoes. They both adopt hats, of a not dissimilar appearance. But when it come to their approach, Gertrude attempts the superior brush-off, as practiced by generations of Ward Sisters, and Mrs. Jones becomes a battler from the streets, not to be put off by some hoity-toity.

Gertrude snorts, draws herself up and attempts from her short stature to look down at Mrs. Jones. 'Really, who do you think you are?'

'Well, you've got a nerve, talking like that. And me from the village; who might you be, Miss Barge-in-here-know-it-all?'

Gertrude is drawing herself up to put this irritant in her place, when Donald comes forward. 'How can I help you, Mrs. Jones?'

'They sent me round the village. I'm exhausted, been on my feet since seven. You wouldn't have a glass of water, would you? Or a cup of tea?'

She is ushered into the nearest seat, poured a cup from the pot; she gives a sigh of satisfaction. 'Always a genleman. Who's this then? You aven't bin looking after yerself, Donald, letting the likes of her in 'ere.' She sniffs, looking at Gertrude with a grunt of disdain.

Before Gertrude can speak, Donald asks, 'How can I help you?'

'We haven't had your answers, have we?' She gives a nod of satisfaction, a large gulp of tea.

'Oh, the survey. Haven't felt up to it recently.'

'Well, that's no excuse.'

Gertrude comes to stand in front of her, looking down at her, a severe expression. A look of doubt crosses Mrs. Jones's face, a moment of fear. Perhaps she has been in a hospital at some time, and the faint memory of a battle-axe of a Ward Sister brushes over her memory.

'You tell me why Donald is having a hard time in the village,' says Gertrude.

'Well...,' she stutters, avoiding her look, appealing to Donald. 'Don't you see?'

Gertrude stares at her, forcing her attention. 'Have you been spreading rumours?'

'Whatja mean? I don't spread rumours... not me... I wouldn't... it's not decent.'

'So, what have you been saying? Telling people what rubbish?'

'I only asked. Didn't tell no rubbish. Asked why those men were asking all those questions.'

'What men? And what did they tell you when you asked?'

'Oh... oh, they said some awful things. Like Donald wasn't really who he says he is. Some sort of spy, someone said.'

'And you told that to a few other people?'

'Well, I couldn't not tell... what do you mean? I don't tell stories.' She pulls her hat down over her eyes.

'So you've been making trouble for Donald.'

Mrs. Jones shrinks under her gaze, slides sideways off her chair and sidles towards the door. 'You 'ave some funny friends,

Donald. I'll see meself out.' She pulls the door open and is gone with a surprising burst of speed, the door standing open behind her.

'We are going to have to do something about that, Donald. Leave it to me; you are not in a fit state to deal with a little thing like that. Police and spies; what nonsense! I'll sort out your villagers.'

– 16 –

What Gertrude gets up to in the village, Donald only hears about later in dribs and drabs. But one thing is clear to us; she doesn't improve Donald's standing in the village; she makes it worse. So much for the "friend". Poor Donald.

After lunch, Gertrude goes out, a feeble excuse about buying more eggs from the shop; Donald knows that there are plenty of eggs in the fridge; he put them there himself. We know how efficient he is at stocking his "bivouac". Donald doesn't see her for several hours; he finds it hard to settle, to write or research. He looks at his battle; harrumph, he will only be interrupted. Gertrude doesn't seem interested in the battle; there is the hint that Donald is playing with toys. It has unsettled him, this uncalled-for intrusion into his life; he takes being sociable as just one factor in life; there are many other things to occupy himself. Many would call him unsociable, but we know better, and can appreciate how hard it is to concentrate on "work" while this wretched woman is here, nagging, organising, getting in the way.

Gertrude returns. 'Well, I see what you mean about putting you in Coventry. But I think I've dealt with it. You should be back on a sound footing with everyone.'

Donald frowns; it sounds most unlikely that a stranger to

the village can raise the reputation of a villager. 'Really? Even at the pub?'

'I went in there, sorted them out. Told them it was all a lot of nonsense, and they should be ashamed of themselves. Lot of boys. Really, I said, chasing an old man away as though he was a problem.'

Donald didn't care for the "old man", but said, 'Did you meet Jac?'

'I went to the shop; she seems a capable sort of person. I told her I was a cousin staying with you and she sent her good wishes.'

Donald wonders at this; it doesn't sound like the sort of thing Jac says. 'Did she still have that raised pie on the surface? It's marvellous.'

'I didn't see any raised pie, and it's not the sort of thing you should be having.'

Over the next few days, affairs settle into a sort of settled existence. Gertrude cooks meals, that Donald misses on occasion, much to Gertrude's ire; he tires of her "healthy" food and seeks more traditional fare elsewhere. Donald replaces the contents of his kitchen, once or twice a day, to hear Gertrude patiently, but not without a verbal description of what she is doing, rearrange to her satisfaction. The dog stays indoors, apart from brief morning constitutionals, but is forbidden all rooms except for the kitchen and her dog bed. Donald spends much time reading, indoors and out of doors and has no idea how Gertrude can be occupied indoors. But he knows that she goes out every day to "recover" Donald's reputation. Donald notices no change in his relationship with the villagers; if anything, it seems to have deteriorated further.

There is a knock on the door. Gertrude reaches the door ahead of Donald, and stands on the threshold, to prevent anyone entering. Donald makes out a policeman's cap over Gertrude's shoulder and invites him in; Gertrude, with a scowl at Donald, stands aside but indicates that the police officer is to brush his feet on the mat.

It should be made clear that Donald does not wish to engage with the police. But frustrated with Gertrude's dominance of his home, he takes the opportunity to allow a policeman to break the tedium of life. He recognises the man who questioned him after he had called the police and invites the officer to sit, offers him tea and remarks on the weather while Gertrude pushes her way through to the kettle and prepares a tray. After further preliminary chat, relating to the village but avoiding the shop, Donald asks what he can do for the officer.

'Well sir, as you have been the object of a burglary recently, it is the practice of the Force to ascertain whether you believe that you were well served by your police.'

Donald stares, and laughs. 'You mean, you are conducting a survey.'

'Well, sir, we wouldn't put it quite like that. Any comments you choose to give will be treated in the utmost confidence and will only relate to your specific case.'

'How are you doing with your metric conversion?'

The officer smiles, shakes a finger. 'Ah well sir, you will have your little joke.'

'No joke intended. I seem to recall that you were having difficulty in relating millimetres with centimetres. Of course, I can run over the figures now if you like—'

'No, no sir. That won't be necessary. The sergeant at the desk assisted me. Now sir, did you say that the police responded with reasonable speed to your call?'

'Funny you should mention that. It occurred to me that the police responded so fast that they must have been in the village.'

'Well, that's a fact sir. We had been summoned to… er… to a call-out. Another matter all together. Not related.'

'And yet when you arrived, the culprit, the oik that you removed was not hand-cuffed; or even treated like a criminal. What has happened to him? Will I receive a summons to Court at his trial?'

The policeman wriggled in his chair, gazed out of the window, asked for another cup of tea.

'Haven't you done enough?' said Gertrude, hands on hips, standing over the policeman. 'Can't you see that you have disturbed him? He is already suffering from grief, and now you–'

'That's all right, Gertrude. Why don't you go out for a while?'

Gertrude stared at Donald, shrugged her shoulders with a furious gesture, tugged her hat down, put on her red coat and went out, slamming the door.

There was peace for a while. The birds twittered, a mower started up nearby, a tractor passed through the village at speed. Two fighter jets passed over at speed.

'You must get a lot of them,' said the officer.

'I think that you are not being entirely straight with me.' Donald stared into the policeman's face.

'Why? What do you mean?'

'The two culprits, the two burglars, the two louse of the lowest order; you know them?'

'Oh no sir. Most definitely not sir. We don't mix with that lot, they bring down the reputation of…'. The man stared at Donald, coughed, looked down, looked out of the window, went red.

'So you, and I, know who they were. Special Branch.'

The policeman looked astonished. 'Well, how did you know that sir?'

Donald waved his question away; he was not going to breach the secrets that MI5 had placed him under. All the same… 'So why are you here today?'

'Well, sir, I don't think I'm at liberty to—'

'I'm getting very tired of being told that.'

'All the same, sir, it is above my pay range.'

Donald was suddenly furious. 'How dare you!'

The policeman looked shocked, open mouthed, as though he had just chatted up the Super's wife not knowing who she was. Donald can be quite frightening when the gloves are off, and his gander is up.

Donald returned to the attack. 'So you can't or won't tell me why you are here and yet you wish to know how I feel about the break-in.'

The policeman wriggled again and made to get up.

'Oh no you don't. Let's play a little game, shall we? I ask a question, and you give me a truthful reply.'

'Well sir, I don't know if—'

'First question. Did you receive the instruction to visit me from your Superintendent?'

The policeman registered relief, smiled. 'Why yes sir. That was exactly how it came about.'

'Is this a normal kind of request from him. Or her.'

'Well, come to think of it, no sir. She didn't tell me why but I was to ask you about the break-in, I was to remind you of our response and I was to report back.'

You will recall that Donald is not a fast thinker and that he tends to stick on the same subject. Now, his mind was running in unaccustomed fields. Suppose you looked at it like a kind of strategy game, then the Super's instruction came from someone above. The Police Commissioner? Most unlikely. I wonder, he thought.

'Tell me. You have had Special Branch in the station, haven't you?'

'Well, now you mention it, there were two men—'

'Oiks! Of the worst sort.'

'And they were the two here in your house.'

There was a pause. The policeman looked shocked. 'Oh blimey, I wasn't meant to say that.'

'And they get their instructions from a man, an older man in a tweed suit, a wise old man who seems to know everything. You have seen him?'

'Well, it's funny you should say that, but yes sir, we have had a visitor who seemed to have the run of the station. Including the Super's office. And his 'phone. And us running around to everything he wanted.'

'Including visiting me.'

The policeman stared. 'Now sir, how did you know that?'

$$- 17 -$$

Gertrude returns.

It is clear that she is not happy. She offers no further information about the villagers or her exploits. She sits down at the table.

'I don't think I'm wanted here, in this village.'

Donald sits, says nothing. We sympathise with Donald; his first feeling is a great wave of relief, only marginally tinged with guilt, after all Gertrude has done and expressed. We would feel the same.

'And now the police! We never had the police to our house, I can tell you. It isn't decent; what will the neighbours say?'

'I can't help that, I'm afraid.' Donald struggles to avoid sounding smug; a little flame of joy is lit in him.

'Well, Donald, I think there is little that I can do here. I've decided; you will have to come back to my house.'

What?! In shock, he struggles to think of reasons why he can't leave. 'Er…, I can't do that, I'm afraid.' Anything to avoid leaving, anything to avoid spending more time under Gertrude's care, as we can appreciate only too well.

'And why might that be? I can take good care of you, see you eat and sleep well…'. Gertrude is standing over him – an accustomed position – her hands folded over her generous body.

Donald shuddered. For some days, he has put up with her choice of meals, her interference, her meddling in his life and he has had enough. But good manners prevent him from being open, telling her that he can bear her company no more; it's not in his character, is it?

'I can't go. I have… er… village things to do. You saw Mrs. Fortesque, she will call on me… needs my advice. And so on.'

'Are you so important?' She says. 'From what I've seen, they would be glad to see the back of you.'

'And' – the flame bursts forth – 'I can't possibly leave my old dog, and she can't go to a kennels. Too old.'

Gertrude sat looking at him; he felt her mind revolving in smaller circles towards an unaccustomed defeat. 'Now, will you be all right?'

'Dear Gertrude' – she shudders at the term; after all, it is the first time he has used it – 'I have managed very well here for some time, and shall do so again. It was nice to see you' – he wondered if a thunderbolt would strike him down – 'and you must get back to your life.'

'I shall leave in the morning. Perhaps you could take me to the station.'

After she has left and he has rearranged his kitchen – again – and aired the spare room, he wonders about the policeman's visit. Mr. Smith is behind it, he is sure. It is a nudge, to prevent him thinking that he is out of it, free of all association with the spy thing.

What is he to do about it? Summon Mr. Smith and tell him it's all nonsense? He has said that already. What do you do, when you are accused of a crime and it's not true? Reminded him of school days, the boarding house. Someone had raided a tuckbox; one of the worst crimes you could carry out, an assault on the only privacy a boy had. Stolen: A chocolate cake and a Swiss penknife with multiple attachments. Naturally, Housemaster left it to the House prefects to tackle and they made their own biased investigations, particularly among the less popular boys. Including himself. And a bully pointed the finger at him. And instant denial lead to a peculiar loathing expressed by his colleagues; junior boys would walk past, telling loud tales among themselves, all suggesting that he, Donald, would face the most terrific beating imaginable. Sniggers and taunts; life was not worth living, particularly after the penknife was found in his games locker, deep in his PT shoe bag. After that, the Housemaster was involved, Donald was summoned and Housemaster took a more sanguine attitude, addressing the House at House Prayers about those that bullied and picked on the weaker ones and how the weak would inherit the Earth and more of that kind. The chocolate cake was returned, a large slice taken, and for a while Donald's life was easier. A few boys even apologised to him, a few accused him of being a sneak.

Breakfast. He is boiling the kettle, watching the blue tits on the nut feeder, and he becomes aware that there is a stationary figure in the lane. A man, brown raincoat and hat, not tall, standing hands in pockets looking at him. Donald feels frozen, screwed to the floor by the man's eyes; the man does not move, does not wave. Who is he?

The kettle boils; he fills the teapot, looks up and the man is gone. In the space of a few seconds. He thinks about running into the lane; where has he gone? And realises that he is too late. The lane will be empty. Or peopled by an old couple who will ask him if he is quite well; whisper between themselves, dark suggestive looks. His hand shakes as he pours a cup, unsteady as he gets the milk from the fridge. What is happening to him? We should be worrying for him.

There is a loud knocking on the door. He stares at it, as though it might open of its own accord. He is deafened by his heart which is hammering, a rhythm that threatens to burst out of his chest. An unpleasant reminder of a science fiction film. But first the man, and now the hammering?

A voice, loud and impatient. 'Oy, you there Donald, you going to let me in?'

He shakes himself, feeling tension flowing off him; his heart relaxes into an uneven rhythm, before returning to normal. Or as normal as he is ever aware of it. He opens the door to Mrs. Jones.

'I ope you've lost that old lady of yours.'

'Good morning to you, Mrs. Jones.'

'She weren't your sort, if you don't mind me saying.'

'Why is that, Mrs. Jones?'

'We...ell, she weren't no lady. Not like yourself at all. Now, I don't know what you two got up to, but she sewed a bit of trouble in the village, she did.'

'What do you mean, Mrs. Jones?'

'What do I mean? What do I mean? I mean, how long are you going to keep a poor old woman standing on your doorstep without offering her a cup of tea?'

They are sitting, a fresh pot between them.

'Yurs, there was trouble around that woman, I can tell you. Call her a friend, do you? She didn't do you no favours.'

'What do you mean, Mrs. Jones?'

'We...ell, one doesn't like to gossip, but you should hear what people have to say.' She grunts. 'Wouldn't have a little biccy, would you?'

The biscuit tin open in front of her. 'According to your so-called friend, you've got mixed up in some very unsavoury business.'

Donald was silent; what was the point in denying anything? It would only sound like a pathetic bleat against the forces of public opinion. His heart resumed an uneven beat, as though to remind him to desist from stressful activities.

'And then, there was that fight.'

'What fight?' He stared at her.

'Didn't you hear?'

'No. Not a word.'

'We...el, weren't the sort of thing that we like in our village. No, not at all.'

She stopped, but Donald could see that she was dying to tell all, and he poured her a fresh cup.

'There was these two men in black suits; you might have seen them around. Nasty types, them. Asking all sorts of questions about you—'

'Me?'

'And suggesting you were a criminal of some sort, though they never did say what sort. We...el, they was sitting on that bench on the Green, smoking an' that, and your Kevin goes over to them. Loud words; I've never heard such language. They were telling him it were no business of his.'

Donald is having difficulty believing the story.

'We…ell, then they were all standing, an before long, there was a bit of rough an tumble. I reckon Kevin came out on top. He is big lad, he is. Those two took off. But that don't explain why those two have been haunting the village, asking all them difficult questions.'

'I haven't been up to anything, Mrs. Jones. You can tell that to your friends, to anyone, but if they don't want to listen, there's nothing I can do about it. I'll carry on living quietly here.'

Mrs. Jones gives him a look; it changes from deep suspicion to a kind of wonder, as though she has recognised that the truth is not always the most obvious thing.

'Now, Mrs. Jones. What can I do for you?'

She looks surprised, coughs, takes another biscuit as though to delay being thrown out. 'It's that survey.'

'I've had enough to deal with, without that survey.' He nearly says that a man is watching him; she might spread the story that he has lost his marbles. Harrumph. His heart has taken a rest, resumed its normal low beat rate.

– 18 –

After she has gone, he sits, gazing out of the window. Will the man appear again? The telephone rings. He rises, goes to answer it; there is a slight buzz on the line, but nobody responds to his agitated demands for response. Is there somebody there? Can they not hear his heart beating?

When he returns to his chair, he sees the man in the lane again; the telephone rings again. Again, nobody there, a slight buzz. By the time he has returned to the window, the man is gone. He goes back, takes the telephone receiver off and goes into his sitting room, away from the front window, away from the telephone, and sits gazing at the wall. What is happening to him? He has never known anything like it.

We know that Donald is a man of limited imagination, and a slow thinker. He is not inclined to paranoia; he had to face some complicated problems in the Army, some caused by himself it is true, and he has never felt bowed by fears that some unseen enemy is undermining his position.

The day continues in the same vein. Vacant phone-calls when he replaces the receiver, occasional sightings of the man in the lane. He finds it impossible to concentrate on reading or watching television or writing. He spends the day making notes, a record of these unexplained intrusions, and goes to bed early.

It is around four in the morning; the birds are waking, the sun is thinking of lifting over the horizon. And Donald is sure, doubly convinced, that someone is walking round his house with no attempt to walk stealthily. He is fully awake in a moment, grabbing his dressing gown, unsteady on his feet. His heart goes into take-off mode and he collapses back onto the bed. He gasps, coughs. Stands and goes to the window, peering both ways.

Nobody. The birds commence their morning chatter, loud exchanges of condolences and threats. The sun warms the tops of the trees.

Unsteady on his feet, he makes his way to the kitchen and fills the kettle. Automatically, he switches it on. Gazes out of the window. At least there is no man in the lane. Hah! After a few minutes, he comes to the realisation that the kettle has remained obstinately cold. He stares at it. Switches on the radio; nothing. Tries the light switch. The cooker clock is dead. He walks through the house, his mood darkening. Looks at the electrical consumer unit; all switched on, all saying "no problem". Is it a village black-out? Most unlikely. In Cambridge, there were never electricity cuts; the very idea suggests the 1950s, years of his youth when one expected to manage through difficulties of this sort. But hold. This is the new century, a year or two post-pandemic. He is isolated.

He picks up the telephone; dead also. Why? The telephone always worked, through flood and… whatever. Bending down, an instinctive groan, he traces the wires connecting the telephone to… aah, of course. The hub thing. Also dead. He supposed that it would be possible to connect an old 'phone to the telephone socket; he doesn't have an old telephone. One always had the telephone, in any emergency, flood, fire, or cats up trees. And now… he supposes he could reconnect an old-fashioned telephone but it is an awful fuss, wires everywhere, and anyway, there will be electricity, sometime… and he doesn't have an old telephone. It is another unseen threat; somebody or organisation is trying to defeat him, bring him to his knees.

The day has a pall of weariness already. And yet the sun shines, the birds twitter, and he could rise, go out into the great beyond, walk the Common, greet the cattle and breathe. He contemplates becoming a new man; it is too much to handle and he returns to his bed and slumbers unevenly, turning away from the light, thinking about… about anything but the problems that crowd him, and it's very difficult. He turns from one to another, without coming to any conclusions. Anger simmers beneath the surface; he is used to tackling problems, solving problems, even creating problems for others to solve. But these problems are beyond him.

When he surfaces, the sun has been covered by cloud, the birds have fallen silent and he can hear the radio blaring away; he remembers fiddling with the knobs, trying to get some contact with the great beyond. Someone out there must be alive.

A slow start to the day. He gropes his way through breakfast and clearing away. He enters the electricity cut in his diary; he is convinced that it was aimed at him. Electricity cuts do not happen these days.

Scrabbling around on his desk, he finds Mr. Smith's card. Should he call him? What could he say about Max, and the fight? He might have heard about it already.

He dials the number. It is answered immediately.

'Mr. Smith?'

The voice is monotonal, without regional inflection or accent, as if the speaker is imitating a machine. Perhaps it was a machine. 'Who are you calling?'

'Er... Mr. Smith gave me this number.'

'What is your business?'

Donald counted to three, slowly. Gazed at the ceiling; was this how MI5 operated? Talk about an opaque operation. Speaking very slowly and loudly, he said, 'I don't know who you are but Mr. Smith, or whatever he is called, gave me this number and pressed... I repeat pressed... me to call him. Is there anything there that you do not understand?'

There was silence at the other end. Then a few clicks, a purr, and finally a voice. Female, warm and welcoming. 'Is that you, Donald? Good to hear from you, Donald.'

'And who are you?'

'Mr. Smith is not available at this time, but I would be happy to pass on a message.'

'What are you talking about? I would not be happy to give you a message. It was my understanding—'

'Sir, can I help you? Then I can give Mr. Smith some indication of your call.'

'Well, you can indicate to Mr. Smith that I called. I had understood that this is Mr. Smith's personal line and yet—'

179

'I'm sure that Mr. Smith shall be very happy to talk with you. May I say that you called and were unable to mention the subject of your call?' All this in the gentle tone of a nurse before one is put to sleep before a serious operation.

Donald felt his heart beginning to respond to the situation; it is saying why are you doing this to me, and can't we just stop… stop everything… I'm sure you wouldn't want me to stop. He put the receiver down. Breathed slowly.

The man is in the lane. It has started to rain, but he stands there, drips falling from his hat, his coat darkening with the wet. He is quite still, the same spot as before. Donald turns to the kettle, and back, quickly. The man has gone; he knew he would do that. It is getting irritating. He will tell Mr. Smith just how irritating it is, when he can talk to him. It does not cross his mind that the man might be a mirage, a creation of his over-heated mind. But perhaps he is real; Donald will continue to be haunted, pursued by his own demons.

– 19 –

The telephone rings while Donald is entering this last sighting. He suspects it is one of those dead calls and ignores it.

It stops after three minutes; but starts again after another two. Donald picks it up. 'Now look here, I'm going to report you to BT, you can't go on disturbing me like this, it's illegal, and—' He realises that someone has been speaking, for some time.

'Is that Donald?' It is the same gentle female voice.

He was tempted to say that he was the burglar, or the man in the lane, or the two men in black suits. 'Harrumph! You again. Please don't waste my time.'

'Certainly not, Donald. Hold on, I'll put you through.'

Clicks and burrs, a purring sound. Donald wonders if the

calls are recorded at the other end. The 'phone tap has not been removed, in spite of his demand.

'Donald.' The voice is clear, a warm friendly tone, a slight Scottish burr.

'Is that Mr. Smith?'

'It is.'

'I didn't recognise the voice. Are you Scottish?'

A brief laugh. 'A long time ago.'

'I didn't notice it when you visited.'

'It must hide at times, the accent.'

'Damned odd. Never met such a thing before.'

'You called, Donald?'

'Yes, but got that girl of yours.'

'You must be referring to my superior.'

'Your superior? She didn't say.' Donald tries to remember what he has said and whether he has made things worse. Though why he should worry about things getting worse he can't quite see; everything has been done to him, not the other way round.

'She is running the operation. She would have been glad to talk to you. Actually, I hope you don't mind but she is listening in on the call. Your contribution to our operation is invaluable, as I am sure you recognise.'

Donald was silenced. His contribution? He had been trying to get out of it, whatever "it" was. Why couldn't they see that?

'You must have something for us, something useful.'

Donald paused. He wondered what it was that he had wanted to talk about and felt flummoxed. Things had floated out of his head; he should have made a list and now he feels lost.

'We can take it slowly, if that helps.'

'Yes. That would be good. I've been getting a lot of intrusions, interferences if you see what I mean.'

'When did they start?'

'When? When? Why, you know that. You visited me shortly after it started. The two men in black suits who you were said were Special Branch. Bounders. Assaulted me in the road, broke into my home and made the most awful mess. Has England become a police state, the sort one reads about in the papers?'

The voice is soft, female, comforting in intent. 'Donald, I must apologise for the treatment that you have suffered. It was unwarranted and excessive. I believe that Mr. Smith has already indicated that, because you were in the locus of an outage of material, it has been necessary to investigate your actions. I'm sure you understand our need.'

Donald is working through "locus", "outage" and "material". He is happy with the first and the third, though material seems an odd word for information, somehow so solid, but the second seems wrong. 'I suffered an outage of electricity, but I think you were looking for another word. Possibly occurrence.'

There is silence from the other end. After a few minutes, she returns. 'I would not presume to correct you, Professor. However, I was referring to data that had been lost in transmission, lost to foreign forces. I apologise for our terminology; we sometimes forget that it is not as transparent as one would expect.'

Donald reflects that there is nothing transparent about what is going on, except that he is innocent and so is Jac.

'I wonder, Donald,' Mr. Smith sounds a little impatient. 'I wonder if we could proceed with the nature of your 'phone call.'

'Yes. Well.' Donald attempts to put his mind in order. What came first?

'You mentioned the matter on the road and also the unwarranted incursion into your home.'

'But that was just the start of it.'

A pause. 'And what came next?'

'Your black suited men, your Special Branch, have been maligning me. And the village people believe them, their appalling stories. It is insufferable and I understand that they are under your beck and call. So it is you who have been trying to cast me as a criminal character.' Donald's voice had increased in volume, until he was bellowing down the 'phone. A blackbird, which was enjoying a juicy berry, took off with a loud shout of alarm.

There was a pause. 'We should do something about this matter. And do all we can to rectify the wrongs.' The female voice was firm. 'But we still have the little matter of treachery that we are investigating.'

'Who is the man?' Donald cut in sharply; they were not going to get away with it.

'What man are you referring to?' Mr. Smith was solicitous.

'That man whom you sent to spy on my activities.'

'Do you mean the Special Branch men?'

'No, no I don't.' Donald felt his heart rate rising. They were out to provoke him. 'When will you stop provoking me? First you blackmail me, and now provoke—'

'Donald,' the female voice is firm again. He can imagine an Ice Queen, lording over her empire. 'I don't believe that you have been blackmailed.'

'You are much mistaken. Ask Mr. Smith.'

There is a pause, before she comes back. 'Mr. Smith has no knowledge of what you are talking about. I assure you, we are not in the business of blackmail.'

'Then ask Mr. Smith why he threatened me that Jac might be taken by the Georgians if I didn't give him some information, information that I am completely incapable of giving because I don't know what information he wants and I don't know anything about this treachery. Indeed, I only know about it from yourselves. Or Mr. Smith, I should say. Perhaps, it is all a myth and I am being persecuted for no reason. Though why I should be persecuted I cannot think.'

'Persecuted?' Both Mr. Smith and his boss speak together.

'And I suppose you organised the electricity cut and the endless phone calls with no-one on the other end and the man in the lane. And you haven't told me about him.' Donald is exhausted, hardly able to continue the call. He slumps down in a chair. There is a knock at the door; he ignores it.

A silence follows; Donald doesn't care. He puts the 'phone on speaker and switches on the kettle. As it comes to the boil, he hears a voice from the telephone. 'Hang on, hang on,' he says. 'The kettle has only just boiled.' More silence. He makes a mug of coffee, sits again, picks up the receiver. 'Now, perhaps you can answer my questions.'

Mr. Smith. 'One moment. He's on again.' A pause. 'Could we ask you a question first?'

'Why? Haven't I given you a long enough list of complaints?'

'I thought we might get to the nub of it.'

'Why should I be interested in your "nub", when you will not deal with my problems?'

'When you left the shop, before you were stopped by—'

'Stopped? Accosted is a better description.'

'Before you were accosted by the Special Branch boys, you posted a letter.'

'And now you are going to talk about some piffling matter instead of my problems? I'm tempted to put the 'phone down; you have been no earthly use at all.' His voice has increased in volume again. 'Perhaps you could tell me who to complain to?'

'Donald, I'm sorry that we have caused you so much trouble; it really was not intended. But please, could you help us? I appreciate that we deal in "piffling" matters; our work is often tied up in "piffling" matters. Do you remember posting a letter?'

'Good gracious, you expect me to remember a little mundane thing like that?'

'I was hoping that you would remember it. You see, if it had been a letter of your own, it is likely, not necessarily but likely that you would have posted it before going into the shop.'

'And?'

'So you were observed posting a letter after you came out of the shop and I believe that it was given to you by Jac.'

'Wouldn't she have posted her own letter?'

'One would have thought so. But she gave it to you, we believe. So naturally, we wonder whether you are linked with Jac in some way in this business.'

Donald was silent. He was trying to remember what he had done as he came out of the shop; the Special Branch boys had eliminated any memory with their aggressive attitude. After a while, he said, 'It was those Special Branch boys. Don't remember a thing about coming out of the shop, except their aggressive attitude. And their dress; don't Special Branch have any pride in their appearance? I couldn't believe it, the state of their boots.'

'What about in the shop? Do you remember anything then?'

'Damned if I do. Eggs, butter, something or other. I don't know. But you saw it all; I pulled it out for you; don't you remember? Hang on, Mrs. Jones came in before me, went on about a bad egg.'

'Perhaps after that.'

'Damn. I wouldn't have remembered that. The bad egg!'

'But before that?'

'After that? After that? Why, I did my shopping of course.'

'And Jac didn't give you an envelope to post?'

'Did she? I don't remember.'

'So the envelope might have been yours.'

'No. Not a chance. I don't write letters at that time of day.'

'So it might have been from Jac.'

Donald chews it over; can't remember posting a letter of Jac's, and now they say he did. 'Well, so what if I did post a letter. What's so special about it?'

'Sadly, the Specials did not catch the postman emptying the box. We don't know where the letter was going.'

At that moment, Donald has a flash of memory, a picture of the whole, complete with Jac's poems and a Cambridge address. Does he reveal all to MI5?

– 20 –

In his past, he has always been a truthful person, ready with a truthful answer, not so quick to provide truthful information, quick by his standards. Even if teaching history has been a series of stories with alternative outcomes, to Donald it is a running sequence of truths. He leaves it to others to make contrary interpretations; they are welcome to it. It is hard enough extracting the history from ancient documents, some heresay, without questioning the efficacy. The Army valued truth, both in the field and in the barracks; what was the point in conveying some intelligence if it was not truthful? In the barracks, there was no room for deception or subterfuge. Orders were orders. And further back into his youth, he recalled his trouble at school, already reported, that came about as a result of establishing the truth. And even earlier, there was a difficult time in front of a Punch and Judy show, when he had spoken up in opposition to the crowd of other little people around him, telling the baddie the truth and giving Mr. Punch away. Well, hadn't his parents told him to speak the truth. Always.

He is thrown; he staggers, his voice goes quiet. There is a little prompting from Mr. Smith. He ignores him, chews over the problem. Does he reveal to MI5 that Jac is posting poems to an address in Cambridge? Looking at it from one side, Jac is his friend and he is convinced that she is innocent of any crime, particularly treason. The poems are, in any case, love poems sent by a caring and faithful lover who is going a further step and having the poems bound into a book for her so that they are not lost or dishevelled. Bound for her to keep for a lifetime, perhaps an embossed leather cover. He dreams of what it would look like; Mr. Smith calls on him again.

On the other hand, there is treachery afoot and it is very unlikely that MI5 would waste its resources unless there was very good reason. And it is his duty to help MI5, the national security organ. But surely they know that Jac was originally a Georgian and would know of the Georgian stronghold in Cambridge.

What can he say? 'Hullo, hullo. Are you still there?'

Mr. Smith is a little terse. 'Please carry on. Do you recall if you posted a letter for Jac?'

'Actually, I've thought about it and I don't remember a thing. Those damned Special Branch boys. Harrumph!'

'Do not recall posting a letter? Even though you were observed doing just that thing.'

'I was observed?'

'By Special Branch. And we—'

'Special Branch? The two men blackening my name in my village? And you trust that source of information? Really, it gets worse and worse.'

'Well, we would love to know where the envelope was addressed.'

'Well, I'm sorry to disappoint you, I don't remember. If I was observed posting a letter, why didn't you say so? All this going around the posts. Harrumph! And if I did post a letter for someone else, I would not be so impertinent as to look at the recipient.'

'That is very disappointing.'

Donald rallies; back to the reason he called in the first place, if you please. He stands, straightens his back, adopts a parade ground bark. 'Now, who is the wretched man who stands in my lane and stares into my house?'

'We have no idea.'

'No idea? You have had a good idea about all the other interferences upon my person in this village.'

'Can you describe him?'

'Average height, brown raincoat, brown hat.'

'Average? That makes it difficult for us.'

'Piercing eyes. As though he is trying to hypnotise me all the way from the lane.'

'We will look into it.'

'The electricity cut?'

'Not our remit. Sorry. Talk to your supplier.'

'The telephone calls?'

'All too common these days. Don't give them anything.'

'So, when it comes down to it, you are not able to help me.'

'And when it comes down to it, you will not help us.'

'Correction, Mr. Smith, cannot, repeat, cannot help you. When will you get it into your heads? I don't know anything about your problem. Good day.'

– 21 –

Poor Donald. It just seems to get worse, more complicated, and we can't help him; nobody can help him. Putting his defence of Jac's love life aside, Donald decides that the telephone call has been unsatisfactory; we would agree with him. He has not been treated with the respect that he believes to be his right, having served the country and retired with his reputation intact. Harrumph! It troubles him that the village is poisoned against him, that all dealings with his friend Jac seem to be cloaked in a dark cloud of official suspicion and a feeling of not knowing the whole truth. However, the visit from his cousin Gertrude has left him full of resolutions. The good thing that Gertrude gave him was a drive to get things done, not wait for others to do them.

An aircraft passes overhead at speed, the noise bouncing between the walls, the echo lasting long after the plane had gone. Village sounds reassert themselves by degrees; the birds, stunned by an avian louder than themselves, make an effort to match the noise of the aircraft. Traffic on the main road seems to be suddenly busier; children start to cry from delayed shock. And a sudden breeze picks up, whispering through the bushes.

And through Donald's mind, a refreshing blast that clears some of the fog of confusion from him. When we are accused of something, it makes us feel damned uncomfortable, and to start examining ourselves so that a little neurosis can convince us that all is not well and that we have possibly been a traitor without noticing it. He is painted with a pall of suspicion and MI5 seem to be doing a good job of it. But damnit, he is not a traitor and if he is concealing Jac's love life from authority, it is only reasonable; she is entitled to some privacy. They would drag it into the light, belittle and besmirch it so that it became valueless. And then reject it as being of no use to them, like a spent pen.

And then, as if out of his thinking, the telephone rings. He lifts the receiver, and listens; is it one of those damned nuisance calls? Let them speak first. He could hear breathing, measured, not excited. After a minute or two, a mild voice. 'Donald, are you there?'

Not a false call. 'Jac, bless you. How are you?'

'I do not hear a thing.'

'No. I… er…'

'Donald, you sound as if you are not all there.'

'Sorry, old, er, sorry, Jac. Bit on my mind.'

'You all right?'

'Of course, of course. Life carries on. Now, the men in black suits?'

'They outside the shop. Is not good for trade. People don't like men in black suits who stand outside, if they are in the way. People become funny, stay away. Not good for trade.'

'I know.'

'And trade in a village is all there is.'

'I know. Are they there all the time?'

'No. Come and go. Like rats.'

'Rats?'

'Yes. You know.'

Donald does not know. He doesn't want to know about rats. He has been told that they are easier to find, out here in the country. Boys in the pub talked about rat shoots with glee. Digging them out with terriers or ferrets. Always more at the grain harvest, they said. And he remembers the sayings, you are never more than a yard from a rat. Comforting. And rats desert sinking ships. Perhaps not the most tactful thing to say to Jac just now.

She says, 'And you? Are you still there? Things are better, yes?'

'Good heavens, er… no.'

'You do not complain?'

'I've tried.'

There is a pause. 'Donald, I would not ask things of you.'

'They don't seem to get the message.'

'No. Is hard.'

'And now there is a man in the lane, staring at me.'

'Oh goodness. You sound... busy.'

A pause. Come on Donald, get it together. Stiff upper lip, and all that. 'Oh Jac, not really. Why would you not ask things of me? Come, I would always help, if I can.'

'Well, you tell me of stress, all these things happen.'

'My dear, they are all as nothing compared with your problems. Piffling concerns.'

'Really? My problems not so great. They question me, they let me go.'

'Shocking. Not at all the thing. By the way, can you tell me about the fete?'

'The fete?' Jac sounds suddenly weary; perhaps she is regretting calling Donald. His notes his mind wandering, difficulty in concentrating on one thing at a time.

'Yes, you know, the village fete.'

'What about the fete?' Her voice is certainly weary now.

Donald does not hear it; he rides over it. 'They want me to do a re-enactment.'

'Why? What is actment?'

Donald becomes aware that this is not the moment to discuss the fete with Jac; he has got it wrong, again. 'The shop? You mentioned the falling off of trade.'

'Yes.'

'Well, get it out. What did you have in mind?'

Jac is businesslike, almost brusque. 'I stuck. Have trouble with help in shop, with men in black suits. I am...what would you say... tied to the counter from seven to seven.'

'I am sorry to hear that. Can I help?'

'Well… possible. But I must be here. Tomas is coming; he come for twenty four hours. It is marvellous to see him. He come for the fete; help me.'

'Help you?'

'Yes. I do teas and drinks. You know. You been there.'

'Actually, missed it for one reason and another. You know me.'

'And they want you do something?'

'What do you advise?'

'That Mrs. Fortesque. Beware. She always get what she want.'

'I suspected that. Comes over a bit of a battleaxe. She has got me doing an enactment.'

There is a pause. Perhaps Jac has given up trying to extract from Donald what an actment is.

'Can you give welcome to Tomas?'

Donald can feel the stress rising; a battle to organise, children to be marshalled, Mrs. Fortesque kept happy, space to be protected, feed and relieve himself, perhaps even a few moments' rest – after all, he is not so young – and now Tomas to be greeted. Harrumph.

A pause. He can hear her breathing, a little rough and uneven. 'Of course. Splendid. You deserve a bit of company. His company.'

'He has no car.'

$$- 22 -$$

We watch as Donald gathers his thoughts, and feel for him. When the poor man is in a quandary, what he needs is time; Donald is not a quick thinker. What does he know? He does know that Jac posts her love poems to an address in Cambridge and he has not told MI5. He does not remember the address but he knows where it is on the map. But MI5 probably know of a local Georgian stronghold; they don't need his help. Except they don't know... or do they? He does know he will help Jac and protect her private life. As long as he is convinced that she is not guilty of treason. And he is convinced of that.

He knows that she loves Tomas and believes that Tomas loves her. They are a couple that intend to spend their lives in England; they would not wish to prejudice their futures. He does not know if Tomas works in the unit that is leaking information but he knows that MI5 are interested in the shop; they have told him that the leak goes to Georgia and Jac and Tomas are Georgians. Is this a coincidence? Beware of coincidences. Perhaps Tomas is suspect, an unwitting cog in the espionage machine. But good grief, what harm can it do, Tomas coming down for the fete weekend? He, Donald, can't be accused of aiding and abetting; curious concept, aiding straight forward, but abetting; what does that mean? Must look it up. Did Essex aid and abet Queen Elizabeth...

Come on, so much to think about. He takes a break, staring into space. Birds call, tits feed, cats creep. The sun disappears behind a cloud.

Back to the problem in hand. He knows that MI5 suspect him of holding information that might convict Jac of treason and equally, apart from the Cambridge address to which he posted a letter, he knows nothing. Apart, of course, what they have chosen to tell him and he made it clear that he didn't want to hear it anyway. Official Secrets Act, my foot! Harrumph!

Jac wants him to fetch Tomas so that Jac can be with him for a night or two. What might happen? The Special Branch men might stop him and take Tomas. And he would be accused of assisting a traitor if Tomas is guilty. Which he might be and might not. It is all too confusing. However, he feels that Jac's happiness is more important and Tomas should come. Somehow. Not his business if he is suspected.

He does not come to these thoughts and conclusions logically, even if they have been put like that. His mind goes into a fog and he is unable to answer Jac, except by promising that he will fetch Tomas. The thinking follows the commitment, goes on long after the call has terminated. Donald is sitting in the kitchen, gazing again at nothing in particular, lost to the world.

So lost that he is not aware of the bell. Not aware until there is a hammering on the door. He groans; he doesn't think he has finished the thinking, come to any resolution. He rises, opens the door a crack.

'Really, Donald. You are the hardest person to tie down.'

Ah, it's the hat. Mrs. Fortesque. And maybe he does not want to be "tied down". 'I'm a little busy at the moment.'

'But not too busy for me, I'm sure.' A little false falsetto snigger, and she is stepping forward; he has no choice and steps back as she pushes the door open. 'I've always thought, what a sweet little home,' she says as she looks around, a fixed smile on her face that never reaches her eyes, which are an unreal blue; he hadn't noticed that before.

Donald suspects that her own home is large and wonders what she really thinks of his "little home". Probably just the size for lodging her husband when he becomes tiresome. Not much larger than a stable for her pony, if she has one; he wouldn't be surprised. Except, not a pony; that would be too small. At least a hunter. He is able to examine her. Her tweed suit is well worn but undoubtedly of good quality. As are her brogues and lisle stockings. And the silk scarf around her neck, a horsey pattern. The hat; is it a joke? A sort of cap, it could be described, with a sort of parapet; some material that Donald can't identify, and a false flower peeps over the top, also unidentifiable. Her similarity to the Colonel's wife strikes him again. Her grey hair emerges beneath the hat in tightly controlled curls; any departure from a disciplined existence is apparently not acceptable. She is a battle-axe, a good description; he can imagine her going into battle in any committee and being on the winning side. Even being an old-fashioned magistrate, the sort to terrify some local errant boy. He can imagine her demolishing an argument at a village council by force of personality rather than by reason or logic. And should she find fault with a neighbour…

She is sitting at the table, opening her large leather bag – a saddle bag? – and spreading papers around. 'Now Donald, I know it's tiresome, but I need you to sign some papers.'

'Papers?' What on earth did she want? Him to sign over his house? A giant sigh; we can feel for him, hassle after hassle. Surely, he is too old for this sort of treatment.

'The fete. You will recall that there are a number of issues around your display.'

Donald remembers nothing, no issues, nor even what he said he would do. Or had she done all the talking? Really, it was most tiring. His mind drifts… horses… would Mary have enjoyed riding?…

'I… er… Remind me what it is that you wanted me to do.'

Mrs. Fortesque raises her head and examines him; she has produced a pair of spectacles, frameless with a cord around her neck. She peers at him over them, coughs, and speaks. 'Now, Donald, I'm sure that you can't have forgotten everything. The fete; I am the Chairman, and I have taken it upon myself to brief you personally rather than delegate it, as one must so many matters. I felt it was the right thing to do in this case, to deal with you personally; we're all so grateful that you can spare the time to educate us… no, inform us and guide us in the proper manner. You wouldn't believe how many matters there are,' and she proceeds to list the "matters" that a village fete involves, including the police, local Health department, the separate stalls, the childrens' sports, toilets, parking and so on. And shows just how busy and important she is. Donald is not impressed; he has lived among those who thought themselves busy and important most of his life. Even thought himself important for a short while, until the Colonel…

Donald sits in a blur of information, little of which penetrates his mind. He is thinking of Cambridge and Tomas, of Jac and the Special Branch. Eventually, he interrupts her. 'Did you say police?'

She does not care to be interrupted; she freezes, casts him a glacial look, a habitual practice with those who dare to interrupt her, wonders about continuing her list. And you should understand that, in a moment, she becomes afraid suddenly that she might lose Donald altogether. His contribution could be an important attraction, such as other local fetes did not have, and could have a major effect on the outcome of the fete; she was not to know of how major it will prove to be. The fete has to be successful; anything less is not acceptable. Poor Mrs. Fortesque. 'I'm sorry, Donald. Perhaps I went too fast for you the other day.'

Donald is silent. As though he has woken up, he is listening now.

'What I thought was that we had agreed on was a display of your medieval warfare with a little re-enactment, with local children taking the part of your soldiers.'

'Good gracious. How on earth am I going to organise all that?'

'Oh, it won't be difficult. You will be coming to a committee meeting and it will all be organised for you.'

'I… I don't think that would be a good idea.'

'Well, why on earth not?'

'You are not aware of it?'

'Aware of it? What are you talking about?'

'I find that the village has put me in Coventry. I know why, but I am innocent.'

'Well, if you are innocent, you have nothing to fear.'

'If only it was as simple as that.'

'My dear, you come to the committee and we can sort it all out. A great opportunity.'

Donald thought about the opportunity. Perhaps it would work; it depended upon who was on the committee. He forgot his concerns about the display.

'So,' Mrs. Fortesque was forceful. 'I need you to sign these insurance papers. Just a formality, I'm sure.'

'Why?'

'Why what?'

'Why am I obliged to sign insurance papers?'

'Well, if there is any accident, you know, if some boy is hurt, a question of liability arises and therefore you have to be insured against such an eventuality.'

Donald noted the words; insurance speak. It went with the part, the chairman of a committee, the organisation. It was building; he felt it in the air. 'I think, with respect Mrs. Fortesque, that it will be more than I can manage and you should leave me out of your arrangements.' He turned away, wondering what he should do next. The battle? Or perhaps the book?

Mrs. Fortesque did not become a chairman without facing such small oppositions and overcoming them. She laughed, the same melodic clatter as before. 'Dear Donald, please, you really should not worry yourself. All will be organised for you; I have just the person to act as your lieutenant. And the children will

197

have to have child carers; it's the law, to protect them from any untoward approaches.'

'But, all the same, the village—'

'Don't worry about the village. We have all had our problems with the village and they pass away with time.'

Mrs. Fortesque is not held in high esteem in the village; her bullying manner, her snobbish approach and her lack of consideration for anyone below her station in life have not proved popular. Donald doesn't know that, but he is getting a measure of her. And yet she is valued, for doing the work that others have no inclination to undertake. She takes the chairmanships that are onerous, the posts that involved clashes with District Council, the Police and other outside bodies and the roles that require so much work that most villagers shy away, though are vocally always ready to help. Help, but not manage. She looks at Donald; he has not offered her coffee and he is not looking well; a little peaky. What he needs is a good meal.

'Donald, I have a suggestion. Why don't to come to dinner at my house tomorrow and we can talk about things. No pressure. You are happy eating meat? So am I. Good. I'll see you at seven.'

And with that, she sweeps up her papers, slides them into her bag – saddle-bag?– and departs, Donald sitting at the table, watching her without comment. He no longer feels like the battle, or the book; he feels rather like going into hibernation and allowing weeks to pass.

– 23 –

He intended to send an apology. What was he thinking of? Can't get involved, village people, exposing himself to more criticism, more odious rumours. He can't possibly accept her invitation, will say he's already booked an appointment, not specified, but finds that he does not have her address or telephone number; she has described where she lives and it is a short walk. He resolves to go for a short time only and is sure that there will be nobody of interest to start an interesting discussion. Preferably not village matters, nor politics, nor the fete. He must not get involved with those subjects. Oh, these villagers. He wonders what to wear.

It is a mild evening. Quiet. The sun is low and heat radiates from walls. The scent of roses and evening primroses hangs in the air. Birds are mostly asleep; a few bats flit over his head. Voices sound clearly and there is the purr of lawn mowing and the hub-bub of drinking parties in gardens, the pub overflowing into its own garden and the street. Cats congregate on the Green, a collective competitive caterwauling, broken by occasional dogs. He walks through the village. A few couples and others pass on the way to some idle entertainment; the odd person bids him a good evening but mostly villagers ignore him. He is getting used to this treatment; it reinforces his tendency to retreat into his own little world, cut off from society, except for occasional contact with Jac and the few persons who do not bide by the prejudices of the populace.

A modern house, three bedroom type, plastic picture windows, a porch with columns and a pediment, quasi-Corinthian capitals. He wonders what medieval remains were buried forever beneath the foundations, and hovers in the porch; the door is opened. A small man, bald, stands back, bows slightly; no words, a smile of greeting. Donald steps forward.

The hall is warm; oak boarding stretches away from him, the walls redecorated with those little pictures of hot countries that you buy when on holiday. A small chandelier brushes his head. Across the floor comes his host, a flowing full length green silk dress, some sort of silvery necklace that makes a soft clashing noise. The lipstick is bright, the eyes tastefully touched up, the hair firmly in place. A fixed smile.

'Donald, how good to see you. So glad you could come. Come into the lounge.'

She takes his arm and directs him through a glazed door into a room. It is of generous size, two sofas, armchairs, a huge television screen, pictures including photographs of grinning young people in university robes, a mirror over the fireplace, with an electrical fire with pretend coals. And flickering flames, no heat.

He finds himself in the middle of the room. Before him is a group of people, standing with drinks in hand; he doesn't know any of them. He hasn't seen them in the shop, the church or on the streets. They all turn to look at him, blank looks of disinterest. The bald man brings up the rear, offering him a drink while Mrs. Fortesque introduces him. He doesn't remember the names for more than a few moments; why should he? He won't meet them again. He supposes that Bald is Mrs. Fortesque's husband, before remembering that her husband has died. The others are obviously village members; they share that irritating familiarity of teasing and abusing each other. There is a squirrely sort of man, short, a toothbrush moustache not unlike his own, hair slicked back, an unpleasant look on his face. Avoid him. And then there is a woman in a long Indian sari with lots of beads and long hair, who laughs a lot, and another woman who looks worried, quick fretful movements, hands clasped over a glass of orange juice. Perhaps she came with the squirrelly man. And a couple in the background, whispering to each other.

He accepts a large gin and tonic and notices that the men are all in dark suits, the women all in long dresses. He looks down at his own clothes; he has forgotten to change. Corduroy trousers, hacking jacket, Newmarket shirt and a tie. At least he is wearing a tie. And at least his shoes are clean – they gleam. A quick survey reveals that Squirrel does not know how to keep his shoes clean. Harrumph; he won't be staying long.

Squirrel goes into the attack, or so it seems, the way that he bends forward, curls his top lip, screws up his face. 'You live in the Lanes.'

Donald makes no response; whether it was a question or a statement is of no interest to him. An unpleasant little man; reminded him of a Quarter Master in his last regiment. He, Donald, won't be staying long.

The Sari breaks in with a false laugh that causes the chandelier to ring. 'Oh, don't take any notice of him. It's been a long day at the Council and he likes to stir things up when he's a bit tired. Though how he gets tired there, I have no idea.'

She earns a furious look from Squirrel, who splutters over his drink, thrusts the glass at the bald man for a refill and renews his foray. 'You were in the army, eh?'

'Harrumph! And you,' said Donald, nettled by his tone. 'You were in the Boy Scouts? Eh?' He regrets it immediately, astonished at his own rudeness and that he is wasting time on this little man.

Sari hoots with laughter. 'You tell him. Spot on. Boy Scouts to a city college to the Accounts office at the Council.' She must be Squirrel's wife or partner. For the present.

The man looks at her with loathing. 'Well, at least I didn't drop out of university to go gallivanting around India.' He attempts to pull himself together, with a joke and a half-smile. 'So, Donald, I hear that you are suspected of spying on our country.'

There is a shocked silence.

Eventually, Donald smiles. He should have expected this kind of comment and he doesn't have much of a sense of humour. Now is the time to leave; but he is irritated, spurred to return the attack. 'Spying? That is an interesting accusation. Where did you pick up this bit of nonsense? The gutter?'

Another shocked silence.

Donald has had enough; he cannot think what has happened to his manners. He never acts so badly; except, maybe, there were one or two times when under the influence in the Officers' Club. He turns to leave but finds Mrs Fortesque coming through the door. He sidesteps her but she smiles and opens her arms. 'Donald, so good of you to come. I gather you have had an interesting life; where did you live before here?'

He hesitates, fatally; the moment passes. She takes his arm, directs him to a sofa and sits with him. He mutters that he lived near Cambridge.

'Such a beautiful city. You are lucky. Did you work there?'

Donald stares at her. 'Taught medieval history, actually.'

'Gosh. Of course, I did know that. Silly of me. Now, will you excuse me while I attend to the kitchen?' She summons Sari to sit in her place, making tacit signs that she is to prevent him from leaving, and slips away.

Sari bobs down next to him and gazes into his face. 'You must have had such an interesting life!'

There is no answer to such a statement. He starts to get up but she clamps onto his arm. 'Where do you get such excellent clothes? My husband always chooses such rubbish; I wish I could dress him better.'

Donald is getting increasingly unhappy. The room is full of idiots. What is he doing there? He hates making a fuss, a display of bad manners, but really. He looks around. Squirrel is whispering in a corner with Nervous, and Bald has disappeared to the kitchen where Mrs. F is rattling pans. Sari ignores Donald now; she sees him as a dead loss, gets up and gazes out of the window, her back to her husband. Donald rises, looking for somewhere to put his glass.

The nervous woman looks at Donald, a sharp look of alarm on her face. She is about to speak when Mrs. Fortesque returns and shepherds everyone into the diningroom. Donald is swept up in the crowd, unable to politely separate himself and escape.

A small room; they have to manoeuvre around each other to reach the seats that Mrs. F indicates. Bald man pours wine, offering red or white. Donald accepts red, noticing that everyone else has white. There is no conversation, since Squirrel's blunder and Sari's failure. Mrs. Fortesque returns with a dish of slices of smoked salmon, little sprigs of parsley, small slices of lemon. She passes the dish around.

The first course passes with little talking; Mrs. Fortesque has placed Donald on her left and attempts conversation, questions about the army and his university career, all of which he fields with a few words only, almost no information. The nervous woman is seated next to Donald and she says nothing, gazing at her plate, eating little, sipping water; Donald is out of practice at dinner parties. He wonders whether he should be making polite conversation with her when she peers up at him, and says, 'Is it true?'

'Is what true?'

The other conversations around the table die.

'I mean… er… is it true what they say?'

'I am not aware of what they say.' Donald speaks stiffly, sitting bolt upright, surveying his escape route. It would be difficult in this small room to escape without bowling over his hostess. The little bald man is at the far end of the table and would not be able to come to Mrs. F's aid. Squirrel he would have no difficulty putting down, even though he is about thirty years younger. The women he discounts.

Mrs. Fortesque bores over the other woman's question. 'Now, really, we don't deal in rumours here, do we?' An ingratiating smile. 'Donald, really, we are all good friends in the village. I'm sure you know that. Let us talk about the fete. Rupert here,' indicating the Squirrel on her right hand and opposite Donald, 'is my right-hand man, and will be very glad of your input.'

Donald looks at Squirrel with loathing. Now he knows, with a large measure of relief, that it will be impossible to involve himself; the man is a jack-ass. Squirrel is about to speak, but Mrs. Fortesque senses the problem, clamps her hand over Squirrel's arm, and steers the conversation onto other matters. 'Tell me, how is the Greens Committee going to deal with the dog mess? It's not healthy and it's so unsightly.'

Squirrel chips in. 'These damn dog owners. They ought to have their dogs shot when they allow that. The dogs or the owners, heh?' A mirthless laugh. Looks of embarrassment around the table. Donald wonders how many dog owners there are here.

Bald utters for the first time. 'We all take our black bags with us, you know. It's the visitors.'

Squirrel throws up his hands. 'Rubbish. Seen it many times. Now what I want to know,' leaning forward and staring into Donald's face, 'is why the Greens Committee is not cutting the grass often enough.'

Donald can think of a reasonable answer but he is damned if he is going to respond. He stares back, without comment. Squirrel splutters, his colour rises and he grabs his drink, a large gulp, puts the glass down choking. Mrs. Fortesque looks at him, a little sigh. Sari asks Bald a question, a clear voice, about his dog. Squirrel directs a sneer in her direction; it is like water off a duck's back.

Outside, a dog can be heard barking, a long drawn out howl repeated over some minutes. A few heads are raised, and there is a discussion as to which dog is barking. Squirrel suggests that the dog should be put down; he is ignored.

Mrs. Fortesque has withdrawn, Bald is clearing the table, and she returns with a casserole, plates and vegetables. 'Now, can I dish out?' She proceeds to fill plates, which are passed round and round the table until one reaches Donald. He leaves it in place.

As they start to eat, there is a murmur from Nervous next to him. 'Oh dear, oh dear. I did tell her. I don't eat meat.' She sat gazing down at the stew, her hands twisted below the table.

Mrs. Fortesque stares at her. 'It's all right. It's not beef, you'll be able to eat it. It's deer.'

'Oh no, you don't eat deer?' Nervous produces a minute handkerchief, mops her eyes, pushes her chair back from the table.

Sari looks sympathetic, as she tucks in. 'I'm sure it's very healthy. I read that we need some red meat, for our blood. You know, the corpuscles.'

'As though you know anything about it!' Squirrel casts a look of loathing at his wife.

'Do you get it from the shop?' asks Sari.

The conversation rumbles on uneasily, across subjects such as the shop, the traffic through the village, excessive and too fast, the amount that the Church receives from the Fete profits, loudly protested by Squirrel, more complaints about dog mess, all avoiding the matter of the fete. Donald sits in silence; he didn't come here to listen to village talk. It's boring and he has other things to think of. As they rise from the table, Mrs. Fortesque grabs Squirrel and pulls him into the kitchen, slamming the door. A loud conversation can be heard, Squirrel becoming quieter, Mrs. Fortesque more demanding; until there is silence. Donald thinks it is unlikely that the two are having an affair but he comments to Bald that he has a very strong wife.

'My wife? Oh dear me no. My wife died some years ago, and Mr. Fortesque died just a couple of years ago. Covid, you know. Caught at the golf club. No, no. She asks me to be her partner at things, like this evening. Bridge, theatre visits, supper parties; you know the sort of thing.'

Donald stares. Poor chap. He can't imagine being a partner to Mrs. Fortesque.

As though reading his mind, Bald says, 'You'd be surprised how lonely it can get, when one's wife dies. I'm very happy to go along with it. It's all right for bachelors like yourself.'

Donald does not let him know that he too is a widower. He wonders if he can walk out of the door without causing offence. He edges towards the hall.

Dinner parties are a trial to those who are unaccustomed to the conviviality, the sharing of tall stories, the joint and vocal appreciation of food that much effort has produced, and the feeling of goodwill that must be shared. We all have experience of them. They are a process that each society, country and class develops in a different way; there are rules to learn and habits to acquire, so that an essential feeling of ease can be acquired. Donald has lost these habits; the army had a fixed form of behaviour to which he found it easy to adapt and the College also had a form that was not hard to learn. These were organisations with a strict hierarchy; it was easier to fit in, follow the rule. But here, one has to learn village etiquette, village priorities of personality, taste and power. For power always exists as an ever-present element. Here it is exercised by Mrs. Fortesque.

She emerges from the kitchen; she has lost that look of quiet control; her moves have become more rapid, almost violent.

Squirrel emerges behind her, avoids Donald's eye and slinks into the room where he tells his wife loudly that it is time to go home. She protests, equally loudly, sitting down and lighting a cigarette. He hovers over her briefly and leaves abruptly, pushing past Mrs. Fortesque with a muttered thanks. Bald takes the opportunity to tell Donald that there is an exceptional malt whisky and would he like a glass. Donald hesitates, finds Mrs. Fortesque blocking the doorway, wishes to avoid departing with Squirrel, and accepts. Nervous comes to sit next to him on a sofa and asks him how he fills his time. When he mentions writing, she flourishes for the first time, telling him of the novels she has written, the universities she has attended, and the teaching that she undertook before retiring. He finds himself drawn into the sort of conversation that he has not enjoyed since he arrived in the village, a conversation where he can contribute his own experience and exchange ideas. Nervous is delighted to hear of his Cambridge Lectureship, his College life and his pupils.

After a time, he is aware that they are the only two people in the room. There is conversation in the kitchen, a separate party. Otherwise all is quiet. The need to escape has died away and he talks as he has not talked for a long while. He does not notice the time until Nervous rises with a jerk.

'Oh my goodness, the time. I hadn't noticed. Thank you for our talk; I enjoyed it very much. I hope we might talk again in the near future. There are a number of historical theories that I should like to bring forward.'

Donald hates historical theories; he avoided them as much as he could in his university days. But he smiles, bids her good night and prepares to leave himself. But Mrs Fortesque comes through the kitchen door and takes him aside, shutting the lounge door behind them, fixing him with a look that he takes time to decipher; he realises that she is about to plead. It must be an unusual mode for her; he assumes that she is accustomed to giving commands, with the expectation that they will be obeyed. But he will not work with Squirrel; the man is an idiot, and mayhem would ensue. He can't see his display working to his satisfaction.

'Donald, I wonder… how can I introduce the subject?'

Donald knows very well what subject she is wanting to introduce and steels himself against being drawn into her fold. He looks at her, his gaze as blank as he can.

'Well, I must be on my way. Thankyou for a delicious meal.' He turns to the door.

'You see, Donald, there are two matters that concern me: the first is the reputation of the village. I'm sure that you feel the same way. Our village is special, unique, and we are sensitive to how we present ourselves. Perhaps you haven't been involved in Committees that promote the village yet. But we cannot sit on our backsides and expect the village to thrive without a certain level of attendance to our reputation. I'm sure that you can understand.'

Donald is silent. He has never felt any need to 'promote' the village; perhaps there are others who do that, it has never occurred to him. He is not sure how important it is to 'promote' the village, apart from the value of properties and the facilities that the village provides.

'The other matter that concerns me is your reputation. No, do not stop me. I am aware, yes, even me; I am aware that you are being accused by the jetsam and flotsam of this village of being a spy. And this accusation has spread; I was devastated to hear it mentioned in my lounge before dinner. I had thought it was limited to those who have nothing better to do than have idle gossip. I apologise for my friends, most earnestly.

'But, if you are to redeem your reputation, would it not be good if you were seen as the leader of your display, a display that our village would be proud of, I've no doubt. There can be no other person who has the special knowledge and experience.'

Donald reeled under the weight of her arguments. He reflected on his situation, his insecurity and on MI5 and their accusations. Noting his hesitancy, Mrs. Fortesque pressed him to come to a Committee meeting.

'At least you will have the opportunity of putting your concerns to the whole Committee. There, why not? Wednesday evening here at eight. Shall we leave it at that?'

– 24 –

They meet at the pub. The shop has closed for the day, and Jac appears tired but relaxed. It is a quiet evening, a minor hum of conversation around the bar. They sit side by side, in silence at first.

'Do you pick up Tomas? I am grateful.'

'Jac, I have already committed to helping you. Has anything happened?'

'No; the same thing of Special Branch. You don't believe, they ask my customers. Is not permitted; what do I do?'

'I don't know.'

'But I tell you, again and again, and Special Branch, I do nothing. Nothing, I tell you.'

'Did you tell them about the poems you post to Cambridge?'

'No. Why I do that?'

'I didn't tell them either. Your private business, that's what I say.'

They sit in silence. Donald is worried, and restless. After a while, Jac notices.

'You have a thing to tell me, Donald.'

'No… no, I don't think so.'

'Something is worry for you.'

'Just a detail that I have been working on.'

'It is?'

'The matter of getting Tomas to you without Special Branch interfering.'

'Tomas innocent. Why a problem?'

'You told me how they kidnapped you, kept you overnight. They might do the same to Tomas and there goes your night together.'

'They have no right!'

'No.'

'You see a problem?'

'What?'

'Oh Donald! Getting Tomas, of course.'

'Well, there is a chance of interference.'

'What we do?'

'Yes. I've been thinking about it.'

'And…'

'And… suppose he was disguised?'

'You mean false moustache? Beard? That would be good? They do not know how he looks.'

'No. But supposing he was disguised as something different altogether.'

'What could that be? The postman? A doctor? I do not understand you, Donald.'

'I'm being pushed into doing this medieval display sort of thing. You know, halberds and swords, a little battle perhaps.'

'You do not want it?'

'Not much. But I used to do it at Cambridge. It shouldn't be too difficult to organise, if they do the organisation.'

Jac sips and twirls her glass; it is nearly empty. Donald goes to the bar, another two drinks. The men make way for him, silent until he leaves them when a murmur breaks out.

'I was thinking—'

'You think all the time, Donald, but how you help.'

'Oh well, if that's what you think—'

'What can you do?'

'Disguise him.'

'Oh, back to that.'

'No Jac. Something else.'

'What?'

'A soldier.'

'What?! A man in the army?'

'Yes.'

'But where you get the uniform?'

Donald smiled.

'You mean… you have uniforms?'

'Of course.'

'What it look like, a young man wear your uniform? You a General, huh?'

Donald laughs. 'No, only a major. But I thought it might put Special Branch off if they saw a uniformed officer in the front seat. You see, they were only non-coms.'

'Non-coms?'

'Yes. They weren't officers.'

'And they let him pass?'

'They would probably salute him. I would have to teach him what to do.'

There was silence for a while, as both imagined Tomas as a British officer.

'It's an idea, isn't it?'

'Oh Donald, is marvellous. I email him, tell him to do it.'

'No, don't. They may be intercepting your emails and we wouldn't want to give the game away, would we?'

The fete committee assemble in Mrs. Fortesque's lounge, after supper. Many of them would rather be at home, or in the pub, but they know their duty. Committee meetings are a regular facet of English village life; we know them, avoid or love them, but Donald has no experience of them. Here, they are all good citizens, all resident in the village; an even distribution of men and women. A cat looking in the window would note the deep seats, conducive to relaxation, and a certain air of fatigue as though all have slaved away over a long day; it would see a few surreptitious yawns, politely concealed, and a few heads that drop and recover with a jerk. Little conversation. And near the door, one man, sitting in an upright chair; Donald is hoping that he will escape early. Squirrel is there, sitting at the far end of the room, silent, avoiding Donald's eye. They wait.

As the clock in the hall delivers a series of electronic chimes, Mrs. Fortesque wheels in a trolley with coffee and biscuits. Bald follows her and proceeds to offer and pour cups, distributing around the room. Donald refuses a cup. Bald asks him if he can get anything else; Donald suggests malt whisky, which arrives in large tumbler with a jug of water. The members of the Committee look on with chagrin, some raising their hands, all ignored by Bald.

Mrs. Fortesque sighs, a dramatic gasp. 'Are we all here? Oh no, Kevin still not arrived?'

Nobody offers an explanation for his non-appearance; presumably, they all guess where he might be. Nobody offers to ring him or go to look for him. Mrs. Fortesque sits at a small table, papers arrayed before her. 'Well, does everyone approve the last Minutes?'

Again, there is silence. She sighs again, signs the Minutes, and says that she will deal with Matters Arising as part of the main items.

The doorbell chimes. Bald goes and returns, followed by Kevin. He looks slightly the worse for wear; his working clothes are as dirty as ever and he sways a little as he enters the room. There is a universal groan as they see him, except from Donald.

Kevin smiles, a big toothy smile. 'How are yer all? Bit like a morgue in here. Surprised to see you here, Donald; wouldn't have thought it was your kind of thing at all. Perhaps I should leave yer all to it.' He turns to the door.

'Now, Kevin,' says Mrs. Fortesque. 'We are all very glad you could come. Here, come and sit near me.' She pulls an upright chair closer to her, flips a newspaper onto it and pats it. He subsides onto it, a creak and a belch.

He looks around. 'Anybody got a drink?'

'Coffee, Kevin?' Bald is standing with a cup in hand. Kevin shakes his head which he then rests on his hand. Bald passes him a large glass of water which he accepts and downs in one.

'Now,' says Mrs. Fortesque. 'Shall we continue? I have asked Donald to come this evening. It would be wonderful if he joined the Committee but that is not the purpose of this meeting. I want to explore the viability of Donald presenting a display of medieval weapons, and hopefully, a small battle.'

A shy lady sits up. She has a floral blouse and silver brooch; she smooths her tartan skirt over her knees, sitting primly upright on a soft sofa, fighting the inclination to relax and drop back onto the cushions. She has a worried frown. 'Does that mean fighting?'

'Well, yes. That is what a battle is, isn't it?'

'But... but... er... do we wish to promote... fighting in the village fete?'

'My dear, I don't think you understand. It will be like a theatrical battle, you know, the sort that you see on stage. The armies will be drilled to avoid aggression and harm; we cannot have those.'

Donald wonders who is going to do the drilling; it sounds a lot of work. And realises that the battle is a foregone matter in Mrs. Fortesque's mind. Harrumph; what does she know?

Mrs. Fortesque continues. 'I have had a word with the schoolmaster; he thinks it is a great opportunity to involve his children and educate them about those times.'

Squirrel comes to life. 'You didn't tell me that.'

Mrs. Fortesque ignores him and turns to the other members of the committee. 'Could we determine whether this committee approves the addition of the display or even part of it?'

There is a silence, broken by Kevin who laughs. 'Reckon you've got them by the short and curlies, missus.'

There is a 'Well, really!' and a few snorts, quickly stifled. Mrs. Fortesque ignores them all and turns to Donald. 'I wonder, would it help, if you were to give a brief introduction to your display?'

Donald shrugs. He looks round the room and meets not a single eye. Except Kevin's, who says, 'Come on, Donald, give us your best.' And wonders again why he is there.

'Well, Kevin,' he addresses Kevin alone. After all, he could almost call Kevin a friend, unlike all these strangers here. And Donald does not like addressing strangers, unless they are his pupils or lesser ranks. 'I'm not at all sure that I wish to do a display; as you can see, there isn't much enthusiasm for it, and frankly, old boy, I get a little tired. But since you asked, you can have a display of weapons, static you know, some description of what they could do. And then you can have a little re-enactment, what Mrs. Fortesque describes as a battle. But as

214

she rightly observes, they have to be well organised to prevent bodily harm.'

'Well, we wouldn't want that, would we?' says Kevin with a laugh. 'Mind you, it would sort out a few of the little perishers in the village.'

There were murmurs of protest, at the thought of the little darlings put at risk.

'But,' says Donald. 'I haven't agreed to put it on. It's a lot of work, and I have other things to do. Harrumph.' He is tempted to stand to attention and bark at them.

'Now come on,' says Mrs. Fortesque. 'Can we have a vote on it?'

Assorted hands rise in a ragged show of support.

'And who would be willing to work with Donald on his display?'

There is a long silence; some are looking away, finding the view of the evening light more interesting, some gazing at their feet, some finding time to update the diary on their phones or make notes.

Kevin laughs. 'Reckon you got a problem there, missis. But Donald, old mate, you can count on me.'

Donald gives a thin smile. 'That's very good of you, Kevin. But we would need at least a couple more hands so it's a non-runner.' He rises, thinking that he has done his best, shown some willing and now he can go home. 'I'll wish you all a good evening.'

He has reached the door before Mrs. Fortesque has laid down her propelling pencil and leapt, positively leapt to her feet and laid a hand on his arm. He freezes, looking down at the hand.

In some societies, the laying on of a hand is deemed to be an assault. Even in Western societies there are instances where it seen to be unsuitable. Donald has had a good relationship with his wife; she looked after his needs, both in bed and in the home, very well. But one thing that he did not encourage was casual touching in public; they never walked hand in hand. In the Army, it was unheard of and could send a man to the Guardhouse. They may say that an Englishman's home is his castle; in Donald's case, his self was a castle, to be assaulted at the great risk of starting a fracas.

But Mrs. Fortesque belongs to that great strata of women who refuse to see any problem in physical contact. The odd hug here, slipping an arm into a friend's arm, even a sisterly kiss deposited on the cheek. And perhaps, in her widowhood, she feels the need for physical contact more keenly.

She looks up into his eyes. 'Donald, Donald, please. Don't be too hasty. You know it would be good to involve you in the fete, good for the village, and, dare I say it, good for you.' She is risking a lot; does she realise it?

Donald looks down at her. He thinks what a tiresome woman she is and removes his arm from her touch. The whisky has slowed him and he pauses, looking around the room. Everyone is silent, watching him as though he is a performing bear that might turn on them in a moment. What a miserable lot, he thinks; no guts to any of them. Except for Kevin, who laughs.

'Good on yer, mate. You tell them.'

Donald turns and makes for the front door. Here, he wrestles with an unfamiliar night latch until Bald comes to his assistance and opens the door. He steps out into the evening air and breathes deeply. What an escape; he would have been foolish to commit himself to that crowd of smug, self-satisfied citizens.

He strides homewards. There is no sign of the Special Branch boys or their black car. Bats soar over his head and an early owl hoots hopefully.

– 26 –

He bumps into Kevin a day or so later.

'You ought to have heard her, mate.'

Donald has never thought of himself as a mate of Kevin but he desists from pointing it out.

Kevin continues. 'She had them by the short and curlies, no question. She let rip, told them that they had a job to do, that they were a load of self-satisfied bastards who should pull their fingers out of their arses and get on with it. Wouldn't have believed the language; she really let rip. Didn't expect it, but I quite admired the old bird.'

Donald somehow does not believe that Mrs. Fortesque will have used some of Kevin's words but he guesses he is getting the gist of it.

'And then she said,' Kevin chokes on a chuckle, 'she said that they were going to have to beg you to do it. And they would be coming round yours to ask. And that squirrelly man, he's a useless toss, and me, we're not to be the ones. I think it'll be that tight arse woman with the brooch and a few others.'

'When were they planning to visit?'

'Dunno, mate. I'd left by then. Didn't get anything sorted that meeting, not the electricity, that's my job, nor the straw bales, nor nothing. Bloody useless. And so she told them.'

A few days later, he receives a submissive sub-committee, who come like the Burghers of Calais to offer their necks. He receives them in the kitchen, is happy to have them stand around as he doesn't have enough chairs and will not, will not allow them in his sittingroom and the battle display; and his books; and his papers. And, after a long debate during which they wriggle with fatigue and frustration, filled by Donald with all the negative factors that would come into effect, and by the good whisky that they brought as a peace offering like the squirrels and Old Brown, it is agreed that the display and battle will proceed, the schoolmaster who they brought with them enthusiastic to assist and offer to make replica weapons and armour out of broom poles and cardboard and to drill the children on the cricket field under Donald's supervisory eye. Other roles, the costume, the setting up of a display, the taping off of a battlefield and the provision of plasters for wounded soldiers, are all delegated to the other members present.

But, even before they leave, Donald already has other concerns to work on and wishes them away without any casual conversation.

– 27 –

For some time, he has been mulling over the Cambridge end of the puzzle. As usual, he is unable to come to any quick solution, but wanders about the problem, breaking off to gaze at the birds outside, to wonder whether he needs to call the gardening boy, whether he needs to shop, and has the milk been delivered. It is bright outside and he is tempted to put off any thinking until the dog is walked, a necessary occupation that calls him away from his other occupations twice a day.

He sits, a piece of paper.

The thinking: He is prepared to believe that MI5 are investigating a leak. He has come to this slowly; he distrusts any service that does not wear a uniform, some recognisable sign of authority. He also believes that Jac is innocent, is sure of it, quite convinced. How could she be involved in something so alien to her wish to be a good English person? There can be no hint of treachery in love poems and the place to which they are being sent, a company of publishers to create a volume brimming of…

He has to stop, breath slowly, remembering far back his wife and their first encounters. Not that he sent her poems. Not his thing, actually. But Jac, well, I mean…

The two things don't add up; they conflict in a way that has brought him into the picture, dragging and protesting, but still there. Right in the picture. You would think that the people in power would be able to sort things out for themselves…

So it's down to him. He has to prove Jac's innocence to MI5, and they can trot off and deal with the leak themselves. He can then face Mr. Smith and tell him to leave them alone. And he would tell him in no uncertain terms. Job done. He feels so satisfied with his decision that he has to turn on the kettle, make coffee, dig out the biscuit barrel, select two digestives and sit gazing out of the window. For a while.

Birds sing, a cat slinks through the garden, neighbours pass by. Nobody greets him, though. His coffee becomes cold as he wonders whether he is doing the right thing; suppose there is some danger… rubbish, harrumph, rally the troops! He will visit Cambridge, his old home, the centre of his teaching life, drop into the College, might even book a room for the night, listen to the old High Table gossip, teasing and so on, look up a few of the bookshops and just happen, between visits to old haunts, tea-shops and pubs, just happen to drop into this publisher and check them out. Tickety boo.

It becomes a deployment of a force of one. He plans the route, his dress, the location of the address that he will be investigating, where to park his car, escape routes should things get a little hot, and other matters like booking a College room, a safe haven if necessary. He assumes that his old College will always provide a safe haunt, the Porters remaining friends. There is a bonus benefit; his College is not far from the location. He considers which day of the week will be best, and looks at the weather forecast, hoping to find a day that is not too hot and not too wet. He fills the car with petrol, checks water and oil. And remembers the dog. Blast. Rings Kevin, and wishes her on him. Good man, Kevin; promises him a bottle of the best. Whisky, of course.

He feels prepared. Of course, he cannot scout the location; he has no idea how many offices will be within the address, but he assumes that a polite and forceful approach will give him the intelligence that he needs. And he will return to the village to vindicate both Jac and himself from the outrageous accusations that have hampered his life, ruined his reputation, and interrupted his research. At heart, he believes that that will be the outcome. How can it not? And then the deep satisfaction of calling Mr. Smith.

It is a cheerful sort of day when he sets off; buzzards and swifts soar overhead, the sun shines through a pattern of white puffy clouds, and a gentle breeze cools the air. He hums a military tune, punctuated with harrumphs and hurrahs. Notices pigs in large numbers rolling in the mud, dog-walkers in profusion, and a low flying pheasant that just misses his windscreen. For a change, Donald feels uplifted; he has escaped the village and its problems, he has a task to undertake, and he is doing something useful, something that benefits both Jac and himself as well as the village, not that they would notice. The journey is not long, not long enough to merit a stop to rest and recuperate on the way. He is content, too content to make a regular surveillance of his surroundings and the following traffic.

Before long, he is drawing close to Cambridge; the traffic increases and he is obliged to halt at traffic lights, negotiate roundabouts, cruise at a sedate pace into the centre to his designated parking place in the College. A few words with the Porters, all delighted to see him. Strange thing that; do they get tired of the dyed-in-the-wool academics? Always seemed to love his few military tales. Not that he told them anything important, of course. Promises to return for the night, look forward to a few more tales of naughty academmics. With a light heart, for he always enjoyed promenading the streets of Cambridge, he strolls on a diversionary route to his destination, avoiding a direct approach as a sensible precaution. Because, in spite of all the diversions that he has looked forward to, the problem is like an itch under his skin, and he wishes to satisfy his curiosity. It has risen up his list of priorities; get it out of the way, and he can enjoy himself.

A town pigeon, tired of bombing tiresome tourists, follows a gentleman of a certain age, hacking jacket, cords and a cap, steering his way between the crowds of tourists, occasionally standing aside to let others pass, perhaps dropping into old haunts, pubs and shops where he will be recognised, or picking up a book from a pavement stall to peruse briefly before replacing, until he turns into a narrower street, where the pigeon, in disgust at losing the opportunity of a discarded beef burger or a part of sausage dropped by a meandering tourist, returns to an easier target, particularly the ones with brightly coloured clothing that leaves much uncovered.

Donald has memorised the address, but to be sure, he stops and reads the scrap of paper he recovers from his pocket and wanders on, checking the house numbers. He notices how the buildings are in better repair than before; the Colleges must be dispensing some of their riches. About time too.

The street was empty; he was sure of that when he came into it. It is a narrow street, single carriageway, narrow pavements on either side, the houses built up to the pavement; a residential sort of street, probably all student residences. Not his College. He walks on. The houses become a little larger, still in a terrace with three storeys but with semi-basements, and a short set of steps rising to the front door.

Ahead, he can see one particular house where there is a group of men standing around, some sitting on the area wall, some on the steps. They are not students, at least, not of this university he believes. Their clothes are rough, workingman clothes, worn it seems with pride; Doctor Marten boots, dungarees, utility trousers, caps and heavy jackets, surely too hot for the day. As he approaches, their conversation ceases and they stare at him. Perhaps they can help him; they must work for the publisher. Mind you, funny sort of place for a publisher; didn't Jac say they bound her poems?

Donald has been in many places in the world where he has been stared at in an unfriendly manner; it's the fate of Army men. Similar to policemen, he guesses. There to keep the peace, as often as not, but derided just the same. And, dammit, it's happening again. He is not disconcerted; where would one get if one balked at an unfriendly stare? He stops at the foot of the steps; checks the number, slowly. Yes, this is the house, without doubt. He makes to climb to the front door.

One man, possibly still in his youth but tall and square, a big man, puts his leg out across the steps. 'Where you think you go?'

Donald pauses, looking at him. The accent is not English; he is running through his knowledge of Middle European accents, then further East. But not as far as Pakistan or Afghanistan. Ukraine? Bulgaria? And then it clicks; they are Georgian, aren't they? 'Excuse me, but are you Georgian?'

'What it?'

Good gracious, this man learns his lines from movies. 'I believe that there is a publishing business here.'

'No publishing business, mister.'

'I have the address. It was given to me by a Georgian.'

'Who you?'

'No, not me.'

The man appeared irritated. 'Who you?'

'I beg your pardon, but I have business here in the house.'

'Your name?'

'You won't know my name. Nor will I tell you the name of my Georgian friend. But I am here on her behalf.'

There is a burst of conversation in a tongue that he knows not at all. It is excitable and there is clearly an argument between the man on the steps and another in the street. The others appear to be taking sides. Fists are raised, some confrontation. Eventually, the man on the steps turns to Donald who has stood on the bottom step entertained by their argument. Good gracious, was what he wanted so complicated?

'You follow me.'

The man goes ahead up the steps, Donald following; he looks back. You might have thought that there has been enough warning, the unfriendly welcome, the foreign language by a group of men that appear to occupy the building. You might have thought that Donald, having carried out a recce, would undertake a sensible retreat, hold his fire, delay coming to conclusions about the address while keeping it under observation. But he does not believe the man that there is no publishing business in the house; why he has the address from Jac. And Jac would not mislead him; after all, he is helping her with the accusations, and helping her with Tomas. And she is innocent; of that he is sure. Obviously some mistake; these boys are just hanging about. Though one of them must work here. The others stand together around the foot of the steps, watching him. Through the front door; the house is dark within, stairs rising before them, room either side, doors shut. A little light seeps through a dirty window on the stairs. Up the stairs they go to the landing.

'Excuse me, where is the publishers?'

The man ignores him.

'I say, can you tell me, please, which room is the publishers?' Damn rude, these people, he's only trying to establish that the address is correct.

'In here,' the man says, pointing to a door.

'What's in here?' Donald is wondering where he is; it's confusing. He has expected a friendly welcome, a simple explanation, and a speedy exit. There's no helpful label on the door, no indication of a business at work. But the man seems to be helping him.

'In here. He.'

Donald shrugs, opens the door and goes in. The door is locked behind him.

– 28 –

It takes one back to training; Sandhurst, a few decades ago. Prepare for capture and interrogation; what was it they taught? In all his Army career, he has never been captured. Come under fire, many times. Been scared shitless, a few times. But never captured. It is a new sensation. But bugger it, he is in Cambridge in the twenty-first century, and what can happen? Really? What has happened?

It's all a bit sudden. Why, he should be outside enjoying the city, looking forward to dinner in Hall. His heart has increased its rate and he is breathing deeply. He leans against the wall. It is difficult not to feel sorry for Donald; he is well-meaning, has not assaulted or threatened anybody, though he was tempted with the oiks.

The room is quite dark, stained curtains drawn over the window. He can make out a single bed, an old metal frame, made up scruffily, an upright chair, a small bedside cupboard. Nothing else; the floor is covered, in places, with dark stained lino. The walls have not seen a fresh coat of paint for thirty or forty years. In the centre of the ceiling hangs a pendant fitting, no shade, no bulb. Cheerful house, he thinks. He steps across the room with care, and pulls the curtains aside. The light level improves, but not much; the glass is filthy, a heavy accretion on the outside. The view is of an adjacent wall, brick, in need of repointing. If he peers upwards, he can see a slip of sky, still bright. But peering to the side, he can see no further than the brick wall. Which needs repointing.

He returns to the door, knocks loudly, calls for attention. Harrumph. The house is silent; he can hear no signs of movement; it is as though the Georgians, if that is who they were, have left altogether. He moves the chair over by the door and sits down.

You would think that an Army man, particularly one who has taught young people, would have developed a measure of patience. It must have been necessary at some time in his careers. But Donald has lost those skills; when he retired, he wanted to fill his time without waste and he has pursued that philosophy assiduously. Conversations that bore him are terminated abruptly, books that bore cast aside, places that bore never revisited. This place pulls him back into former years and he racks his memory as to what is a balanced and considered way forward.

Escape; every British officer's duty. He recalled the tales of Second World War soldiers who had been imprisoned in Germany. Some had escaped, many to be recaptured. Some had escaped to be shot. But all had had the drive to get out, to prevent the lassitude that came from sitting in one place too long. Escape. What shall he do first?

He tried the door; the handle was quite loose but the lock held firm. He peered through the lock hole; the key was in the lock. Wasn't there a clever way of knocking the key out and recovering it under the door? But he has no tools on him. The window is closed, a normal sash lock. Ah, more hope here. He releases the lock, and pulls on the bottom sash. And pulls; oh bugger it, it's stuck fast. He is tempted to break the glass, but peering down, he sees a fall to a concrete side path below. There would lie a broken leg at the very least, possibly a broken pelvis. He's too damned old for this game. He checks the floor, but finds no loose boards. The walls are solid, plastered. And only now, does he ask himself why he came on this hare-brained mission. What has he learnt? He is too old for this nonsense. Ought to be locked up in a home. No, not yet, but ought to stay closer to safe homes. Who were the young men around the door? Probably Georgians, though he has not recognised their accent. Should he have brought Jac with him, to communicate in their own tongue? The one thing that he is sure of is that the poems are being posted to this building and that there is no publishing business here. But perhaps there is a friend who takes them elsewhere. All too complicated. Harrumph.

He tires of the chair and inspects the bed. Filthy sheets, blankets with holes. He stretches out the cleanest blanket over the bed and sits down. After a while, he lies and thinks of the village, the Green committee, the fete, all those awful people among whom he lives, and wishes he was back among them. He wonders if Kevin is feeding his dog properly and taking her for a walk; she likes a walk in the evening. He sleeps.

What time does he wake? It's too dark to see his watch. The sky is lit with the night-time glow of all cities, and the background noise of traffic and pubs is almost non-existent. There is the hoot of an owl and the screech of a group of persons returning from a club or pub or party, or whatever. It's not at all like the village. He sighs and returns to the bed.

Waking early, he resolves to be more active. He is hungry and thirsty but not without brains. The house is still quiet. He looks again at the lock. And the floor. A tool to wiggle the key. Looking around the room, he can see nothing. He examines the bed more closely.

There is something that all girls and boys learnt from adventure stories; how to escape from a locked room. We know he thinks slowly, but he is not without enterprise. He is thinking of the books of his youth; perhaps children don't learn these things any more. Pity. Donald's favourite was 100 Things a Boy can do on a Rainy Afternoon; damn good, full of useful things, like how to get water in the desert, and how to make the perfect apple pie bed. Of course, the circumstances described were always simple so that the end could be achieved with the minimum of fuss and frustration. But all the same, there are techniques that survive the ages, tricks that will work in this electronic age as they worked before. Donald thought back to his youth and smiled. His memory, so poor in relation to people's names and what he did the day before, recalls perfectly the techniques described.

The mattress is an horse-hair stuffed type, stained and pitted with use. Beneath that, the bed has an old arrangement of springs and a wire lattice. Steel wire. There is a loose end, about six inches long. He tries to bend it; yes, it bends. He works it to and fro until suddenly, rather sooner than he expected, it comes loose. He examines his treasure. It has a slight hook at one end, where it came out of the lattice; the rest is almost straight. He puts it under his shoe, which has a good leather sole of course, and straightens the wire, leaving the hook in the end. Now the door. It is not difficult to tear a piece of lino from the floor; it is so rotten that it takes no effort. He slips the lino under the door, beneath the keyhole. Now the key.

He had seen it done at college. He had laughed and believed the lesson a waste of time; sadly, it was one technique from the book that he had not achieved. He had even had a go, unsuccessfully. Well, he was not going to fail now. The problem was, how can one look through the key-hole while manoeuvring the wire? Does one wiggle it hopefully? He examines the key, as much as he could see.

A blessing; he nearly whooped in joy. The key lies vertically in the lock; it will need no more than pushing.

At that moment, he hears someone on the stairs. He creeps over to the bed and lies down. The door opens. He sits up.

'Hey! What are you doing? Why have you locked me up?'

It is the man who locked him in; he says nothing but puts a bottle of water and a packet of sandwiches by the door. And leaves, locking the door. In a moment, Donald is at the door, peering through the key-hole. The key is not vertical. He swears silently. The house becomes quiet; he hears the front door slam. Inserting his tool into the lock, he wiggles it. No success. He looks again. The key is almost upright. He wiggles again, looks and sees that the key has turned further, well past the vertical. He swears, curses himself for being a fool and tries again.

It takes about half an hour; his back aches, his knees protest, and he has run out of swear words. But eventually the key is vertical in the lock. He checks his piece of lino; pulls it back, pushes it into place again. His gaoler did not notice it, it seems. He starts to gently push the key out of the lock.

He is sweating, the water and sandwich forgotten. The key resists his push; he realises that he must lift the end with his hook and try again. It slides away, gratifyingly, and slips out of the lock; there is a slight tinkle as it lands on the floor. He cannot

228

stoop so low to see it below the door but it is an old four panelled door and there is a good gap beneath it. He slides the lino back towards him. It jams. It would. He releases the pressure, moving it back a little, moves it to one side, tries again. Again, it jams. He moves it the other way and it slides smoothly towards him, the key coming into view as innocently as though it belongs in his hand. He silently blesses the author of 100 Things a Boy can do on a Rainy Afternoon.

And pauses. How tempting it would be to unlock the door, gambol down the stairs and emerge on the steps; to be surrounded by his enemy. What shall he do now? He is so excited, and elated at his success, that he has slow himself down, allow the heart to assume a more even pace.

It is morning. He has been imprisoned for a little less than twenty-four hours. What did they want of him? Perhaps they had no idea. He is thinking of such matters, wondering why he has told nobody where he was going, who they thought he was, whether they knew Jac. Or Tomas. For a little while, he feels foolish; what has happened to his planning? It must be old age… not the way to think. Only as old as you think you are; and so on. After all, he is a British Army officer on an intelligence sortie; and he will never give in.

As he has these positive thoughts and stands a little straighter, thinking of taking on rations, he hears a thundering on the stairs. They are coming to get him.

A man stops outside the door, shouting in an Eastern European voice. He rattles the door handle. Presumably one of the Georgians. Why don't they come in? It takes him only a short time, not more than two or three minutes, to realise that they don't have another key; he is in possession of the only one. He smiles though realises that there may be no more bottles of water or sandwiches. And he is feeling devilishly hungry. The rattling ceases, a thundering on the staircase, and quiet returns. What would be a good hour to attempt an escape? Probably the evening. He resigns himself to rest, lying on the bed, trying not to think of food or home; but not succeeding. Then remembers the sandwich and water that he had put aside.

The day passes slowly. He hears a school bell, the chatter of small children, a whistle followed by silence. How simple life was, the years at his first school. A little trouble with one of those boys who grew rather faster than the others, a brute who persuaded others to hand over sweets and favours; he recalled doing his arithmatic prep for him, so easy that he could not understand why the brute found it difficult. But he did not argue the issue. He hears a dull roar of distant traffic, the odd bird call, unidentifiable, and occasional conversations, some within the building. But he has the key. He snoozes; patience is called for and his army life required a great deal of patience.

The light drops, the sounds of the city recede and he becomes alert. Now is the time. He gathers himself, sitting on the bed and putting on his shoes. As he rises, there is a huge outburst of noise. Shouting, both outside and inside, English and presumably Georgian and then shooting, a few shots that silence the shouting. Followed by the thunder of steps on the stairs, even greater than before, shouting on the landing, a warning that he cannot take in and his door explodes inwards, hanging on one hinge, the frame ripped and savaged.

Unfortunately, Donald has been standing inside the door, attempting to decipher the sounds. He does not have time to retreat and is blasted away behind the door. Lying on his back, he has difficulty in understanding what is going on; his head aches and in the darkness there seem to be a number of even darker figures around him. Not for the first time, he wonders whether his wisdom had deserted him when he undertook this mission.

A number of black dressed men stand around him, firing questions; they take a little time to realise that he cannot respond. They wear black boots, black combat trousers, black blouses and black helmets with visors. They are armed with hand-guns. Still deafened by the shooting and the explosion of the door, Donald regains some feeling and stares at them; one reaches out to take his arm and he twists away.

'Who are you?' His voice is a rough gasp; shock and fatigue has reduced him. He feels quite frail, unable to encounter any more excitement. He holds out the door key. The man stares at it, laughs briefly, and throws it away.

'Come.' The man reaches out again, and this time, with a man on each arm and one behind, they manoeuvre him out of the door, down the stairs and out of the front door. They pause; there are more black dressed men, holding a variety of weapons and two black vans. Oh God, a foreign army; where are they taking him?

And then he sees that at the foot of the steps, one of the Georgians is kneeling with his hands over his head while Mr. Smith patiently asks him questions. There do not seem to be answers; the man cowers before Mr. Smith but says nothing. The sight of Mr. Smith brings tears to Donald's eyes; the relief is too much and he sinks onto a step, hugging himself.

Mr. Smith gives up his interrogation and speaks briefly to one of the men who takes the Georgian into one of the vans; Donald can see that there are other prisoners inside. He looks up to Donald on the steps. 'Well, I suppose I should thank you for leading us to the traitors' lair.'

'Leading you? I came alone.'

'Of course. But you could have saved us, and yourself, a great deal of trouble if you had given me the address. As it is—'

'You don't understand.' Donald sounds fretful.

'Perhaps we should speak on another occasion.'

'But—'

'No, not now. Take him home, will you?' He addressed one of the soldiers. For a moment, Donald thinks he is to be incarcerated in one of the vans. But he is led past to a black car, with aerials on the roof. The soldier, one of the two who released him, removes his helmet and grins at him. It is the older Special Branch man who burgled his house and escaped.

Donald stops, resisting the hand holding his arm. 'No, I have my own car.'

'I don't think you will be suitable for driving, sir. Just now. Get in, will you please, sir. Anywhere you like.'

The front seat. It is suddenly the most comfortable seat that he had ever sat in. He mutters, 'How did you know where to come? I didn't lead you.'

'You were under observation, sir.'

'But…'

There is no more and before they have left Cambridge, Donald is asleep.

– 29 –

And now, to set aside the Georgians, the industrial espionage and Mr. Smith, we can return to village matters. Donald recovers from his ordeal and is immersed in the fete. He was shocked by the imprisonment but rallies; after all, he is an old Army man. No time for dwelling on the past. He forgets Mr. Smith and the Special Branch and even the Georgians.

We might find it surprising, this change in priorities and circumstances. But he is being pushed, corralled, even trained by Mrs. Fortesque. She knows nothing of his Cambridge adventure and would probably dismiss it as a boys' adventure. The fete is all. She has obtained his services and he has become one of her puppets. Not that she would ever dare to suggest such a thing to him; she is aware of his independence and determination to avoid collision with village people and she negotiates with care. But all the same, he is at her beck and call, all day and most evenings, and he is committed to a good showing; to do anything less would not be acceptable in his own eyes, to maintain standards, though he cares less for his reputation in the village. Why he finds himself going along with the plans he is not at all sure; had he not done everything to resist being enrolled? It is the result of his Cambridge adventure; he will not admit it, but he feels the need to be closer to his neighbours, to overcome their hostility and join in.

He finds himself attending on the school-master, who has assembled a motley gang of volunteers, aged ten to thirteen, girls and boys, and is drilling them, training them in the art of warfare as advised by Donald, who stands on the side-lines, avoiding any confrontation with master or child. There are some children who appeal to him for procedure, ignoring the school-master; they hold him in high esteem; he is a soldier with active experience. There is a girl in particular, a tall stringy thirteen-year old, who likes to stand next to him chattering, but she is cajoled back into the relevant army. The field of war is the cricket ground; from time to time, they are interrupted by a cricket practice but as many of the children have fathers in the team, there is less trouble than there might have been. They are visited by Mrs. Fortesque who checks on procedure and by another lady who has been enrolled to produce costumes, mainly adapted grain sacks. Helmets and weapons are being constructed at school from thin cardboard and broom handles. Donald has been approached about costume but not referred to after a preliminary consultation; his descriptions were beyond

233

the imagination of the local lady, who is following the pattern observed in Hollywood films, adjusted to her budget and means.

There is a constant problem that the master faces; some of the children do not wish to play the vanquished and will fight for supremacy. And at the suggestion by a few boys that the girls play the vanquished, there was almost a walk-out. It requires the greatest tact and patience on the half of the school-master to overcome this problem, partially by pointing out that the vanquished have a glorious moment to exhibit dramatic deaths, drawn-out scenes of exaggerated gore with sachets of tomato ketchup. Donald, on the side-lines, avoids any part in this problem; at university, there were always those who were content, even willing, to play the defeated, wounded and killed soldiers. He has not had young children for a long time and has forgotten the rivalries that echoed through the home, disrupting domestic harmony; his years away in the Army did not aid his involvement and his wife had to be consoled from time to time as she became the one alone who exercised parental tact and force.

There is one unfortunate occurrence; Mrs. Fortesque attends at a late rehearsal when the semblance of blood is on show. She is shocked, appalled that the villagers and their visitors, almost guests in her eyes, are to be submitted, in her view, to the types of vulgar trickery that mock the dead of wars. The school-master argues, without success; he is not capable of standing up to her. Donald stands like a rock; he has not cared either way about the bloody tomato ketchup. He never had it at College and he sees no real reason for it now but he has grasped the need to reward the children with a little dramatics and been happy for the school-master to encourage it.

'Is that your final instruction?' He speaks gazing over her head, as though he could not care either way. The master and

234

children begin to crowd behind him, almost entirely silent apart from a little jiffling to get a better view which is some sort of a record for twenty children of that age.

Mrs. Fortesque does not recognise the opposition; she is not accustomed to being opposed and makes the mistake of thinking that she will always succeed. You might find this surprising, after what she has been through persuading Donald to take part and give of his time and expertise. But he has been her puppet for too long, and she has forgotten. 'I find it uncouth, and it may cause some distress.'

'Some distress?' Donald is making her do the work.

'Well, does it not glorify war?'

'Does it?'

'Well... I mean... it's blood, isn't it?'

'And you think we can have a bloodless battle?'

'I think you know what I mean.' She attempts to freeze him out, struggling to meet his eyes. It does not help that she is a little shorter than him and he continues to gaze elsewhere.

Donald's thinking has not quite caught up; he doesn't know what she means, but pursues a logically aggressive line as he was taught at Sandhurst. 'Are you suggesting that the battle, that you have strenuously persuaded me to display, does not involve the sight of blood?'

'No, not at all. But your display is only a small piece of theatricals, isn't it, and therefore the blood is not really necessary.'

Donald does not care for the words "only" or "small piece" or "theatricals" or indeed "not really necessary"; he could refer her to the numerous Hollywood films, and other attractions that have no problem in a little gore. But does not; hasn't thought of them at that moment. He flinches, coughs, looks round at the assembled children, meets the master's eye and turns back to gaze over Mrs. Fortesque's head.

'Harrumph. That is incorrect; it is not a small piece of theatricals. And you neglect the educational aspect, a huge benefit for the children. And perhaps for the master. And perhaps for the village. But evidently not for you.' He lingers on the last word, and sighs. 'Very well. Enough; we shall cancel this… erm… "small piece of theatricals" and leave you to find an alternative entertainment.' He turns round, his back to her. 'I'm sorry, children. The fete does not have the appetite for your excellent work.'

There are cries of complaint, a few tears from both boys and girls, and the master looks stricken, gazing at the ground.

Donald continues, his back firmly against Mrs. Fortesque. 'It is a great pity, considering your work, the skills that you have displayed in overcoming certain problems of acting, the fact that costumes, helmets and weapons have been made. Perhaps we should offer the display to another village fete. Yes, I think that would be a very good idea and then all your good work will not be wasted.'

He hears a gasp behind him, a stuttering, and then feels a hand upon his arm. As you know, Donald does not care to be handled. He moves brusquely to the right, still back to her. He is prepared to walk home, to have done with it all; he feels some sympathy for the children and their master but he is becoming rapidly fatigued by the whole matter. It crosses his mind; he determines to be absent on fete day. After all, he has made every attempt to be helpful, on his own terms of course, but enough is enough. He does not consider what the fall-out of not appearing will be, and wonders which whisky he will enjoy when he returns home and how his table battle is proceeding.

The sun is setting and birds are returning to their nests. A blackbird flies overhead, shouting an alarm when he sees the crowd below him. Donald yawns.

A small voice behind him. 'Excuse me. Could you help me? To understand?'

Donald stops. He is non-plussed; and weak before women who plead or weep. He looks at the children, the master, and turns to face Mrs. Fortesque. 'What is so hard to understand?'

'I mean... er... why can't the display... I mean battle continue without blood?'

He bends towards her, fixing her with a glare. 'Harrumph! Perhaps you would be so good as to inform me of a battle where no blood was shed.'

Mrs. Fortesque is silent; her eyes are starting from her head. She is controlling herself as tightly as she can but it is an unaccustomed posture; her body is rigid, shaking slightly, but she has not retreated a single step. She was taught, at her girls' school, a grammar in the North, to stand one's ground, particularly in the face of one of the opposite sex. She makes a slight gargling noise. No man has confronted her like this since she was a girl when she told her father that as a woman she was entitled to his respect in allowing her through a door before him. She was twelve. She is beginning to experience the same feelings that she felt then, when she was dismissed to her bedroom and missed supper. No such problem raised its ugly head all through her marriage; her husband was obedience itself.

Allowing a few minutes to elapse, Donald continues, speaking slowly as though to a child. 'Now you need to understand. It is important that people, and I mean both children and grown-ups, appreciate that war is not a pretty business. People get hurt, both those on the field of battle and others. And getting hurt often involves blood being shed, sometimes a little, like a cut, and sometimes a lot, from which people die; that is the nature of it. Now, if this is all too much for you and you want us to present some sort of fantasy, sadly you have come to the wrong person.

237

Or should I say, people.' He turns away, as though to bid farewell to the company of children and their master.

There is a cough and Mrs. Fortesque abases herself so far as to walk round him so that she can address everyone. 'Please listen to me.' A few groans, some theatrical gestures from older children who have been watching too many soaps. 'I believe that I have misunderstood the whole business. Naturally, I am concerned as to how your... er... battle will appear and I feared that some observers might feel that we are going too far, too far in showing all aspects of battle. But I was wrong. I am sorry to have caused distress, and I hope, I do hope, that you will put it all behind you. And continue with your splendid display.'

How much it costs her to reverse her opinion we will never know. Certainly, the school-master looks surprised; at first, the children do not gather the import of her speech and stand looking confused. But the older children, or at least the few who have listened, spread the word through the crowd. There is a burst of shouting, laughing, and clapping; glad smiles on every face except Donald, who continues to look grim. It has all cost too much; he is exhausted. In the future he resolves to stay out of village politics and to avoid Mrs. Fortesque. But that is the future; he will not disappoint the children; the battle will go ahead.

When he returns home, there is a telephone message waiting; please will he call Mr. Smith.

– 30 –

We know that it is a constant problem with older men; the threat of a breakdown, heart, stroke or prostate, when pressure increases through stress or simply excessive labour. It is not always possible to foresee these momentous occurrences, particularly with men who feel the need to drive forward, maintain a full physical and mental life. Donald looks at the telephone; he hears the message, and his mind closes down. He has confronted Mrs. Fortesque, he has held the balance of the battle in his hands, he has worked to stimulate the children, and he has been imprisoned. All recent in his mind. He has not faced such a trial for some years; university was soft, a holiday after the Army. Of course, there were all sorts of scrapes in the Army, though he was rarely under fire. More a question of dealing with non-coms and their petty complaints, and with superior officers and their petty complaints.

He feels a great fatigue, his heart is rattling a little and he slumps into a chair. With the minimum of food, but the addition of a good malt whisky, he retires to bed. Sleep evades him for a while; eventually he falls into an exhausted slumber and dreams of a medieval battle in which Jac and strange hooded characters flit through the battlefield without harm; he cannot determine which side he is on, where he should be. In the morning he is still dreaming, while the telephone rings, once and then twice more.

It is midday; how did that happen? The telephone is alight with messages. He ignores it, lets the dog out, apologises to it for a delayed walk, makes a jug of good coffee, opens the paper, sits and admires the birdlife in the garden. A cat appears and is sent on its way with a stentorian roar. The telephone rings again; after ten rings he can ignore it no longer.

'I called a few times, hoping to speak with you.' It is Mr. Smith.

'I was busy.'
'May I call on you?'
'Do we have matters to discuss?'
'Certainly.'

Donald groaned inwardly; after his Cambridge adventure, he had thought that the whole matter was finished, out of his life. It was agreed that Mr. Smith would visit the following day.

Morning the following day, coffee time. Donald has a jug on the table, mugs and biscuits, five minutes early, Army time. He waits. At exactly the hour arranged, there is a knock on the door and Mr. Smith comes in. It is sad, but we can see an older Donald, exhausted by recent events, sitting withdrawn, hands on his lap. The authoritarian army officer is absent. Here is a man who is either advancing fast in years or is unwell. Either way, it is a problem for Mr. Smith. He wants a helpful witness who will help him move forward speedily with the case. Donald is silent, apart from the briefest words of welcome, a welcome so qualified so that it is hardly a welcome.

'Perhaps you are not prepared to talk with me; perhaps a doctor would tell me that I should not be demanding your time.' Mr. Smith sits facing him, leaning forward, an earnest expression, sympathy written across his kind face. 'I'm not sure that you are aware of the matter in that you have been involved.'

Donald looks at him; what matter has he been involved in? He hasn't been involved in anything. What is there to say? He has said it already.

'But, you see, we need more information, we need to understand how the espionage is being executed. I have already indicated that Whitehall will not let us interrupt the research, even though they know that there is a leak. Extraordinary, you may think; but the machinations of our political masters are often curious.'

Donald sips coffee; he is beginning to feel as if he could wander off and leave Mr. Smith ruminating to himself. He feels the call of the wild, his garden. He makes to rise; there was a particular paper on glaives that he was keen to read and in a moment all else has no relevance.

'No, no. Please don't go.' Mr. Smith holds up his hands. 'You see, I am convinced that you know something about the matter that we do not.'

Standing, Donald sighs, looking down at him. Mr. Smith is the quiet urbane man as usual, a meekness that cloaks a blade of steel. Who is he really? Does he grow roses in the suburbs? And belong to a croquet club? Is he religious? Does he have family and worry about his grandchildren? Donald coughs. 'Harrumph. Who are those Georgians?'

'Those Georgians?' Mr. Smith frowns.

'I said. Georgians.'

'I wish we knew. But isn't Jac a Georgian?'

'I should have said that she was English.'

'Well. She hasn't received her papers yet.'

'Why not? Her parents are naturalised, aren't they?'

'Well. Not yet.'

'What is the problem?'

'None that I am aware of.'

'Well—'

'Now Donald, may I bring you back to the matter in hand?'

'I should say that that is exactly the matter in hand.' Donald has a thought in his head, and he will pursue it setting anything else aside. Otherwise, it gets too complicated. 'She works very hard at a job which is essential to this village, even though she doesn't always receive the respect she deserves. And yet your... boys, those uncouth ill-dressed youths you call Special Branch, hang about her door putting off the customers. And you tell me that her papers are still not processed. I find that absolutely appalling. Appalling.' He slumps down in his chair, gazing into his lap.

Mr. Smith blinks, looks a little unsettled. 'Well. I can see what you are saying. But it would be easy to withdraw the Special Branch if we knew what the link was between the shop and the leak.'

'Get on with it, then. Find your link and leave us alone.'

There is a pause.

'Donald. Can you tell me now. Why did you go to Cambridge?'

'To help out a friend. That's all. Private business. Harrumph.'

There is a hammering at the door. Mr. Smith looks up; he looks weary and frustrated but says nothing. Donald rises and opens the door.

'Why, there you are, an' I've been looking for you a'while.'

'Good morning, Mrs. Jones. What can I do for you?'

She edges round him, looking around the room. 'Oh I am sorry,' in a tone that displays no regret whatsoever. 'I didn't know you had one of your men friends 'ere.'

'Mrs. Jones, I'm a little busy, and—'

'An' so am I, or why would a poor ol' woman be a'maundering around the village when she could be sittin' with her feet up watchin' the telly?'

'What is it, Mrs. Jones?'

'I was wonderin' whether you'd be changing your mind about that survey.'

'Now, I told you, I can't be bothered with it now.'

'Well, that's no way to be talking. How is the village goin' to make decisions if you posh people don't fill in the survey?'

'They will manage very well. Now Mrs. Jones, if there is nothing else—'

'Is that a pot of tea there? I get awful thirsty walking round.'

'I'm sorry, Mrs. Jones, but not now. Good day.'

Mrs. Jones adopts a disgruntled look, mutters a Well Really, and slides out of the door, after another thorough inspection of Mr. Smith, who has sat in silence, his head down. Donald makes more tea, sits, pours. Waits. If only he would leave, he thinks. And thinks of all the other things he would rather be doing; the list is long.

Mr. Smith lifts his head, gazes at Donald, a fixed gaze that pins him to his chair. 'You said you were helping out a friend.'

'When?'

'In Cambridge.'

'Who?'

'Jac?'

'Oh yes. I was.'

'What were you doing?'

'Nothing to do with your business. As I said, private.'

'So you keep saying.' Mr. Smith was holding Donald in his gaze. 'You see, I have to decide whether you are assisting this gang, whether you are in fact a traitor.'

'What gang?'

'Those Georgians were not exactly your nice legal immigrants, keen to work here, keen to help.'

'Assisting? A traitor? Part of this gang? Me? And then being locked up?'

'Maybe they had a use for you.'

'A use? What use would I be?'

'Yes. We suspect that there is a link with the shop in your village. Perhaps you are a courier.'

'A what?' Donald rummages through his past; a courier was one of those polite people who carried small packets for businesses.

Mr. Smith maintains his patience with difficulty. 'A courier, someone who carries secret materials for an illegal outfit.'

'Preposterous! Who do you think I am?'

'That is the question that I have been trying to answer ever since we first met.' Mr. Smith is struggling; his masters will not allow direct investigation of the research unit and apart from knowing that material is sent to the shop, he does not know what happens to it and how it reaches the Georgian stronghold in Cambridge, where he has a sleeper in place. Not that he dare reveal that to Donald, who would question as to why he was not released sooner. Indeed, the sleeper was the one who first gave the alarm that the research unit had been infiltrated, but no indication of the link with the shop. For the first time in his long career, he wonders whether it is getting too complicated and whether he is getting too old for the business of dealing with the likes of Donald and Georgian gangs.

'Ridiculous! I was doing a little checking of my own. Just wanted to make sure that her poems were... oh blast!' Donald wipes his hand across his forehead. 'I wasn't going to mention those.'

'Poems?' Mr. Smith was as quiet as usual. Perhaps now he will learn something that will lead him forward. His face brightens a little.

'Just some love poems. But they're private, nothing to do with espionage.'

'How do you know about them?'

'Jac is innocent of this business, you know. I'm sure of it.'

'Quite. But the poems? Can we put our minds at rest about them?'

'I wasn't meant to tell you about them. Harrumph! Bad form.'

'We need not interfere, if we know them to be innocent. As you claim Jac is.' Mr. Smith added, with a little irony.

'Well, she is.'

'And why does she post poems to a Georgian stronghold in Cambridge?'

'It's just an address. Tomas, her boyfriend, writes her love letters; you know the sort of thing,' Donald is gruffly dismissive. 'And he sends her love poems that she wants to keep. Young people, you know.'

'Tomas; where does he work? And she doesn't keep them. Have you seen a poem?'

'Good gracious no. What do you take me for?'

'And the letter that you posted after coming out of the shop, at the start of our connection, held love poems?'

'Could have done, not that I remember posting any letter. As I have said many times. Your people claim to have seen me post a letter but I didn't look in any envelope, of course; wouldn't open someone else's post. Didn't look at whatever any address may have been; someone else's post, you know.'

Mr. Smith falls silent, looking down, rubbing his knees. Donald wonders how old he is. And how many investigations he is pursuing at the same time. He ought to be retired, growing his roses in suburbia. Harrumph.

'If you want to know, I didn't take anything with me.'

'But you knew the address.'

'The address?'

'Yes. The Georgian headquarters in Cambridge.'

'Headquarters?'

Mr. Smith is tiring of the constant repetitions, tiring of Donald's evasions, as he sees them.

Donald has no ideas of evading but his mind constantly drifts away from the present. 'Don't you get tired of all this? Constantly pursuing those who attack this country?'

Mr. Smith looks at him; there is a quiet floating mood over his face, as though he is taken to another place. He smiles. There is no simple answer to a man such as Donald, who fought for the country and must have seen some hard sights, death and destruction. 'Did you not use intelligence in your operations?'

Donald has to think hard, back to the years before Cambridge. There were good times and bad and he has suppressed many memories to rid himself of the nightmares and fears that he suffered in some postings. He is silent.

Mr. Smith looks down. 'Perhaps the hardest battle that one ever undertakes is with oneself.'

'Eh?'

'Oh, fears and doubts. That you are doing the right thing.' He doesn't mention the cynicism that sets in after a time, as one dreadful sight is overlaid with another. War weary was how it was expressed in the army. But the secret service has no easy escape; one carries on until one is posted elsewhere; or forcibly rendered unfit for work. No agent will admit that he is unfit; he or she adopts a carapace, not even a reflection of their own character to ward off the evil.

'Orders, that is what we did. Carry out orders.' Donald is clipped and sure.

'But sometimes, did you not see those orders as contrary to common sense and even contrary to your own ethics?'

Donald shakes himself. 'You spoke of intelligence. I pitied those men. The responsibility and the liability. Some were lost. But we never questioned the material; it was always good.'

'I'm only collecting material.'

'And I'm only helping you.'

'Are you?'

'Yes.'

'Then you can get me something else. If you would.'

Donald feels a wave of cold coming over him, sweeping away his blanket of comforts and strengths. He waits.

Mr. Smith bends towards him. 'I know it's intrusive but can you obtain a poem for me?'

'What? A poem?'

'Well then, you see, we can ascertain whether the poems are involved in the transmission of the secrets.'

'But they are love poems.'

'But they may contain a code.'

Donald is shocked; how can a love poem contain a code? That would be too duplicitous.

'You see, it may be as simple as a book code, and—'

'What do you mean, a book code?'

'Well, both parties—'

'What parties?'

'I mean, both the transmitter and the receiver use a common book.'

'But if it's common, it must be easy to—'

'When I say 'common', I mean they have the same book.'

'But how could they, if one is transmitting and the other—'

Mr. Smith is starting to lose his patience but he knows that it will be useless if he deserts this conversation with Donald now. He still hopes to make use of him. 'What I mean is that they use the same book, but obviously different copies.'

Donald reels, stares and harrumphs. 'That's devilish clever. But, but, hang on a mo, how could you ever decipher it? If you don't have the book?'

Mr. Smith is about to reply when Donald continues. 'And how do you know it's in code?'

'Ah, we have some very clever gentlemen who recognise patterns, and even if they cannot read the code, they will know that there is a code.'

'Damned clever chappies!'

Mr. Smith continues. 'You can understand can you not? If we can identify the transmission process, it will entirely remove any suspicion of your part in the matter.'

So that was it. Provide a poem, and he's off the hook. Bugger and damnation.

– 31 –

There is a time in a man's life when he would just like to lay down the trowel, or pen, or whatever it is, and sit back, contemplate the garden that will always need a little attention, visit the grandchildren, go on cruises and generally cease to have any responsible role in life. We think that Donald has reached that time, and we know he has plenty of good things to fill it. It is vexatious, to put it mildly, to be put into the situation of having to limber up one's mind and limbs, and go forth to tackle a mental, and possibly physical problem. Particularly when it involves deceiving a friend.

For a long time after Mr. Smith's departure, Donald sits in silence, ignoring the alarms of the blackbirds, the roar of F15s overhead, and the haunting call of the buzzards, trying to bring his mind to focus on the central problem. The trouble is that his mind will take a path of its own; it will meander away off the straight and narrow into pleasing diversions concerning aspects of medieval warfare or battlefields in England that he means to visit or even what he is going to cook that night and therefore what he will need to buy, and… and so on. And in any case the problem to be solved appears to be intractable.

Eventually, he drags himself to his feet, gazes for a short while out of the window, and goes in search of a scrap of paper and a pencil. It is remarkable how when one has such simple needs, of such simple basic items, that they become invisible. And in searching for a scrap of paper on his desk, he becomes distracted by notes that he has made for his next chapter; and articles from magazines that call for attention, relevant information for his research, important. So it is an hour or more before he returns to his chair, with scrap and pencil, to make notes, to determine a procedure for answering Mr. Smith's requirements. But by this time, it is lunch-time and with a gasp of exasperation, he lays scrap and pencil aside. For mealtimes are sacrosanct; on her death-bed, his wife made him promise to hold to them, not to allow the hours to drift so that he became weak and ineffectual. And he is aware that recently, he has not made good on his promise a few occasions. Particularly when imprisoned. Though that was not his fault. Or was it?

So it is afternoon before he is sitting again, scrap and pencil at hand, and wonders where to start. Perhaps a map. A road that may not be straight, but starts at the top and finishes with handing a poem to Mr. Smith. For it will not do to hand it to anyone else, particularly not the SB boys, who don't look reliable at things like that; why, they couldn't even polish their boots. He wonders whether his boots need a polish, glances down at his feet, and is perusing his ancient slippers when he becomes aware that the map has not advanced. At the bottom, is Mr. Smith; how will he hand it to him? Perhaps he would like it posted, but maybe not. Should he 'phone him? Would this be a breach in security? He could speak in code, book code; perhaps book code is no good in speech. And what book do they share?

Really, this is no good. He is not progressing at all. Suppose he asked Jac for a poem; what would she say? She would ask him why he would want to see her poem, she would be offended at the intrusion on her privacy and she would probably not wish to talk to him for a time. Even if he tries to explain that it would clear both her and him of any suspicion; she will not believe him. Well, it doesn't sound very credible, does it? Dead end. We can feel sorry for Donald; it is not a predicament that any of us would wish to face.

How can he obtain the poem without her knowing? Impossible. She simply places it in the post-box outside her house. How often has he posted an envelope for her? Once.

Why can't MI5 obtain the contents of the post-box? Don't know. But Mr. Smith didn't suggest it as though he wants Donald to make the effort to clear himself. Damned cheek; why should I do anything?

Would Tomas give him one or could he take it off Tomas? Both sound totally implausible. He may be picking Tomas up for the fete weekend but it is a couple of weeks ahead. Dead end.

Poor Donald; he is at his wits' end, and pours a generous Scotch. To dull the senses.

Oh well, he can hover, he supposes. Might be able to steal it.

He takes to dropping into the shop at varying hours, three or four times a day. Jac is bemused; Why Donald, she says, what is eating you? Have you a worm that is starving you? He picks up extra items at random, some luxuries, some he will never use. And meantime, his shelves, fridge and larder are overflowing with goods. No deal; there is no sign of an envelope to Cambridge. He becomes depressed and ceases his manic energy, falls back to his regular times at the shop, once a day, early in the morning. Jac wonders, are you well? And he shrugs, carries on as normal, until...

One morning, he is feeling tired. In the shop, he picks up his paper and vegetables, shrugs off an enquiry about his health and is making for the door when Jac calls out, 'Donald, if it isn't too much trouble, could you put this in the letterbox for me?' And hands him an envelope addressed to Cambridge, the right address, the Georgians.

How does he feel? Elated? No. Mildly depressed that he is

doing the dirty on his friend. He 'phones Mr. Smith. In an hour, a courier is at the door, gives a codeword agreed and insisted on by Donald, and bears the envelope away. Donald has extracted a promise that the envelope is delivered as normal. He rests; now he should feel free of the whole matter. Until he remembers that he is picking up Tomas and Tomas may be one of the traitors. Not proven.

Picking up Tomas; is this a treacherous activity?

– 32 –

The weekend approaches and the day to pick up Tomas arrives. Jac is so pleased, she hovers around him in the shop, offers him refreshment for the journey, a drink perhaps or a sandwich; has he something to wear if it gets cold or a raincoat? Is it too much trouble?

Donald has to remind her that he is only driving about twenty miles and that he should be back in one and half hours; or thereabouts. He has set aside his concerns that Tomas might be trouble, but he will do his best to deliver him to the shop. An easy journey.

And so it should be. How often have we set off to run an errand, exepecting to be back before long?

His car, little used, develops a noise before he has left the parish. He panics; this is not how the day was meant to unfold. Fortunately, the garage is open and he drops in. A nice man points out the stone in the hub cap, removes it, sends him on his way without charge. The sun shines, the wind is low, the programme on the radio is interesting; his heart has returned to its normal rythm. He bowls along thinking of his next piece of writing, of Jac, of the village, but not at all of the fete.

Onto the dual carriageway and he is immediately engulfed in

a problem, unforeseen before he joined the slip road. The traffic crawls and there is no clue to the blockage. The radio palls, and he becomes frustrated. After half an hour, condensing from two lanes into one, they are directed up a slip road and into the local town, where the through traffic crawls around the shoppers. The locals do not relish invasion by "main road" traffic, and make their objections known, by crossing the road at a snail's pace, by uttering loud and uncouth comments about "strangers" in the town, by making various signs, none of which Donald ever uses. Past the church and through a succession of junctions, traffic lights, generally red, and bends, they emerge onto a local road. Donald is not well acquainted with these local roads; he would like to stop and ask directions but the continuous flow pushes him along until he is ejected onto a tee junction where he has to guess the direction of the city.

He guesses wrong. Of course. But realises before long, turns round and weaves his way into the city, adjusts his knowledge of the roads and eventually arrives in front of a terrace house near the university. So far he has been on the road for one and a half hours and he feels tired and looks forward to a welcome, perhaps a cup of tea, and a speedy departure. He wishes he had accepted the offer of a drink and something to eat from Jac. Perhaps he could ask Tomas. But the house is not welcoming.

Around the pavement gate, as at Cambridge, is a tight group of young men. He identifies the Georgian tongue from Cambridge but he is not prepared for the blatant hostility that he feels emanating from the group. He sits in his car, waiting. Nobody comes to him. They stare, chatter among themselves and present an unfriendly front.

He gets out of his car. 'Excuse me, I am here for—'

'We know you is.' One of them spits in the gutter, just missing his wheel.

'I think there might be—'

'Look, we pay you last week. And now you here for more.'

'But I wasn't here last—'

'And you don't get more. We call police, perhaps.'

Donald is getting a little angry; why, he is here to do a good turn and he is being treated like… well, he doesn't know what they are talking about. It starts to rain and he stands there, no raincoat, undecided as to how to proceed. Harrumph. He gets back into his car, and watches the Georgians getting wet. Serve them right.

It could be that he dozes for a while; the radio has changed programme. Certainly, he notices that the rain has stopped, and he tries again. As they start to talk, he holds up his hand, clicks his heels and harrumphs. There is a pause and then sarcastic applause.

'Now, fetch me Tomas.'

'Tomas not here.'

'What do you mean? I am here to pick up Tomas.'

There is a huddle, a whispered conference, and one goes into the house. A pause as they watch him. The man comes out of the house with one who is older and the others make space around him, deferring to his seniority. A tall man, wearing army fatigues, a black eye-patch over his left eye. Donald, who has served overseas, finds this a little dramatic; reminds him of a certain Israeli general.

The man bows. 'Good morning. You wish to see Tomas?'

'No. That is, yes.'

'And can you tell me the reason for your visit?'

'Who are you?'

The man smiles, and shrugs. 'Perhaps Tomas is too busy to see you.'

'You know, I'm getting pretty fed up with this. You see, these men—'

'Were only doing their duty.' The man speaks quietly, almost apologetically as though Donald should know what is what.

'Do you always treat visitors like this?'

'Are you a visitor?'

'Well… actually, no. I have no intention of… visiting you.'

'Why are you here?'

'I'm here to pick up Tomas.'

'Who are you? You will not tell me.'

'I'm damned if I'll be cross-questioned like a criminal. What is the matter with you all?' Harrumph.

'You are police, yes, come to pick up Tomas?'

'No, I am not police come to pick up Tomas. I am friend of Jac.'

There is a pause. And a substantial change comes over the man's face. 'Ah, now I understand. You should have said.'

'What do you think I said?'

'A friend of Jac is a friend of ours.' And he spoke to the others in their tongue and they crowd around, clapping him on the back and press him into the house, ply him with coffee that is so strong that the spoon almost stands up and tell him tales of courage and skill that Tomas has done. But no sign of the said Tomas.

An hour passes; more tales of great courage, of bravery and distinction. Donald doubts their tales, but does not argue; Georgians mean trouble, and he is not looking for trouble. Or imprisonment. He is plied with coffee, strong drink and small cakes, a Georgian delicacy. He is beginning to feel exhausted, and the coffee has generated a storm of heartbeats. There is a silence as the door opens and a young man enters. A rapid introduction in Georgian and Donald has his hand shaken by Tomas who sits, accepts coffee and a drink. And a small cake. Will they ever leave?

Donald rises. 'Well, my friend, time to go.'

There is a process of departure. Now a woman appears and all have to shake Donald's hand, clap Tomas on the back as though he is going into battle. Some crude innuendo about Jac, put down severely by the older man.

And they leave, after Tomas has looked over Donald's little car, muttered some comment, and fitted himself into the front seat, refused the seat-belt until Donald sat waiting in silence. Donald wonders whether Jac has feared the worst, that there has been an accident, and how would she learn of it. So much time has passed.

Donald is struggling with driving; the cakes and drink and coffee have rendered him a little weak and he loses the way a number of times. There is a small incident when he tries to drive down a one-way road the wrong way and comes face to face with a police car; the police wait without comment while he achieves a three-point turn in the road, narrowly missing the parked cars on either side and drives off in front of the police car. He is at last set on the right road out of town. Tomas is quiet; he gazes about himself, looks at the fields with interest, says little.

Donald feels that he should prepare the young man for the village. 'Now Tomas, you should know. Jac has been watched by the police; they are suspicious of her for some reason and they will be suspicious of you.'

'What they grow in that field?'

'Er...' The field is long past. 'Was it wheat?'

'Why suspicious? What do I do?'

'It's not a question of what you do... have done. More a question of who you are.'

'Who I am?'

'Yes.'

'And who am I?'

'Can't help you there.'

'Can't help?'

'Can't help.'

'With what?'

Donald is becoming confused. 'I said, I can't help you.'

'But you help me.'

Silence. Donald breaths deeply, misses a turn, carries out another three-point turn before they are set on their way again.

'I'm doing this for Jac,' he says.

'Jac can look after herself.'

'No doubt about that, Tomas.'

'Why you say "no doubt"?'

'Well… er… I have seen how she holds herself.'

'Holds herself? Are we talking sex here?'

'Certainly not! How can you suggest such a thing?'

'Well, not understand.'

Donald tries to organise his thoughts, difficult when he is only trying to describe a feeling; and drive. 'She… er… manages everything very well.'

'Ah. Good.'

'But she needs your help.'

'She no help from me.'

'But she is your girlfriend, yes?'

'Pff! She is a girl; she do as I say.'

Donald is shocked; there is a great disparity between Tomas's expression of love, and Jac's. Didn't Jac say that they were in love, exchanged love letters, emails, telephone conversations and he sent her love poems? They drive for a while in silence, Donald thinking that it is not his business but concerned for his friend and unhappy about not saying more.

He harrumphs. 'She's looking forward to seeing you.'

Tomas says nothing. Is there a sniff? Donald tries again. 'She has been missing you, she said.'

'Ugh! She can look after herself.'

Donald remains concerned for Jac. However, he is committed to delivering this youth and he will deliver this youth; he hopes that Jac will be able to look after herself. A few miles outside the village, he pulls up beside the road. 'Now, you have to get ready.'

'Ready? What you mean?'

'If the police see you arrive, they will make trouble.'

'I can fight them.'

'And you will lose and Jac will be taken away and – good God, man, what are you thinking of?'

Tomas is silent, a sneer on his face, gazing out of the window. Like an unreformed juvenile.

'Here, put these on.' Donald drags a tunic and a helmet out of the back seat. 'These are your uniform for the fete battle. Best try them on now. And keep them on until you see Jac; she can approve them.'

'Why she prove?'

'Get on with it, man.' Donald is tired of the whole trip. He wishes to be at home, reading or sleeping. Much of the day has passed and the battle is the next day.

Eventually, with some complaint and a reminder to put the helmet on the right way round, they start off again. As they drive into the village, there is a black Mondeo with whip aerials parked by the side of the road. The two men inside give Donald a long look and then the medieval soldier beside him a further long look.

'You see?'

'Hunh. I can fight little men like those.'

By this time, Donald is almost prepared to cast Tomas to

the lions, watch him being damaged and hauled away by Special Branch. But his respect for Jac prevents him from pursuing this attractive line. 'Oh, good God man, have you no sense?'

He drives on, parks by the back door of the shop. The Mondeo has followed them; he gets out, leaving Tomas sitting impatiently in his seat and waves to the men in black. One of them returned him to his home after the Cambridge expedition. 'Shall I see you at the fete? I'm putting on a battle.'

A gruff response. 'Not our business. You recovered?'

Donald smiles. 'Yes, quite well, thankyou.'

The men nodded; the older one smiled. Neither enquired why there was a dressed soldier in his car. After a little while, they move off. Donald raps on the back door and when it opens, he waves Tomas through it as quickly as possible; a smile exchanged with Jac who says, 'Where have you been all day? I thought—'

He shrugs, gets into his car and drives home.

– 33 –

A red arc over the horizon, sunrise again, the sign for a cacophony of bird chorus, a renewal of friendships and foes. The day of the fete, perhaps also a renewal of friendships and foes.

The sun rises further; warming rays are cast to reach the little village. The ray illuminates the Green; it has changed. It is decorated, banners and strings of bunting, a few tents, but no stalls or tables. Yet. Speeding beyond the Green, a ray illuminates the front of the shop, as the blinds are pulled. Jac yawns; before starting her work, pulling the newspapers into the shop, setting up the displays in front of the shop, flowers and vegetables.

The church clock chimes six, but everybody knows it means eight. The sound of vehicles increases as tractors pulling trailers bearing stalls and tables and straw bales for seats arrive from three directions. A motley gang of helpers emerges from streets, alleyways and doorways, stretching, yawning, shouting friendly abuse at neighbours. Kevin's pickup arrives, a blare of music as he launches himself onto the Green, scattering helpers in all directions as he pulls up in front of the Organisers tent. To unpack loud speakers, cables, microphones and an odd assortment of folding chairs.

Mrs. Fortesque is to be seen in all quarters, clipboard in hand, hat firmly in place, barking instructions, waving her hands, universally ignored by all and sundry; why, they have been erecting the fete for the last thirty years. They don't need a busybody telling them what to do.

There is a diversion that brings them all to a halt, to gather around an old man with a long white beard, a filthy long coat and a stained cowboy hat. He is standing by an upturned orange box, flicking a pack of cards in his calloused hands. Facing him is Mrs. Fortesque, hands on hips, hat askew, a furious expression on her face; she is quivering from head to foot with rage, her clipboard bouncing off her ample bosom.

'May I ask, who do you think you are? You are a disgrace to the fete, to the village.'

There is a broad mutter laced with laughs from the crowd gathered around. The man looks at her; he is much the same height but he tilts his head back to give himself the feeling of being taller. This effect is somewhat spoilt when he leans forward and ejects a stream of tobacco juice onto the ground at Mrs. Fortesque's feet. There is a roar of approval; Mrs. Fortesque steps back, peering down at her brogues. There is a spot of juice on the right shoe; she resists the temptation to rub it on her left leg; the restraint costs her a great deal. She repeats her demand, who are you.

The man ignores her, turns to the crowd. 'How are yer all? Bin a few months since I seen any of yer.'

A wave of happy smiles and grins breaks across the crowd, as though they anticipate a performance that they know well. As yet, there is silence as though they are deciding who will speak on their behalf.

Mrs. Fortesque steps into the silence. 'You will remove yourself from the fete immediately. Do you understand?'

The man looks around, exchanging nods and smiles with a few, and turns to face her. 'Now missus, who be you? I've been at this fete these last thirty years and I reckon I've not set my eyes on the likes of you before.'

'I am the fete organiser. All the stalls have been booked and scheduled; their places allotted, their budgets allocated. Now, you have neither booked nor been allocated and I should be grateful if you would remove yourself. And that.' Her nose wrinkling with disgust, she points at the orange box.

The man laughs. 'I don't know who you is but I reckon I belong here. More so than you.' He looks her up and down and reaches to feel the cloth of her twin suit jacket; she steps back abruptly, almost falling as she catches a brogue on a tuft of grass. His breath floods the air between them and she clutches a lace edged handkerchief in front of her nose.

For a moment, there is silence as neither side is prepared to submit. The pause gives the man the edge. He looks round. 'Now, mates. Do I not come to your fete every year, keep you entertained, take your spare change and have you come back for more?'

There is general laughter, a few hoots and calls and one or two nod and say that it's true, he does always come.

Mrs. Fortesque rallies. 'And what is your stall?'

The man looks around, smiles and turns back to her. 'I don't need much space, do I boys?'

'Yes, but what is your stall?'

'Oh, tis a gentle little pastime, nothing to trouble you.'

'But what is it called?'

'I don't rightly know.'

'You don't know what you do?'

'Tis just cards, you see. A simple little card game.'

'Is this gambling?'

'Now, that's a big word and we don't know it here, do we lads?'

'Well, is it?'

'Not how you would see it. Eh, boys?'

There are smiles and nods around. Mrs. Fortesque looks at her watch, frowns, pulls up her schedule and turns to the crowd. 'We are running ten minutes behind schedule. Please, return to your stalls and complete on time.'

A few people turn away; the majority wait to see the outcome of her battle. She sighs loudly, stamps her foot, turns her back on the man and stomps away, checking on the stalls as she goes.

At ten o'clock, all down tools and disappear into the pub.

Mrs. Fortesque is outraged. 'Where do you think you're going? Hey! Come back!'

'Breakfast time,' she is told, as the Green is deserted, for half an hour or more. Her schedule is in shreds; she stands in the middle of the Green, tears in her eyes, sure that the fete will be a disaster. And at whom will they point the finger?

– 34 –

Buzzards circle in the blue sky, looking down on the village; they see a hive of activity that frightens away their prey. The fete is as busy as ever it has been. The stalls are thronged, children

261

run around shrieking at their parents and the tea tent buzzes with conversation and a few merry complaints from the long queue that stretches around the corner. The icecream melts, the china is smashed and raffle numbers are called over the loudspeakers by a man who has imbibed deeply in the beer tent. On the perimeter of the Green lie a few good ol' boys who have succumbed to the heat and the beer and snore peaceably, undisturbed by the noise and activity. In short, it has all the signs of a successful village fete.

Mrs. Fortesque hovers in the middle; her work is almost done, until it is time to clear away. She can do no more to influence the fate of the fete. In a corner between the tombola and the china smashing stalls sits the old man with his orange box, a steady stream of punters losing their cash to him and returning to lose more. Mrs. Fortesque ignores him entirely; he is invisible, non-existent and she will not countenance any comment that is made about him. She feels, with justification, that he should submit a large part of his winnings to the profits of the fete but she will not confront him again. The last encounter was sufficiently bruising. There is already a serious thorn in her side; Donald has not been seen.

The medieval stall was erected in the morning. The schoolmaster is in charge, supported by a large number of his children who demonstrate the weapons, thoughtfully constructed of cardboard and broom poles but realistically painted complete with gore and rust. Parents gather around, some with concern across their faces, others passing by, delighted to have their offspring off their hands. And now Mrs. Fortesque's lieutenants are erecting the poles and safety rope to enclose the battle zone. More children are gathering, now all dressed in their costume and the schoolmaster is ticking them off his list. But still no sign of Donald.

Five minutes to the hour of four and he wanders up to the stall. A cheery handshake with the master, claps a few children on the head and draws them all around him. Mrs. Fortesque has rushed up to him as he appeared on the road, jabbering in her frustration and excitement but is dismissed with a casual look over her head; she has withdrawn to a safe distance, outside the enclosure, to watch the proceedings.

From the shop emerges a rather taller child dressed in the same costume, helmeted already, who casually joins the children around Donald. They withdraw a little; the stranger is unknown to them and his size frightens them. They will not wish to face him in battle and in any case, their roles have been defined, argued over and practised.

It is not clear as to why Tomas has been persuaded to take part in the battle. Donald has had the thought that, having been seen by the Special Branch boys, Tomas should take part rather than conceal himself in the shop, and prevent the Specials from from becoming suspicious of a person who entered the village to take part in the battle and who did not appear. Jac has not shared his concerns; she felt that Tomas should remain out of sight, preferably upstairs, and not draw attention to himself. Neither consulted Tomas on the issue; unknown to either, he is looking forward to a good fight. When told that it was a children's battle and that he should not harm any child, he scoffed and told them that as a child, he had battled many times, broken bones, torn skin, bruises and black eyes; Georgians are fighters, he said, a history of survival against heavy odds. He takes his place at the rear on one side.

The clock strikes six, actually at least two hours before that, and the armies take their places. There is heroic shouting, the wielding of bizarre flags and banners, the shaking of shields. At a discreet sign from the schoolmaster, they advance towards each other at a slow walk. There is, after all, a limited amount of space to operate and the sooner that the armies clash the better.

With a great deal of childlike shouting and waving of swords, axes, halberds, glaives and other barbaric weapons, they clash, split, wave back and forward and a satisfactory number of children exhibit awful death throes, shrieks and groans, collapsing with jets of tomato ketchup on their costumes, their clothes, their helmets and the ground around. Most parents laugh, applaud and show regret that they missed such activities in their youth; but some have long faces, even shock, mutter and indicate that they would like to interrupt proceedings to rescue their little darlings and mount a public objection to the whole affair. They don't; they hover, looking around for the organiser. Mrs. Fortesque is nowhere to be seen.

The battle proceeds; the schoolmaster has decided that a quarter of an hour will suffice to show the awful effects of war and exhibit the environment of a medieval battlefield. Donald has done his bit and withdrawn to the tea tent. The children have other ideas, ignore signs to withdraw and are encouraged by the attention that they are receiving, even applause from some quarters. Their blood is up, the temperature has risen and it will be difficult to bring it all to a safe and peaceful end. They are, as many parents will attest later, over-excited. Don't we all remember over-excited children?

It will end in tears. Of course.

It is always difficult when larger children are combined with smaller children in some physical activity. There are many who will recall the confusion on a school playing field of being faced with a brute of a boy or girl, wavering before a certain beating. The schoolmaster, being aware of these problems, has rehearsed the battle in detail, ensuring that smaller children are given as good a chance as larger and that those who were to die were selected from both large and small; it added to the drama to have a David fell a Goliath. Though no projectiles are permitted in this battle.

It is a small thing that happens, really. A little boy, over-heated, over-excited, challenges a young stallion almost twice his size. The rehearsed moves already completed, the youth selects a simple action, pushing the young unfortunate backwards onto the ground, treading on his sword as he does so and snapping it before lolloping off to find further victims.

The small boy bursts into loud tears, shouts of anger, which brings the whole battlefield to a standstill, surprise and in some quarters, humour written over the faces, though unseen in the helmets. But one soldier, the one who was a great deal taller than the others, steps forward and scoops the little unfortunate boy off the ground and turns back towards the schoolmaster; unfortunately, in the process of stooping to the ground, his helmet falls off.

There has been no mention of the Special Branch men. It would be reasonable to assume that they will have been given the day off; it is after all a Bank Holiday, and haven't we been told by them that it was not their business? But they have been chastised by their superior for failing in their duties; they failed to obtain the contents of the postbox, they failed to obtain the poems from Donald and they upset Donald in searching his house so badly. Whitehall is not pleased with MI5 and MI5 is not pleased with Special Branch. And their superior in Special Branch is certainly not pleased with them. They are on duty.

They avoided any of the work in erecting the fete, by loafing around the perimeter of the Green, observing the arrivals and deliveries. There has been nothing to alert them to the smallest degree; they retired to the beer tent for an extended break, a liquid lunch, and staggered into the sunshine shortly before the battle. They look forward to going home and, finding a couple of empty seats on a bench, settle for the last hour of the fete. The loud cries alert them but it is only a child and children are wont to cry. They glance over at the battle; their bench is quite close.

There is the crowd of small children, there are the concerned parents, there is the schoolmaster, all already identified; and there is a stranger, albeit in costume. He stands out like a pine tree in a deciduous wood. His features and his expression are foreign; his size does not accord with the average size of the children. All of the Special Branch men's attennae go into full alarm phase, calling for action stations. Struggling with a degree of disability due to a high level of alcohol in their bloodstreams, they lurch into what they might officially call – and report – as an investigation but what amounts to an attack.

There was no question of Tomas being recognised; he has not been identified by any of the authorities. Donald and Jac thought that he should be disguised purely as a precaution, to deflect curiosity. They reckoned without Tomas' character and inclination, as we do. Seeing two men in black suits advancing on him within the roped enclosure, Tomas adopts his preferred method of enduring investigations and advances with his weapon; he has not considered that a quiet word or two might suffice to satisfy the Specials. He has handed the small child to the schoolmaster and recovered his weapon. The glaive is a long pole with a spiked blade on the end; of course, it is only a broom pole with a cardboard blade, painted by the children with realistic gore and rust. The Special Branch men, seeing the size of the weapon, the gore and rust, hesitate, assume that the weapon is a viable threat and draw handguns. Tomas is not in the least disconcerted; he swings his weapon in the direction of the two men, just missing a girl's head on one side and a parent on the other. He advances on the men who are unable to fire for the simple reason that there are people all around, many of them children, and because they have had it impressed on them that a live person is essential for terminating the case. They find that their hands are hampered by holding weapons that they cannot use and fumbling with their holsters, are unable to duck Tomas' weapon that cracks against their heads, shattering the blade.

There is a pause. Already hung-over on the strong local bitter with sharp headaches beginning to assert themselves, they clutch their heads while looking at Tomas' weapon and by degrees attempt to catch the pole. Tomas throws it in their faces; they duck. He runs.

Tomas has always boasted about fighting, boasted of conquests and defeated foes. But he recognises the futility of attempting to defeat the two men and is unaware of the poor state from which they are suffering. He picks a course through the heart of the fete, causing the odd collision, a series of shouts of complaint, some glancing blows and many swearwords, many that he is not acquainted with. The Special Branch men stumble after him.

The villagers have not forgotten the two men who insinuated themselves into their village, casting derogatory comments on one of their neighbours that, for a while, were believable but are now seen as false, a slur upon them all. Seeing the two men attempting to barge their way through the crowd, unexpected jams occur before them, backs turned, children manoeuvred across their path. They are not concerned about the slight young man who has previously passed their way. He is a visitor; not a polite one for sure but a visitor who has been forgiven his haste. But the two Special Branch men are in a different category altogether. Generally disliked, they were encouraged to drink their fill in the beer tent; their fill included the slops from the taps surreptitiously laced with spirits. And being in no hurry to get outside and enjoying what they thought was an excellent local brew, they had dawdled to the amusement of the local men and the barman's profit.

And then, a foot is carelessly extended through the press of mostly male backs and the younger of the two Specials extends his full length on the ground, his face in a discarded ice-cream, his uniform in something worse. The older pauses, looks down in disgust, shrugs and gives him a hand up. Dark mutters from the crowd around. Their quarry has disappeared into the back alleys and yards of the village, never to be seen by them again.

– 35 –

Tomas believes that he is discovered. His poems, written to include the coded information that gave his compatriots the secrets of the research, can be written no more. He must leave; leave the university, leave Jac and leave the country. He can never return to the university town, nor to the enclave at Cambridge. It might be thought that leaving Jac would cause him some distress; not a bit of it. She was a useful cog in the machine, so innocent of the espionage that she could never reveal the part that she played. Tomas contacts Cambridge, receives the assistance he needs to leave the country and departs for ever.

The leak continues; other methods are found for transmitting the information and the Special Branch and MI5 take a further six months to uncover the source of the leak. Jac is questioned once more; she is inconsolable about Tomas who has not been as she had thought and takes time to get over the shock of his changed character and his sudden departure. She endures a further night of interrogation, the two Specials confused by her anger, her righteousness, and her English. She is released, after Donald has discovered that she is being held, and 'phoned

Mr. Smith with threats of exposing the whole drama, whatever punishment he might bring down on himself.

One might think that she has had enough of British justice, and return to Georgia. But she was young when she left, and she feels that she belongs in her new country, that she has inhabited for some twenty years. She remains at the shop; it is her home.

And Donald? He has missed Tomas' escape, the failure of the Specials to catch him, and their ensuing humiliation. He enjoyed a cup of tea and a slice of sponge cake in the tea tent; the lady in charge gives him a big smile, a large slice of cake, and assures him that there is no charge as he is an organiser. He wonders if his time in Coventry is at an end, and whether he might involve himself further in the village activities. Perhaps not; it has been rather tiring, and he has his book and a battle to pursue at home. And he could not endure another evening with Mrs. Fortesque, although he can pass her by in the street with a friendly nod; that is as far as it will go.

At that moment, a crowd of the parents of his battling youngsters come into the tent and surround him with cries of congratulation, applause for the design of the weapons, costumes (that he has had little to do with), and the fighting. The poor school-master, who has been burdened with the majority of the organisation and work, stands silent behind them.

When, oh when, they ask, might he organise another battle? Perhaps on a larger field, like the football field, with larger armies? And perhaps a talk one night on medieval warfare?

Donald smiles, utters not one word, and withdraws home. His dog is delighted to see him and a glass of Scotch taken as he sits in the evening sunlight restores his sense of balance. The village settles to its accustomed summer evening, the cry of children, the roar of lawn-mowers, and the chatter from the pub. But not one bird call; like Donald, they settle for an early bed.

This book is printed on paper from sustainable sources managed under the Forest Stewardship Council (FSC) scheme.

It has been printed in the UK to reduce transportation miles and their impact upon the environment.

For every new title that Troubador publishes, we plant a tree to offset CO_2, partnering with the More Trees scheme.

For more about how Troubador offsets its environmental impact, see www.troubador.co.uk/sustainability-and-community